MERCY UNDERCOVER

A DET. BRENDA SAYERS STORY
with Special Commentary

A. R. LEONARD

ISBN 979-8-9923146-0-1

Imprint: Nita Nae's Books

Publishing Company: Lulu.com, 2025

Printed in the United States of America.

A. R. Leonard © 2024 c/o Nita Nae's Books
Detective Brenda Sayers - Mercy Undercover
 With Special Commentary
Nita Nae's Books—Truthful Imagination © 2015
4859 W. Slauson Avenue, Ste. A - #354
Los Angeles, CA 90056

Book design & cover by: Nita Nae's Books & BookBrush.com

MERCY UNDERCOVER

DETECTIVE BRENDA SAYERS

With Special Commentary

A. R. Leonard

Available

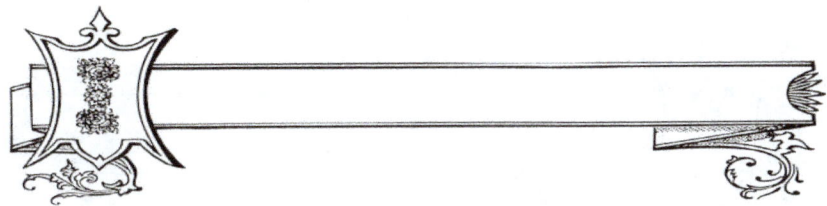

Amethyst in Love, (Amazon, 2019) eBook only
Unconditional Counsel, (CFP, 2020/Lulu, 2025)
Apocalyptic 7—Salvations Cry (Lulu, 2021, Rev. 2025)
Embrace the Dawn: To Live Again (Amazon, 2024)
The Ghosts of Slavery's Dance (Lulu, 2025)

Future Books

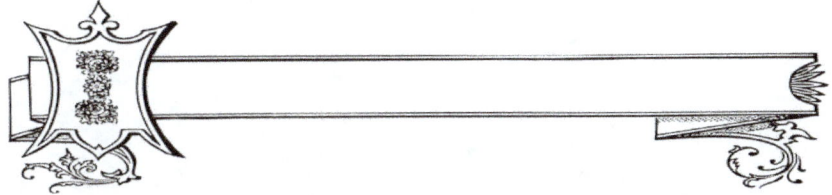

Unconditional Counsel 2: Fate Unbroken (WIP)
Apocalyptic 12—Angels of Heavens Army (WIP)
The Container (WIP)
Opposing Fruit (WIP)
The Heart of an Untold Legacy: A Father's Story (WIP)

Dedication

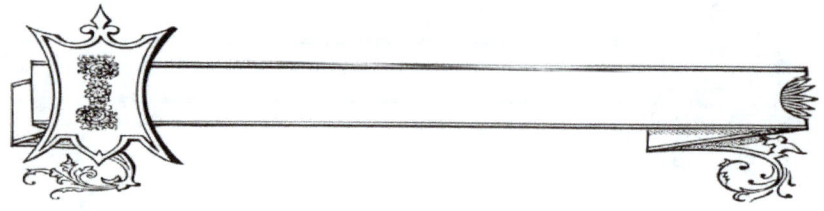

To Nevaeh Smith, Amari & Jazzlynn Smith, my great-nieces, and my new grandbaby Ezryah Makana.
Know that you are the future until Christ returns.
Keep God first until then, and remember that you are loved.

Introduction

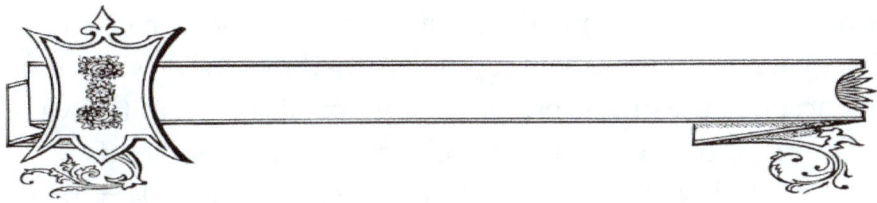

In this fictional story, police officers carry out their jobs in various scenarios to protect and serve. This book aims not to dispel the notion that there are no rotten apples on the police force, but to foster the notion that there are excellent officers who carry out their jobs daily with integrity, heart, and sacrifice. Even though we hold them to a higher standard of conduct, police officers are human beings, just like you and me. As a civilian, I too had my pre-conceived notions that something was wrong with the police, because of what I saw on the news and mainstream media. God gave me the opportunity to work and learn what they do daily. It is much more than what we see on tv on the evening new or in tv shows. I must give much respect and gratitude to those who do their jobs with sincerity of heart. Don't get me wrong, as we've seen in recent years, police are human and are subject to corruption, scandal, and just plain bad decision making, but we can't lump them all in with the dirty bath water. Trust and believe, I have seen the corruption within the ranks, but I have also seen the compassion, laughter, and heartache when an excellent officer dies in the line of duty. Their EOW (End of Watch) serves as a reminder of their commitment, whether through death or retirement.

Even when an innocent bystander loses their life for no other reason than being in the wrong place at the wrong time. Those excellent officers/detectives want to catch the bad guys or gals. I've also seen community members do and say illegal things on camera, which would make you cringe. So, I've seen both sides of the coin. I've had to call the police because a guy was tweaking off some drugs and jumped my fence into my backyard for no reason at all. He turned out to be wanted as an accessory to murder. So, life as an officer is not always easy, but most dedicate themselves to want to do good.

I started writing Mercy Undercover back in 2004, when I had no inkling that I would ever work with LAPD and all the wonderful and not so wonderful officers that I have worked with and those who have come across my path. I especially want to thank Ret. P.O. III, Stuart Guidry, for his honest answers to my questions. Also, to the SLOs at 77th, for their tireless work in the communities they patrol.

Although the nature of this story is serious, the banter and fun I had with the special commentary in between were hilarious to do. I've grown and matured since 2004, and I've had to change my thoughts and realities about life. I've learned lessons from my youth to never repeat. That's why I put the Special Commentary in, not only for you, but for me to remember my mistakes in relationships.

I hope and pray you enjoy this story of God's Mercy Undercover. Don't take it all as fiction, but there is truth within and behind the story. Have fun with the cast of characters.

Contents

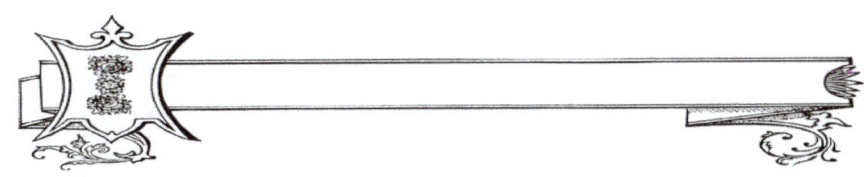

1

 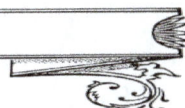

How I Became

In the dead of night, it wasn't our luck the blinding mist hid us. Maybe we could use it to our advantage. It rolls in from the west to give us cover. The cool fog you never wanted to breathe in, but we didn't have a choice. We were going to stand down at first, but this was probably our only chance to have them all in the house at once. Our hearts pounding, and guns drawn. It's the biggest bust of my brief career as an Under Cover Officer (UCO).

A known drug house, gangsters with Mack 10s and I wanted to make sure they went to prison for a long time. My mission—to honor *his* sacrifice. SWAT went in first and I follow with my hand on the left shoulder on our Lead Detective. The suspects gunfire puts one of our officers down. I can only say that Lil Manny's shock caused him to shoot without thinking. We—Farrell, I, and the others—handcuffed the shooter, who wounded Officer Barren and four others at 00:01 a.m.

The heat from my adrenaline didn't subside right away. I ensured those five felt my wrath before the other officers transported them. By no means was I a rogue cop. A personal tongue lashing was my reward for the get-back.

I rode with Officer Barren to the hospital, where doctors would treat him for a neck wound and a bullet wound to his chest, right above his heart and below his clavicle. Once in a blue moon, we'd get hit through the armpit where the bullet-proof vest doesn't protect. One centimeter deeper or lower, his artery would have been severed. Who knows if he would have made it then? It was a good team effort and Farrell had my back. Likewise, I omitted my conversation with the scumbags from the report. I know you ask. How did I get here? What did I do to be investigated by IA (Internal Affairs)? I had given many my personal tongue lashing, but that's not what got me in trouble.

~

Well, it was the 80s, what could be worse? Growing up in Los Angeles, hearing of various lives turned inside out. A wealthy individual is what we hoped to be, in the limelight, an icon, but commonly, pushing up daises or barely making it to have that infamous American Dream. California alone was the melting pot of the United States in many folk's opinions. All walks of life trusted L.A. was the place to be to make it big in show business, the movies, a rapper, a singer, prostitution, or pornography. The disparity was clear: life dealt a good hand to the privileged, but a terrible one to others. Drug traffickers and consumers, pyramid schemes or unsavory acts of brutality to make a quick Benjamin. To be rich, next to hopeless. Some sold out to the man, dying, struggling to keep the high life beyond their means, because why, they could never get out of the game. A portion of the pie was hard to come by. It drove people crazy. Serial killers on the loose, police corruption with tv news exposure on the rise and High School drop-out rate at an all-time high (Yes, I have bars, my boys would say). People on television frequently screamed about police brutality, atrocity, or corruption in those days—some were justified, but not all was bad. Why were the black and brown being racially profiled or killed across America at the hands of the Po-Po's? Was it justified, or the dirty Blue-Line continued to be passed over with little repercussion?

Single-parent homes were the way of life where I grew up. I had the good fortune to have both of my parents together and they loved all their children. It was Compton at first and then we moved when I was three to Central Los Angeles, near the University of Southern California. Leoticious Sayers was an ARMY man, a medic in Germany, when he met my mom and fell in love. Married quickly, two out of the six of us were born with Dual Citizenship, ten months apart. I was the first girl and my dad loved me by placing me on a pedestal I couldn't possibly live up to. Never caused them any strain. I performed well in school and gave them no reason to worry. We never grew up in poverty and didn't want for anything, except for the occasionally expensive toy. Not rich by any means, but a middle-class family, the fourth child from my mother's womb, out of six. Three sons before me and one more son and another girl followed me.

As a baby, the identified chubby one of the family, my aunt would turn her nose up at everything my parents did for their children. She nicknamed me Peach, plump-tomato when you cooked me and not awkward looking. My curves hit in the right place. I always seemed to catch unwanted attention from men, even at an early age, creepy. A bit of a loner, having had few friends growing up. I was a tomboy for a reason. That reason was to stop the gawking of the older, because of my early development in body frame.

Although, I never turned down the opportunity to play street football or climb trees with the boys. They never saw me as their equal until one day I tackled Simon and planted him on the dark-gray ashy asphalt and made him wish he had never tried to oppose me. Not realizing or caring what I did to myself, I gained weight as my grandparents spoiled me almost to death after I visited them for one summer in Philadelphia, PA. My father's words, not mine. It wasn't until the summer of 82, when I returned from PA, that my dad didn't even recognize me walking through the LAX Airport. Livid beyond words, I couldn't blame it all on my grandparents. They were functioning alcoholics and left me in charge of my youngest siblings while they went to work in their deli store.

Many summers later in High School, my weight was never an issue. Although my figure was the last thing I cared about at that stage, the thought of boys fast approached. Just getting through the tenth grade was enough without the added attention of peer pressure. I guess my anti-social personality didn't sit well with others or being sheltered most of my life caused me to not like hanging around too many individuals. As I got older, I found out it was genetic from my father. He didn't like crowds at all. Meeting my best friend in the tenth grade, I guess the traditional saying goes—*opposites attract* was true in our case. Karen Jefferies was wild, loud, and free, but only when she wasn't at home with her family. They lived in Imperial Courts and her momma didn't play. She had a spirit, nothing and no one could tame. We did everything together and most people would have thought we were sisters. Going on to the eleventh grade, I suspect her spirit rubbed off on me a bit. We had fun and yet, despite my lack of enthusiasm about my past school year, I started getting interested in boys. Not sexually, mind you, but just having fun in High School, and looking at my existence for what it was. What does a sixteen-year-old know, anyway? We both wanted to go into the medical field and attended Lincoln Medical Magnet (Now Bravo) High School. Therefore, we volunteered as Candy Stripers at U.S.C. General. Yeah, the one on Soto in East L.A. We would go to hospital and school dances, and party down as frequently as we could fit in. Few guys were interested in me during that period, and the ones I talked to turned out to be flakes.

Interesting enough to experience working in a hospital. We had one patient who walked down the hall with his pale ashy buttocks sticking out. It was amusing until he could no longer hold his bowels. Seeing a trail of undigested cubed carrots and peas left you never wanting to eat a pot pie ever again. Yes, it was disgusting to watch, but it was a small part of becoming old in our eyes. We provided care and companionship to elderly patients nearing the end of their lives, brightening their days two or three times a week.

It was during the height of the AIDS epidemic. We heard many in their last stages of time. Not allowed to work in their rooms, we could only hear their screams and moaning throughout the hallway from the pain they were in from time to time. We could only imagine what they looked like or how much pain they were in. We didn't feel comfortable knowing this was their end and only family could be in the room if they bothered to show. Feeling sorry for them was all we could give, but there was nothing we could do to soothe their pain of abandonment.

So, the summer had dawned its day by ending the eleventh grade on a positive note. I flunked none of my classes. We were always glad when the summer came, because we didn't have to ride those ugly, yellow, breadbox buses. It was sad in the fact I didn't get to be with Karen during the summers too often. One reason was I had to go to summer school and retake algebra on previous summer vacations just to pull up my GPA. The second, math is not my strong suit and definitely wasn't my favorite subject. I passed it with a 'C', and ecstatic I didn't have to take the class over again to graduate.

It was September time again, and school would start soon. Heading to our last year of High School, excitement was an understatement about ending the school year on a high note. I was close in age with my cousin Tanya. I guess I would claim we were hanging partners during the times I couldn't be with Karen. She was two months older, but we were more mature than most of our age. Tanya phoned and said she was setting me up with some guy and he would be calling. I was to be nice and talk to him.

"Why did you do that?"

"Her friend Johnny had a friend he wanted to set up," Tanya stated.

 *Yeah, this was not showing maturity. Like I couldn't find a date on my own. Oh, Hi!! Sayers here. From this point in the story, you'll receive some extra banter from me. Explaining why I did this or why I did that. Why I love men and sometimes want to strangle them too. From here is the roadmap I took down memory lane. I ask you, don't become comfortable and don't feel you have to agree with everything I say — Yes, I want you to agree with everything I say. Just kidding, but here is where the table of my life turned down the gray brick road of life's never-land. There was nothing golden about it until the light shined on me. The accusatory light, the investigation light, the, I told you so light, the forgiving light, and so on.*

"So, you gave him my number?"

"Yes," I could tell she was getting perturbed at me. "Why is this so hard for you to grasp?" I didn't know whether to scream or thank her. "All right, but he better not be ugly. I can't believe you did this." What do you know! Cornelius Owens was ugly, but sweet. We hit it off, and I married him four years later. I had gone to Community College for a year and a half after High School and later dropped out to be the stay-at-home wife. At the end of our third year together, we were engaged and a year after that, married. Two years after, we were getting a divorce. I can laugh about it now. Life had become so unbearable with this guy. He had a life, and I didn't, or at least he didn't want me to have one. He could go out with his buddies and do God knows what. When I would try to go out, he would stay home and beg me not to go. I was one of the lucky ones, though. We had no children or assets to fight over, and if we had, he wouldn't have been a responsible person to take care of his child, anyway. It just never seemed to happen. Only God knew why, but thank God that was never a part of my story.

The divorce was not civil, and we did not end as friends. I didn't hate him, but I loathed him. Which one was worse, you think? Every chance there was to let him know, I did. I loved him, and he sapped everything from me, because I had given so much of myself and got nothing in return. I didn't know who I had become. Supporting him in everything he wanted to do, but again, getting nothing in return but lies and deceit. And get this, a *Dear John* letter on my coffee table. Who does that? I had only heard about white people doing stupid stuff like this.

Not knowing what to do with my life, I had no clue where to start. Being lost emotionally. Depression found me and kept me low, but I couldn't mope around forever. If nothing else, my ex taught me to never depend on a man for emotional, spiritual, or financial stability, which should be the things I should be able to depend on as a wife. The medical field was far out of my reach and there were no career plans.

I had quit school and vowed never to go back. Ruling all Military Services out, I didn't want to become *all I could be.* Therefore, I did the next best thing. I filled out an application for the Los Angeles Police Department. Initially, I don't know why I went the route to Law Enforcement. Watching police shows like Adam 12, Columbo and courtroom drama like Perry Mason and entertaining shows like Night Court gave me little perspective. It was a noble profession, but I didn't know what it would be like as a woman cop. Especially now, with the LAPD under scrutiny all the time.

Everyone in my family, including the dog, thought I was crazy. They were telling me I needed therapy, mental health rehabilitation, and I was going through a psychosomatic breakdown because of the divorce. I mean, what was psychosomatic, anyway? It sounded like some disease you can never get rid of. If so, I was just as crazy as the rest of them.

They didn't like the idea so much, but they supported my decision. Hell, my dad was military and so were two of my brothers—so why not a Police Officer? My parents knew, when my mind focused on something, there was no stopping me, which is how I got married to Cornelius. I felt as long as I had my family and friends who cared about me, I could manage and be anything. My Ex thought I was doing it to have a badge, a gun, and the authority to shoot him and get away with it. He was always entertaining, and it was the only time he was funny. Although, I have to admit, often he was my inspiration to become a cop to better myself and to keep him in fear. After the divorce was final, the determination to do what I wanted for a change and complete what I started was beyond compelling. I had to take care of myself because no one else was going to.

Not understanding what to expect during this transition of my story, I started researching what to do to become a police officer. Surprising to find they do a Preliminary Background Investigation, the Job Preview Questionnaire, and the Personal Qualification Essay Written Test before you can even take to the Physical Abilities Test. You must go through the (Tell me your whole life and leave nothing out, so help you God!) Preliminary Investigative Questionnaire, the Background Investigation, and the Polygraph Exam.

The Background Investigation could take up to 180 days. A Panel Interview, Medical and Psychological Evaluation, and if everything checks out, I'd get certified and appointed to a class. So many activities to become a police officer. There was no alternative route to take but the road others traveled before me to even start the training at the Academy. The Preliminary Background check was the first step, which I finished within a matter of minutes on the computer.

After completing the preliminary stuff to move forward to take the written test, I selected a place and time to take it, which included, having to pass this exam to get to the Physical Abilities Test (PAT) and do the Preliminary Investigative Questionnaire (PIQ). My nerves remained calm until the test date, at which point I packed my good luck bear in my purse. I needed a lot of it that day. Oh! You practice, but how often do the test questions compare to the sample test?

~

The exam instructor came into the room. It was more of what I saw on the other women's faces that caught my eye and suddenly I shifted my gaze to the specimen standing in front of us. Johnny Gill's song, "My, my, my, my, and my," played softly in my head as I gazed at him, thinking, *'He's very handsome and has a nice body.'* He looked to be about 6'3" or

6'4"', medium muscular build, olive complexion and had the most gorgeous hazel-green eyes you would ever want to see on a masculine specimen. You could see his form fitting, black uniform shirt, which didn't hide the muscles in his biceps and forearms. The uniform fit him perfectly in every area.

I had to describe him to you. Yes, the ladies were drooling at the eye-candy. I shook it off, put my head down and lingered in my flash of temporary therapy of sorts, because I needed this. I needed to pass this test. Yes, I was talking to myself and answered, maybe I did need therapy or an exorcism. I couldn't allow the distraction.

"My name is Sgt. Taylor, your exam instructor this morning. I will watch each of you like a hawk." Motioning with his fingers from his eyes to us. Everyone laughs. I thought, *'He could watch me anytime.'* His voice was serious, but his unserious face made the tension go away. All five women out of twenty-five potential candidates in the class were overjoyed to see such a handsome man. If I didn't pass, it was enough just to see him in person. The guys squirmed in their seats, intimidated by his charming, good looks, but they seemed to chuckle at his humor.

Sgt. Taylor continued. "This exam looks at three aspects of your skills: written communication, judgement and decision-making, and behavioral flexibility. This test will decide your ranking and if you get to the next steps, the Physical Abilities Test, and the other steps after, congratulations. You do not have to stay after your exam is complete this morning. You will receive your test scores in the mail. If you pass, you will then get the information to proceed to the next step, which takes place within the next two weeks. I wish every one of you luck, because you will need it. You have ninety minutes to complete your questions and essays. Just a warning, I will disqualify you, if you go past the ninety minutes or talk amongst yourselves during the test. So, please no talking and when the time is complete, please stop," he states.

Under that tough exterior, there was a real sensitive man in there. I just knew it. As all women who have gone through a divorce, not of their own doing, questions what we did for the man to go astray. What will another man see in me that my ex-husband couldn't or didn't see? It had been a year since my divorce was final. I guess my hormones were screaming, 'Do something about this,' and then the doubting questions about reality hit me. Will I ever find the right man, and/or will he ever find me? The vast majority of my daydreaming time was to be on a secluded island with Denzel, Brad, or Idris. I had dated no one in over a year.

We went through the formalities of filling out our names and whatever else they asked us to fill out. "You may begin." Sgt. Taylor said. Snapping back to reality from my inner self-interrogation and examination of my self-worth. I was more relaxed and assured. All I could do was my best. I hadn't completely lost my confidence. I just had a good feeling about the decision I was making. Win or lose, this was something I felt compelled to do, and it was about me now.

An hour and thirty minutes later, "Please stop. You may turn your essay sheets into Officer Briggs. Raise your hand, Officer Briggs." Officer Briggs raised his hand without even looking toward us. His only job was to make sure no one cheated, but he never moved from his seat or looked up to check. I assumed Sgt. Taylor said nothing, since Officer Briggs was less than a month away from retirement. Flyers posted everywhere stated he was retiring after 33 years in the police department.

The last to leave, I stood in the hallway, looking at the glass and brass case of officers killed in the line of duty, finding their youth more disturbing than their deaths. Death was a part of it, unfortunately. It was a vicious cycle, and I was hoping to be that agent of change. "Well, if I go, I at least want to die trying to help someone instead of doing the unthinkable."

Becoming a criminal was not in my nature. I never wanted to go to jail for any reason, not even for a misdemeanor. I lingered around the building and wondered whether this was it or if I at least would have another chance to prove I could follow through. My ambitions weren't very high. I wanted a stable career that was challenging. I have watched Miami Vice, Law & Order, and every other cop show I could watch. It intrigued me, but I never thought it would be me. Although, not understanding what was in store for me if I passed, the thought of succeeding was my number one inspiration to rub it in my ex's face and plant the thought in his head I was stalking him.

Standing at the elevator, I looked up to see Sgt. Taylor coming toward me. It was as if he was walking in slow motion. He stood next to me. "Your Sayers, aren't you? Brenda Sayers?" Looking him dead in his big hazel-green eyes, "Yes." I wasn't trying to be so obvious. "I read some of your answers and they're very well thought out."

"Why thank you. That means a lot."

"I won't be scoring your essays, but you should get something in the mail. No guarantees, though." Flexing his muscles as he's shuffling paperwork from arm to arm. It hurt not to stare, but I endured the pain and then I noticed, "Are you going down as well? The reason I asked is that neither of us pushed the button to go up or down."

"Yes, I have to drop off this paperwork." He then pushes the button going down. We both got in the elevator together and were alone. The doors close. I stood straight and leaned up against the elevator wall with my eyes closed. "Here is my card if you have questions about the test or the next steps. Any tips or pointers I can help with, you just call me." Noticing it was a number on the other side, seeing the initials Sgt. B.T. I screamed in my head, '*No! This cannot be what I think it is? Yes, maybe it is. All you have to do is ask.*' So, I clarified, "Excuse me Sgt. Taylor, the number on the back of this card is your personal number? And this is the number I am to use when I want to ask about anything or get a tip as needed. Do you do this for all the ladies?" He had a smile on his face, as big as a clown. "Oh! Ms. Sayers, only women receive my number to get help and tips and such. And since you assume I do my job to get the ladies, I might have to rethink my decision about providing that help. I will forgo my hurt feelings and continue with my quest to help you in any way I can, if you would like." He leans in towards me. "If you so choose, you can keep the phone number. If not, you can throw it away. I will admit my interest level is high nineties. I can't officially date you until you leave the Academy, but we can be friends and hang out until then." Oh, he was bold and smooth, and just came out with it. Standing there saying nothing and biting on my lip. We reach the bottom floor, get out, and stand there like we were some fifteen-year-old love-struck kids. It was as if I could not move my lips, and then I realized what was there to lose, so I quickly blurted out, "I will keep it!"

Another Training Officer found Sgt. Taylor standing with me in the lobby, "Sgt. Taylor, I need you to sign some forms for the next class." He kept his eyes on me the whole time. "Leave them in my office and I will drop them off to you on my way out." He said to the other officer while he continued to stare at me. I turned to look at the officer. He seemed weird, like he was in outer space or he had been pushing paperwork too long. Turning back to Sgt. Taylor, he had all my attention and interest again and he never took his eyes off of me once.

"I apologize for expressing my assumptions. It was wrong of me." I said.

"Would you go out to dinner with me tonight as a friend? Around seven thirty, if that's all right with you?" He smiled again.

There was no hesitation in my response. "That's fine. See you then." As I walked away, he says, "Oh! Sorry Sayers." I started laughing. "You can call me Brenda since you're paying for dinner." He seemed to giggle like a big ole manly man. "Instead of writing your address, would you call the number and leave it on my answering machine at home? Little papers don't seem to stay with me long." Speaking softly. "No problem. I'll call when I get home." I turned and walked away. As I looked back, he was watching me leave. "Okay, I'll see you tonight," he said. My hormones raged as I exited the building. Was I dreaming? Did that gorgeous man just ask me out as a friend?' Was I being naïve? Did I sound immature? Was I unaware of who I was and what I looked like? Did my self-esteem fly out the window with my ex-husband? What does he see in me? I don't see myself. The thought crossed my mind that maybe I don't know who I am. What am I going to wear? What was I doing? I just met this man ninety minutes ago. We've not talked on the phone, and I am going out to dinner with him. I am too trusting. What are you raging on about? You met him in person. What better way than this? Stupid!

 *You know good-and-well, I couldn't wait to get home and call his answering service. I didn't know the ends and outs of dating an officer back then. I was a newbie.*

Chapter 2

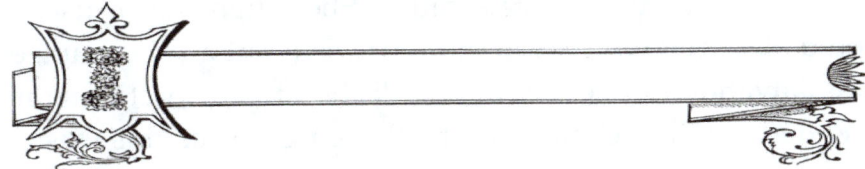

I Digress A Bit

My parents were sitting in the living room when I arrived home. My dad was reading the newspaper with his bifocals hanging off the tip of his nose and my mom was watching television. Walking into my room, I put my bags down and came back to the living room. "I completed my written exam and now it's just a waiting game." They got up from their recliners and hugged me, seeming happier than I was. Gazing at them, my initial thought was they'd try to stop me from going through with it. Instead, they encouraged me to follow my heart's desire. Living with my parents was not the ideal situation I wanted for myself. Since the divorce, it was mutual that I come back home to get myself together and my thought was to help them. A comfort for all of us. They were self-sufficient and took good care of themselves, but they were getting up there in age and I didn't mind me being around for a while. I felt like, after all the times, they had to hear me complain about my life. I owed them something more than sitting around the house wallowing in self-pity. Owing them, my love. Making it clear, it wouldn't be forever.

My mother followed behind me as I trekked to my room to figure out what to wear for the evening. She gave me an enormous hug. "You're growing up. You're not my little baby anymore." I could only hope she realized that long ago. I hadn't been her little baby for a long time now. She was a God-fearing woman. Saved, sanctified, and filled with the Holy Spirit, as Pentecostals call it. She taught all of us we could always go to God in times of need, but all she wanted was salvation for her children. All the kids respected mom and dad for their choices in life. Bringing up six kids wasn't easy, but they taught us well. Respecting one another was big in my family and to always love hard, even your enemies. Do you know how hard that is? To love someone who you can give everything to and get nothing but heartache in return. Sacrifice who you are, only to see the fruits of your labor given to another woman. To understand you did nothing wrong and everything wrong at the same time.

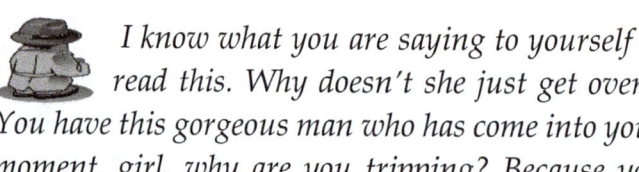 *I know what you are saying to yourself right now as you read this. Why doesn't she just get over the Ex already? You have this gorgeous man who has come into your life. Live in the moment, girl, why are you tripping? Because you know how we girls do. We mess everything up with our own hangups and then want to blame everybody else. And I wanted to stay mad at my ex for as long as I could. I didn't want happiness. I wanted to give my ex-hell, by giving him all the power of my sanity. Okay, okay, I got it, don't you get it too? You've given him or her the power way too long. The power is now in your hands to forgive and move on from what he or she did. The power to move forward with your life is exonerating, because he or she is no longer important enough for you to care. Your Ex should be no more of your concern nor a factor in any of your conversations, unless you are giving your testimony, not gossip. Even if you have children together. He or she has moved on and so should you! I digressed a bit. I'm back on track.*

My mother could read me like a book. Sometimes she would know things I hadn't told her. Sometimes it was scary, and I didn't want to talk to her about it. At one point, we believed God was talking straight to my mom about the things going on in her children's lives. There was no other way to explain it. "Your smile has changed, and I don't think it's because of the test. So, what is it?" As much as I hated her gift of foreknowledge, I kissed her on her cheek and told her, "You know too much. I love everything about you, but sometimes you freak me out, mom. It doesn't matter, anyway. I have a dinner date tonight with a very handsome man. He is picking me up at seven-thirty. Tell daddy to be on his best behavior. You know how he gets when unfamiliar people come around."

"I'll tell him, but you know it will not do any good," my mom said.

"I know, but it doesn't hurt to try."

"He's so full of the devil sometimes, you would think he's never stepped foot into a church before."

"Mom, not that I believe daddy has the devil in him, but some the of those devils are sitting in the pews and preaching in the pulpit right now."

"I understand, honey, but this is an individual walk. You can't base your belief in the people who claim to be walking with the Lord. The Word of God says in Matthew 7: 15-16, *'Beware of false prophets, who come to you in sheep's clothing, but inwardly they are ravenous wolves. You will know them by the fruit they bear.'* (NKJV) Everyone has a choice to make in life: to be a follower of Christ or a follower of sin."

I'd tell her all the time that my dad and the rest of us would be okay. She was still worried about us and our souls. My parents loved each other no matter what happened between them. You could still see the passion that brought them together so many years ago. My wish in the love department was to be like them. Their life had been full, one of excitement and freedom in each other. They had six children, but that didn't stop them from enjoying life, whether by themselves or with each other. Many days, we would camp out in the backyard or make an adventure of going to the grocery store. We loved listening to stories of our ancestors and history, and my father would take our imaginations to those places as though we were there. Some were of glad times and of horrifying tales of deceit and murder. We never doubted the stories my father told us, because he would have our great-grandmother, Nidessa, to confirm what he was telling us when she was alive. The only great-grandma I knew was born in 1899 and just missed being a slave.

My dad is six feet. A good-looking man with salt and pepper hair. My dad had been a functioning alcoholic in his past years. One day deciding to go cold turkey, to never pick up another drink again. I never knew him in his states of drunkenness as I was too young. My mom was beautiful inside and out with her caramel-colored skin and hourglass shape, with long stringy hair like a Native Indian. My mother devoted herself to my father, but she tolerated no nonsense from him or anyone else.

"Is he a nice and respectable man?" My mother continued with her interrogation.

"He's a Police Officer."

Margaret just smiled. I then reminded her when she asked me the same question about my ex-husband when I first met him. She just laughed and went out of the room. I had nothing new to wear except a beautiful dress my mother bought me just in case I went to church with her one day.

Grown up in church all my life, we had to go whether we wanted to. My mom kept us in Sunshine Band, Sunday school, and regular morning service and would go back in the evening for YPWW or revivals. We were full of church and even a member of a gospel group with my cousins. We were footloose and fancy-free back then, but boy how time flies when you are having fun.

Calling Brandon, I left a voice message on his machine. Getting his number to his home was an excellent sign of two things. One, no wife, and two, no live-in girlfriend. At least that was a positive start to me.

Awaiting his arrival, he rang the doorbell at seven-thirty. Either he was a stickler for being on time or he was trying to impress me. I thought it was a wonderful thing. I had been ready for an hour myself. My parents were standing there with fixed grins on their faces. Smiling from ear-to-ear and nothing I said made them stop grinning that way. I opened the door and invited him in to meet my parents. Introducing him to my parents like a respectful daughter, an afternoon delight for my father. I was leery of my dad meeting someone new, but they seemed to hit it off. I expressed we had better go before my father started telling his jokes or one of his lengthy stories. He agreed, and we walked out to his car and he gave me the nicest compliment.

"You look great."

 Okay, I hadn't heard a compliment in a long time.

"Thank you very much." Grinning. Then I thought, *'He could have said I looked beautiful, instead of you looking great.'* I don't know why, I guess I always have to mess up the moment in my head. Just forget what I said before. Closing my door, I could see the looks were there and his body was not too much for me to handle. He was tall, and all I wanted in the physical aspect of a future mate, masculine. He was a gentleman. Despite that, I was skeptical after being with a lying, cheating, no good-for-nothing ex-husband. It was early in the game. This guy might be too good to be true. I reverted to my being too harsh. I didn't even know him, and I was judging him already. He had to have a flaw somewhere and I will not mention what kind of car he drives, because that would seem shallow — Porsche. I sat back as we took off for our destination. Talking more than any two people should on a first date. Let me clarify. I talked, and he listened and chimed in the brief moments he had something to say. I didn't want to have any awkward, silent moments. "Where are we going?" Wanting to know. "To the hills." I guess wanting it to be a surprise. He told me the name of the restaurant before we got there. It was a Japanese Cuisine on top of a hill.

You could look down and see the sparkling array of shimmering lights throughout the city. I stood by the car, looking at the view. He came over to my side and stood staring at me as I stared at the sparkle. I turned to him and he took my hand and led me to the door. We waited for our table. He looked down at our hands together but said nothing. As the hostess said our table was ready, he grabbed my hand and put his other hand in the small of my back and led me to our seat. Oh, my goodness.

 *Oh yeah! He was into me. I just let him lead me like a puppy on a leash.*

Seated at a table with a window, seeing the lights again. The view was magnificent. "This is an exquisite place. How did you know about this place and I didn't? I've lived here all my life." He was playing it calm, cool, and collected. He smiled. "Because you seem like a salad bar kind of woman. You are someone who's not afraid to go to a fast-food restaurant and sneak food in at the drive-in."

 *The drive in…!! Okay ladies and gents, he must not have been on a date to the movies in a long while. A long, long while.*

I didn't want to turn the evening into my hangups, but I said, "I don't know if I should take that as a compliment or not?" He took my hand, and I started blushing. He looks up at me. "I meant it as a compliment. You are an exquisite woman who's not afraid of hard work." He pulled back from me then. "If you had objections, you wouldn't be pursuing a career in law enforcement. From what I have seen so far, you are very intelligent and I'm sure you'll score high. Mine were decent, 10th in my class, so you should be very proud of yourself. Intelligence and beauty run through those veins." He sat back. Good comeback was all I could say in my head. "Thank you for your kind words of encouragement." I said, unable to think of nothing else, but thank goodness, our server came to take our order. I imagined jumping in his arms like a ferocious lion or tackling him like a car crash dummy, showing him what I was made of. Willing to break the rules for a quick, hot second. I hadn't got into the Academy yet. Having a brief conversation while eating, he commented on the fact I wasn't a nibbler.

My thoughts wondered after the comment. Because most guys say they want a woman to eat when they take them out to dinner. But they don't want to deal with the bulge of consequence. Let's get it together men, don't you know by now, you can't have it both ways, unless the women are doing both eating healthy and working out, and if not, you deal with it and don't bash them for it.

Now, before I go any further, no, this is not a story about bashing men. On the contrary, I love men and I respect, honor, and look forward to meeting all kinds. I just know there are men out there not worthy of my breath and women who act like petty girls. I will only discuss the men who have come across my path. The good, the bad and the ugly.

"No, I don't nibble. I eat, but I work out to keep my weight down." I said.

"That's good. It should help with the Physical Abilities Test. If you pass, you're halfway done," he stated.

To unofficially date again was exciting. He was far from what I previously married and dated. It went well, better than I had hoped or even expected. At least for now, off with the suspicions he was a serial killer, I didn't want to get my hopes up too high either. I wasn't down on love. I just didn't want to get hurt again and plummet.

~

He took me to the Redondo Beach Pier, winning a stuffed animal for me was his goal. He gave me a friendly peck on the cheek and kissed my hand.

~

Arriving home, he walked me to the door. The perfect gentleman, asking if he could kiss me goodnight. I propped my giant bear on the door. Of course, I said, yes. Should I even tell you about the kiss? Okay, I will. Oh, man! The kiss was all I expected it to be. Savory, sensual, like a medium rare steak and a loaded baked potato. And guess what, his breath didn't stink. Some men just do not know how to kiss, but I couldn't say that about Brandon. He pulled away because I wasn't. I had to keep my composure. Every part of me was screaming in silence. I couldn't let him know how exceptional he was in the kissing department. Also, I didn't want him to think it wasn't nice either, so I told him it was very, very, very nice. He smiled and stepped back towards the edge of the porch stairs.

"Is it okay if I call you tomorrow when I get off from work?"

"You may."

He walks closer to me. "Sorry, I didn't ask before, but I don't have your telephone number."

I invited him in to give him the number. He stood by the door, waiting for me to return. Coming from my bedroom, he didn't take his eyes off of me and I asked for his wallet. He surprised me when he gave it to me so easily. "I'm putting this in your wallet, so you won't lose it. And just to make sure, I will call your answering machine and your work number and leave it on there, too." If I sounded desperate, no, I wasn't, but I wanted to make sure he knew I was interested!

"Thank you for a wonderful date and I will call you tomorrow." He kissed me on the cheek again and stole a peck on the lips and then walked out the door. He reminded me of Idris Elba without the accent. Watching him was like seeing Denzel walk. I stood there on the porch, in the dark until he drove off. "Wow!" My heart was pounding, so I knew I needed to go take a cold shower and then go to bed.

Chapter 3

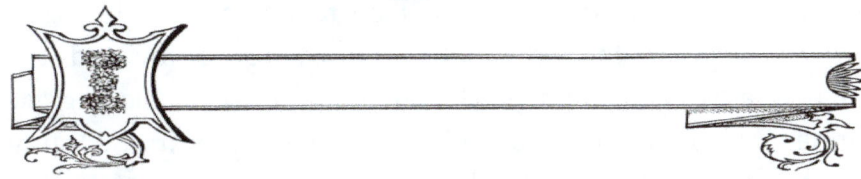

Revenge Through Me

Brandon and I went on several dates within a two-month period. He called me before leaving work. He invited me over for dinner, having something to discuss with me. My intrigue gave way to self-destruction, questioning everything he said.

~

Arriving there around six o'clock, I played it cool and collected. Upon him opening the door, I said, "Hello there." He greeted me in an apron and with a pleasant kiss. His lips were full and sensuous and tasted like Chicken Fettuccini. I followed behind him towards the smell of food where he was preparing dinner.

"Thank you for coming." He was stirring a pot of what, I didn't know, twisting his head towards my way, looking for an answer.

"Why did you think I wouldn't show up?"

"To be honest, I was feeling stupid about the whole talk and should have been upfront about it. Plus, I sounded really serious over the phone and I didn't know if I scared you off."

"To be honest, curiosity took over. I am a straightforward person. I know what heavy conversations are like and I don't scare off that easily."

He was relieved to hear me speak freely. What he had to say to me was really important. He seemed a little apprehensive, shy, or uncomfortable. This was my first time coming to his place, and I felt free to be me. I still didn't explore beyond the bathroom, the living room, and the kitchen, and I didn't dare go near the bedrooms. Placing the dinner into the oven, he asked me to have a seat in the living room. I sat wondering what he had to discuss with me. Sitting next to me on the couch, he took my hand.

"Two months ago, we had a wonderful date and our mini dates in between have been outstanding, and I hope there will be more to come."

"Me too! It's been a while since I had such a good time."

"I know we've talked a lot and we both have had discussions about our ex's, but there is something I did not mention, and you did not ask about it either." I mean, he's fidgeting like he's about to have a panic attack. Caressing his hand seemed to calm him a little. "Honestly, I'm not sure if this is going to be a deal breaker for you. Now, I didn't mention this on purpose until I knew for sure we at least liked each other enough to continue dating. I know we've had some incredible dates, but I feel there is something meaningful between us, and I hope you feel the same way."

"I believe we've had a wonderful time together, and I hope there is more to come. So, what is it you want to say?"

He stood up and just blurted it out, "I HAVE A DAUGHTER!"

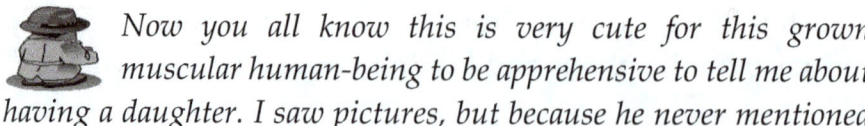 *Now you all know this is very cute for this grown muscular human-being to be apprehensive to tell me about having a daughter. I saw pictures, but because he never mentioned*

a daughter, I didn't pry. Yes, it's rare for a woman to do so, I must say, but it's true. I am not the prying type, because I don't want anyone prying into my life, unless I give them access to ask. I don't know, I just couldn't help myself. At first, I started giggling, and then it turned into a chuckle.

Taylor stood there with his mouth-hung open. I don't think he could believe I was laughing at him. I got up from the couch, gave him a big hug, and told him I was leaving and never coming back. All he could say was, "What?" Some of his veins were popping out, so I had to relieve his pressure. I turned around. "I'm just kidding." Then I gave him the best kiss he had ever had in his entire life, and he responded rather nicely. It seemed like the next few minutes, we were in our own little world and it was getting hot, until we smelled something burning. "My dinner is burning." Taylor ran to the kitchen and pulled the pan out of the oven that was boiling over with cheese sauce. A few minutes later, "Well, it's not burned too badly. It's at least edible."

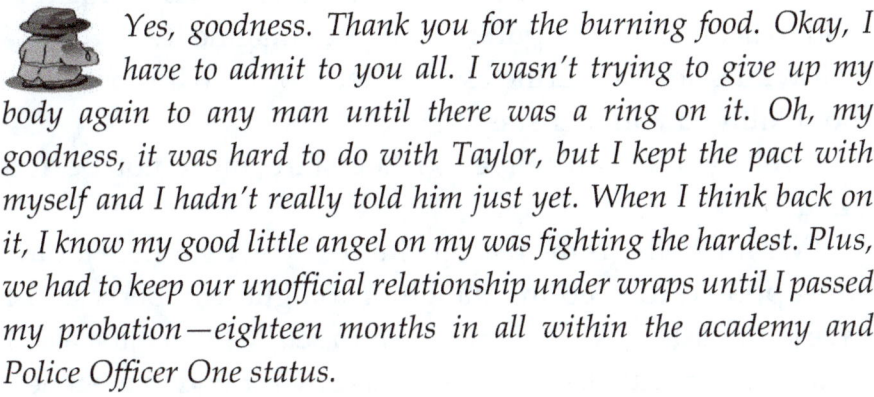 *Yes, goodness. Thank you for the burning food. Okay, I have to admit to you all. I wasn't trying to give up my body again to any man until there was a ring on it. Oh, my goodness, it was hard to do with Taylor, but I kept the pact with myself and I hadn't really told him just yet. When I think back on it, I know my good little angel on my was fighting the hardest. Plus, we had to keep our unofficial relationship under wraps until I passed my probation—eighteen months in all within the academy and Police Officer One status.*

While he was scooping out the good part, I asked him how old his daughter was and how did she react to his other dates? "She's a troublesome four. Time has flown so quickly. It seems like it was just yesterday I held her in my arms for the first time."

However, he reassured me she was as sweet as could be. I know I had heard that from many parents and it was not always the case. This whole conversation reminded me of a little girl who came in a store where I was working. I was nineteen at the time and worked at the Westside Pavilion, Cook's Work's and we sold gourmet coffee and high-end cookware items. This mother came in to buy some gourmet coffee beans and the daughter begged for things in the store. It didn't matter what it was, a Gourd, a kitchen utensil or whether she even knew what the item was, the little girl wanted it and she wasn't taking no for an answer. The mother politely said, "No." The little girl fell on the floor and started screaming I hate you to her mother. It took every part of me to keep from grabbing her. I wanted to spank her silly, despite her pink frilly dress. It was my Aunt Mable moment. She would throw a shoe with bullet accuracy. The mother just kept saying, "No, no, don't do that." Then I wanted to strangle the mother with my bare hands and ask her what in the hell was wrong with her and why is she was allowing this child to act this way in public. Can you imagine it?

Taylor said, "Nevertheless, it's her mother who could just about kill you with her stare."

"Well, you're still alive, so her stare must not be too lethal."

"My little bitty is the reason I invited you over here today. I'm supposed to keep my daughter tonight. Kimberly and I have joint custody. So, when I want to see Ashley, I just ask. I thought this would be a good time as any for you to meet her. Perhaps I'm rushing things. I wanted everything to be out in the open. I don't like to keep secrets. Keeping secrets can get you in more trouble than they are worth."

 *Boy, did I learn that lesson the hard way. Anyway, I wasn't sure if he was rushing things or not. I didn't have any children of my own, so I didn't know whether it was right or wrong for someone to introduce the person their dating so soon to their children. I mean, he had been to my home and met my parents. He knew I wasn't a serial killer, and I was at least stable in the head. Was he rushing it after only dating for two months—who knows? He felt the need for me to meet his daughter and I was fine with it. Maybe he knew exactly what he wanted out of life and included me.*

"Everything is fine, and I would love to meet Ashley, but are you sure she will be up to meeting someone new in her father's life?" I walked up behind him and hugged him from behind to reassure him I was good with it.

"There shouldn't be a problem. She's four, but very intuitive."

"Kids love me anyway, even more than their daddies. Mommies, you can never replace."

"Well, I'm so glad you feel so confident. I definitely want you to be confident when Kimberly gets here. She intimidated my last girlfriend. That's why I'm single right now."

"You don't have to worry about intimidation. I've gone a round or two with the best of them. Growing up with three older brothers, you learn what intimidation is all about."

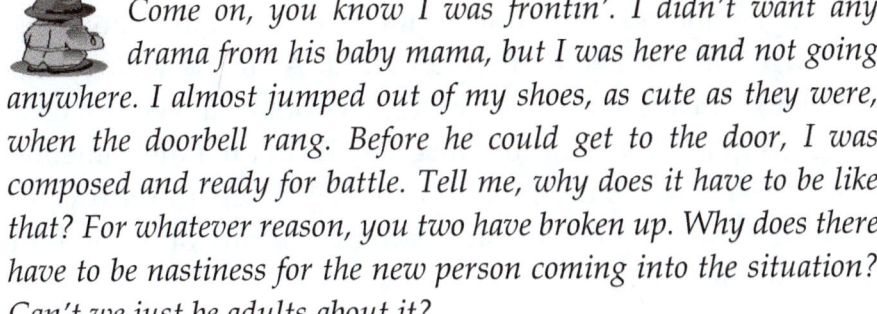 *Come on, you know I was frontin'. I didn't want any drama from his baby mama, but I was here and not going anywhere. I almost jumped out of my shoes, as cute as they were, when the doorbell rang. Before he could get to the door, I was composed and ready for battle. Tell me, why does it have to be like that? For whatever reason, you two have broken up. Why does there have to be nastiness for the new person coming into the situation? Can't we just be adults about it?*

All I could hear was this little voice saying, "Daddy, daddy." This beautiful little girl jumped into his arms and gave him a big hug and kiss. Her jeans and shirt were girlie cute and thankfully, so was her hair. "Thank you so much for the love. Come in Kimberly." It was as if she walked in—in slow motion. I had been seeing this too much lately, and I didn't like it.

"Guess what? I have someone I want you to meet."

"Who do you want me to meet?" She turns her head toward me.

"Ashley, I want you to meet my friend, Brenda." She looked at me, smiled, and said, "Hi, Brenda." She stuck her hand out to shake mine, and I obliged rather quickly, and then she stuck her head into his chest. "Why don't you go and see what I bought new for your room? It's on the pillow." Brandon put her down. She said, "Okay." She ran to her room.

For his ex, it seemed like he wasted no time. "Kimberly, this is Brenda. Brenda this is Kimberly." I just knew right away we wouldn't hit it off. Despite her supermodel looks, she revealed her ugliness the moment she saw me. I said, "Hello," and stuck out my hand to be polite. I had nothing against her. She was no longer a factor in his life, other than being Ashley's mother. She backed out of the door as if I had the plague and told Brandon, "I'll talk to you later." Pointing her finger at him like he was her child. As if she were going to talk to him about this later and it will not be a pleasant chat when we talk about this, because you didn't tell me someone would be here kind of talk. You could see the scowl of disappointment in her twisted face as she probably thought he would be alone.

 *See, I knew what she thought. She thought she could come over all sexy and get back into his life.*

More than anything, if she could have taken Ashley out of the door after she knew I was there, she would have in a hot second. I had to show my lack of intimidation. So, I went to the door and asked her if I knew her from somewhere. Of course, there was no response, so I asked what time she was expecting Ashley home tomorrow. Brandon and I would drop her off together. Once again, there was no response, so I said, "Bye."

 *You let me know, maybe it was wrong of me to say, but I wanted to prove to myself I could handle a family man and whatever family came along with him, because I would want the same type of man myself. I wouldn't want a man intimidated by my ex. That's right, stand up for what's yours—within reason. Don't stand up for him if he's a criminal and has done bad things to people! That's not nice.*

Veins were popping, and you could have melted a popsicle on her forehead, but I gave her a big smile. Walking into the house like I owned it and shutting the door before she could get into her car. I leaned up against the door when I closed it. I glanced over at him. Brandon was giggling under his breath, while looking out the window. I guess vengeance is sometimes sweet. "She finally met her match, and she can't take it. Wow, that was great!" I threw a pillow at his head. He caught it, of course. "Well, I am generally not the type of person who loves confrontation, but sometimes you have to be bold." I smiled because Brandon was really enjoying the moment. I would find out later why he loved her and despised her at the same time. There was no need to dim the lights for him right now in his moment of triumph through me. I was pretty sure, by his reaction she deserved it. Or was he being petty.

His home was beautiful and very cozy. It looked as if a man lived alone, and the décor was rather earthy. Scattering between the kitchen and the living room, I went into the bedroom where Ashley was playing. I started playing with her while Brandon finished scraping off the dishes. Ashley and I got along great, but I guess having thirteen nieces and nephews helped some. I don't think Brandon expected it either. He didn't think I noticed him spying on us, but I did.

Brandon loved his daughter more than anything in the world. You could just feel the love in his voice when he talked about her. He would do anything for her, even leave fieldwork to train new officers, to spend more time with Ashley. It wasn't a decision that was hard for him to make. I just wondered. Would it be hard for him if things got serious between us? To accept the fact, I would be out there on the streets. That was a concern of mine. Of course, it would be a concern if I were seeing anyone. I had to trust my gut and move forward. I had been stuck going backwards. This would be a new chapter. I was looking forward to something finally good coming out of a decision I made. I had to gain my trust back, which was hard to swallow.

After playing with Ashley, I put her to bed and she fell asleep. I found Mr. Taylor napping on the couch with the television watching him. He trusted me with Ashley, which meant a lot. I didn't want to wake him, so I left him a note and snuck out quietly.

Chapter 4

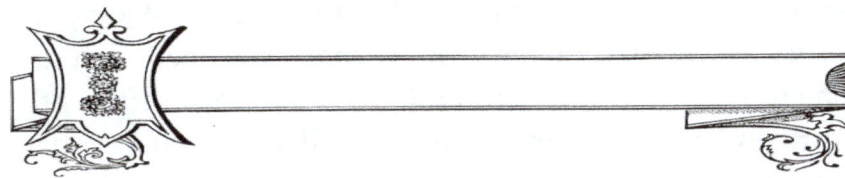

Training Days

 *I forgot to tell you what I had to go through for the Physical Abilities Test.*

Brandon gave me a few pointers, so I took the test and passed. The instructor was blunt and straight to the point. Just the way I like it, at least at first. "Ladies and gentlemen, this is an example of what your training will be like for the next six months at the academy. Thereafter, your training will be in the field for a year. If you think you did well today, then think again. We pride ourselves on having officers in tiptop shape, except for the ones who sit at a desk and eat donuts all day."

Wow, that was a cold shot against his fellow police officers. I think about it now, yeah, there were some who ate donuts on the beat, but it was only because the donut shops were friendly to officers and would give out donuts and coffee when they wanted to—it wasn't always free either and it wasn't all the time—I got a few in my day.

"Believe you, me, by the time we are through with you, you will wish you had never passed the written and the oral exam. Once you leave, training your body is up to you. Just ask Officer Shivers here. This is Friday, so you have a few weeks to think about your career in law enforcement. I want you to think about this long and hard and decide whether this is the career you are ready for. Every day, you are out on the street, putting your lives on the line for those who want to kill you and for those who support you. We do not need Rambo's, Rocky's, Supermen or Wonder Woman. We need men and women who will go out and do their jobs, efficiently, effectively, and correctly. Like I said, if I see you in a two-months' time, expect to work. This is not a game, and it is not an adventure—this is real life. Some of you will not make it through training. For those who make it, I pray you have made the right choice. You're dismissed."

That was the worst garbage I'd endured in life, except for the B.S. my ex-husband gave out every time he came home late. If we didn't know what we were getting into, I don't think any of us would be here. Although, he made some valid points, the other stuff was third grade. Trust me, the talks got better.

~

I did not see Brandon until the next morning. He surprised me by taking me to an early bird breakfast to celebrate passing. He also confirmed he received the same speech. After he finished his shift, he picked up Ashley to hang out with her. The complete process took a while, but all the other exams and questions were happening pretty quickly, but not fast enough for me. The Background process began. They interviewed my Uncle Benny. I don't know why he told them I was crazy at first, but then took it back and told the truth. They interviewed my father, who gave me rave reviews, and they even went to my High School and spoke to my English Teacher, Mr. Matzner. It wasn't clear why they did a background investigation on me. I had no tickets or criminal history. I guess they really want to know if you are crazy or not. After being on the force as long as I was, I was pretty sure some crazies fell through the cracks, like all other places.

Now, all I had to do was get through the Panel Interview, Polygraph, Medical Examination and Psychological Interview in one piece. Brandon reassured me it was going to be tough, but was confident I would get through it.

"I just want you to be prepared, regarding some attitudes you are going to have to face. You'll hear the truth about the mistreatment of women on the force, even if it's whispered. I work with these guys every day. Of course, you know there are those who think women shouldn't be cops. Their thinking is women should leave this kind of work to men."

"Well, I'm glad you don't think that way."

To be honest with me, he tells me the story of Elizabeth Minor. Unfortunately, he did think that way, until one day, he found himself with a new partner. She was smart. She had what it took to be a cop—guts. He didn't like the idea at first, but when you're assigned a partner, it's in stone. At least back then. He didn't want to transfer because the station was close to his house. Anyway, when he finally gets use to the idea of having a female partner, they get a call. A crazy drug addict barricaded himself in a building, brandishing a gun at the window and yelling at people outside. Taylor and Minor were the primaries at the scene. Waiting for backup, the guy yells and demanding they get him dope out the drug locker, and he needed someone to kill his mother. "Yes, I can laugh about it now, but then it was a very different story," he said, smirking. Elizabeth got on the bullhorn and Taylor called for backup. She started talking to the man—trying to calm him down for the time being. He went crazy and as soon as they saw the gun pointing out the window again, they tried to back up behind the car, but he started shooting and she noticed a red laser light on Brandon's head. She jumps in front of him and pushed him backwards and just as she did, a bullet pierced her in the back. The bullet hit her right between the neckline and the edge of the bulletproof vest. "I thought she was dead. He was still shooting, so I had to ease her off me. I got clear aim for a headshot and took it." He rubbed his head. "To me, it didn't seem real in the moment. I looked, and I didn't think she was breathing, but I felt a pulse."

Another police car pulls up as he was calling for an ambulance. Brandon went back to her and told her not to die. He drove behind her to the hospital. Eight hours passed.

I felt the sincerity of his guilt. He didn't say it, but his body language still personified the uneasiness of his words.

"The bullet ricocheted off her shoulder bone, then hit her spine, paralyzing her, the doctor explained. When she was shot, it ricocheted off of her shoulder bone down to her spine and she will never walk again. I couldn't believe it. My partner paralyzed and then the guilt sets in, because she did it for me and I really didn't want her to be my partner. She saved my life and look what she got for it." To come to his senses, it took a bullet in Elizabeth for him to stop being a chauvinist. Or that only men could be police. "I knew from that day on, I could truly understand what the phrase meant when they say you can't judge a book by its cover. She never once misjudged me as a man, she never disrespected me because I was a cop and her partner. I had and still have more respect for Elizabeth than I do for a quarter of the men on this force. Not all police officers are cut from the same cloth. She took a chance at possibly losing her life for me."

"Do you see her now?"

"No, but I talk to her often. Her parents moved her back to Kansas. She needs daily care and has no family here. All I want you to know is you will have opposition, but just hang in there. You are perfect for this job. Learn, do your job, and have your partners back and you'll be fine. You can't take what you hear as face value. Know who you are as an officer and a woman." He kissed me.

He answered my concern. He knew what it's like out there on the street. The possibility of getting hurt or dying was real. He had to contend with someone worrying about him when he was on the street, so he knew firsthand that we were cops and what that entailed. Now this was the test to see if he could handle the job of loving someone else who was a cop.

~

After five and a half months of testing and interviews, I finally received certification, a class assignment, and selected for training in two weeks.

 *I will not lie. It was hell for the duration of the training, but it got easier each week. My first day, I thought I was going to die. I couldn't even talk without groaning and moaning for the first week. All I could do was cry, laugh, push through it because everyone else would laugh at me and didn't think I would make it through. All that time I had been going to the gym, thinking I was working out and if police training was like this, I was certainly glad I didn't choose to go in the military.*

The training taught me something altogether different, but through it all, Brandon was there for me, giving me encouragement when I just wanted to quit. It was just his ever-glowing smile that made me tell myself not to quit and need of a job. I couldn't live with my parents for the rest of my life, and I would never depend on anyone else again. I made the mistake of going that route once before and I would not make that same mistake again.

Don't get me wrong, do I keep saying that? Well, I don't want you to misunderstand what I'm saying. I loved my ex-husband, probably more than he ever loved me, but I stuck to our marriage because I knew nothing else. But one day he came to me and said he loved me, but he was not in-love with me anymore. He was in-love with someone else. Who was I to stand in the way of true love and happiness.

When we first started the weapons training, it was exciting, but also scary. I had fired my father's .038 and his shotguns while growing up, but these guns were much bigger and much more powerful. I had to go to the range for extra practice once or twice a week.

It was the end of training—six months to be exact and I had finally passed and had finished something for the first time in my adult life, except high school.

~

Graduation day, my mom and dad were there, my sisters and brothers, my aunt, and of course, Brandon and Ashley. I cried so much (inside). I just couldn't believe I had made it through. I knew for sure I couldn't have made it without Brandon by my side.

My parents gave me a surprise party. Brandon and Ashley took me out for ice cream. He brought me home around seven o'clock. We walked in the door and everyone yelled, 'surprise'. I had walked into the kitchen to fix my mom a plate of food and when I came back out, "Attention, attention. Can I have your attention, please?" Brandon was boisterous.

I stopped dead in my tracks. "I would like to make a toast. To one of the newest members of the Police Department, a courageous, smart, caring, and very beautiful woman and to you guys too over there, although you're not women. I say congratulations to you and may you have the best of luck and God's covering in your careers."

"Here, here." Everyone shouted.

We all drank sparkling apple cider. I'm pretty sure it was spiked. It was the first-time Brandon had ever mentioned God. It shocked me a little, but I brushed it off.

 *Don't be shocked by my comment. I was down with God. Church was a significant part of my upbringing. I wasn't going to be a hypocrite, though. Why do we say that? God didn't say come to church after you stop being a hypocrite. He said, "Come as you are." He does the drawing and the changing. Sorry, we can't fix ourselves. I shook it off and I'm certain my mother was saying hallelujah, thank you, Jesus, under her breath.*

"Excuse me, I'm not finished. I would like to say to you Officer Brenda Sayers, I met you over a year ago and it was the best day of my life and I also believe I fell in-love with you after our first date together, but I didn't want to tell you back then. I talked this over with Ashley and she whole-heartedly agrees with me. Officer Brenda Sayers, I want to ask you to become my wife?" All I could do was stand there. My ears started pounding and the background noise faded to nothing. He got down on one knee. "Will you marry me, Brenda?" I didn't even know what I was saying, but "Yes. I will marry you." He pulled out the ring. It was so big and beautiful. If someone had shot me, I wouldn't have felt a thing. I was in awe, and I knew I was *in-love* with him too. Ashley ran to me and I gave her a big bear hug. "You're going to be my new step-mommy, aren't you?" The tears started rolling, finally. "Yes honey, I am. And guess what? We are going to have so much fun."

"Good." She gave me another hug and wiped my face.

 *Okay, okay! Yes, it was a beautiful moment, and I cried. You can get your tissues and then come back and finish reading. What was I feeling at that moment? I knew it was right this time. I didn't have to worry. Brandon would be faithful, and he's*

never given me any reason not to trust him, plus now I had a gun too, so he had better act right. He's a good father and man. Was it too soon, though? Like I said, he knew what he wanted. I was the one with the apprehension, but I would not let him get away—just yet!

As we were taking Ashley home, in the car, all I could do was stare at my hand and say I could not believe it. It was so weird. On the way to Brandon's' house, we passed by this little white chapel. We stopped and looked through the gate. A beautiful garden chapel had greenery everywhere, with white trimming.

I said to Brandon, "This is the place I wanted to get married." He agreed. Finally getting to his house, we just plopped on the couch.

"Here, I bought you a present, and this present is from Ashley and Kimberly."

"Kimberly! Are you kidding me? I thought she couldn't stand me."

"Look at Kimberly like her bark is worse than her bite. She gets jealous easily. I had a discussion with her about things she would say about you to Ashley. I told her Ashley likes you—No! Ashley loves you, and she shouldn't try to make Ashley play favorites." He had also told her he was going to ask me to marry him and Ashley agreed. Kimberly and I had many moments. Each time she saw me, it got easier. She finally understood that I wasn't going anywhere. I think my consistency brought her around a bit. Plus, she knew she didn't intimidate me, and she didn't want Ashley to be hurt by her feelings. If nothing else, her love for Ashley was beyond compare. "So, you can take this present as a peace offering and my present you can take as a love offering." He put my legs across his and handed me a blue velvet box that was so pretty. In it was a silver and gold antique bracelet. The inscription said, "To my Favorite Number Two Cop. Congratulations, Love Ashley. This is beautiful. I'll have to thank them in the morning."

Believe it or not, that was the first time we had ever been together physically—it was wonderful. It was as if we were in total sync with each other and together for years. It was all I expected it to be, just plain love, and I definitely did not want it to end. I cried with tears of joy, because I really didn't know it could be like this, but in the back of mind, I didn't want it to turn out like the last time.

I told you he had to put a ring on it. You all thought I was playing games. On the real, too many times I gave myself to men with nothing but a heartache in return. It wasn't just a ring, but it had to be real with both of us. No games, no secrets, no doubting in my mind—he was the one. This was the first time I was absolutely sure of the man he was and my reasonable and non-negotiable expectations—he met.

We had both agreed we didn't want to get married right away. There were no doubts we loved each other. In our hearts, we just knew from experience, rushing was not the way to go. I wanted to get a little more established in my career and he didn't want to do it right away, so Ashley could really get adjusted to everything. Even Kimberly and I started becoming friends. We had the pleasure of going out on some double dates and having dinner together at home. She was finally moving on with her life and we were happy about that.

Yes, the gorgeous lady even became my friend. You are all so messy. Just because you are gorgeous on the outside, doesn't mean you don't have problems. All she needed was a good girlfriend to tell her the truth about herself and I was just that friend, really.

Chapter 5

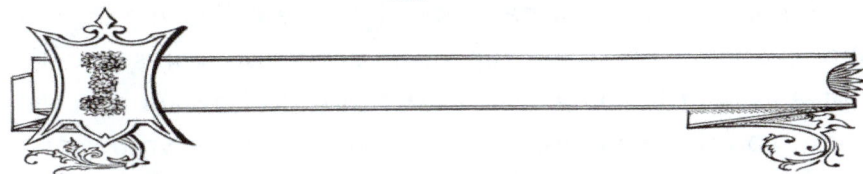

Partner from Hell

After graduation, we had more training to do, but eventually, we got around to getting assigned to our Field Training Officers (FTO). As a P2 straight out of the Academy, you have to worker with a Senior Officer and Mike Farrell was his name. He was the clown of the Van Nuys Station and they stuck me with him. In his early thirties, he had been on the force for twelve years. He was arrogant, pig headed and funny all in one. And this was my first impression of him. I knew he had major issues and it wouldn't take me long to find out what. His carrot top crew cut seemed out of place but fit his handsome freckled face. Farrell was a PIII +1, and he didn't make nice with newbies. "Sayer's reporting for duty, sir." Captain James Hillary—you couldn't get anyone better than him. He was one smart cookie, and you could never get anything past him. I could sum him up in two words, proud and fair. He wasn't arrogant, or pig headed as he moved up the ranks to Captain. This was during the time when the Rampart scandal had just broken in the news, and the Department was truly under scrutiny. He was proud of the work his department was accomplishing under his watch—despite the scandal, he was what every precinct should have, someone who is willing to stand up for what was right and have those officer's backs who were doing what they were supposed to. His only flaw was he liked to gossip with certain people within the precinct and in time I would become one of those people. The first day I met him, he called me into his office. "I have read the report of your test scores and the scores in your training. I am very impressed by your written exam. You received ninety-eight. Although I like your scores, that's not what got you in as an officer. I am happy to welcome you aboard, Sayers."

"Thank you, Sir."

"You will do some training for a couple of days and I am going to keep my eyes on you. On Saturday, you will be here in my office at thirteen hundred hours to meet your FTO... Thank you, that is all."

~

That Saturday changed my life forever. When I met Mike Farrell, I knew he was one I would have to get used to.

"Officer Farrell, meet Officer Sayers."

"Oh! Just kill me now!" was all I heard. His reputation proceeded him and if the Captain didn't know him better, he would have gotten written up for his conduct. We were not off to a good start by any stretch of the imaginary. "A woman! You put me with a woman rookie. Why didn't somebody warn me, I would have transferred?" I stood there as quietly as a church mouse, but not cowering at all. I did not move, although I was seething and wanted to just shut him up, but I couldn't. "Like it or not," the Captain said, "She's your boot. No ifs, no and's or but's about it. You're going to treat her with respect. Oh! By the way, she got better scores than you ever have. Now get out of my office, both of you."

 *You don't know the image I was going to describe to you. Just think Dahmer the serial killer, but much more clean-cut and thicker in body mass. The Captain saved you from my mind.*

~

I had gone over to Brandon's house. The first question he asks was who was my FTO? Not, honey how was your first day on the job out of the academy, but who is your FTO? Perturbed at his lack of concern about me, I let it go and told him Mike Farrell. He just started laughing uncontrollably. Yeah, the joke was on me. I told him it wasn't funny. "You must know him." I said. I could only laugh with him, but I wasn't laughing on the inside. "Yes, I know old Mike. He's arrogant, pigheaded and a clown." I thought, 'I must be in hell.' No this was worse than hell—maybe. My head rested on his shoulder. I wanted to cry so badly, but I couldn't. I think some toughness was settling in. "Don't worry," he said. "Think of it this way. You'll be learning from one of the best." I thought, but then I said it aloud. "That's a good thing, but very soon I'm going to have to put him in his place. I can feel it in my bones." I needed more reassurance than my fiancé's word.

Of course, you can speak your mind respectfully to a Senior Officer. Make no qualms about it. The police are paramilitary and if given an order that wouldn't be second guessed by superiors. You had better do it. I didn't know how long it would be, but I knew it was coming.

My first day with Farrell was difficult for me. I had to endure him moaning and groaning all day. Oh! It was pure agony for the next two weeks. Whatever he corrected me on while doing police work, I certainly listened and took in the instructions, but his attitude got old really quickly. He wouldn't let me drive, and all he could do was talk about how great he was.

After the third week, I had just about had enough of Mike Farrell.

"Please, pull the car over, sir."

"What!? You sick or something?"

"I said, pull the car over and get out—respectfully, sir."

We pulled next to a park that was empty. Only Pigeons occupied it. We hadn't had a call in over an hour. So, I took the opportunity. "Sir, you are arrogant, self-centered and an egomaniac clown. I am sick and tired of you talking about yourself, as if you are a god or something. You are a man, just as I am a woman. I am tired of you ignoring me and I am tired of you hogging the car. I don't want to hear another word come out of that mouth of yours unless it is about police business. Now give me the keys, you arrogant piece of ooh."

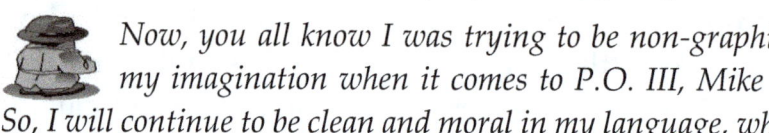 *Now, you all know I was trying to be non-graphic about my imagination when it comes to P.O. III, Mike Farrell. So, I will continue to be clean and moral in my language, which you had to learn to do because of the foul language culture within the police department. Trying to give you the picture of what I was feeling at that moment, I could have shot him, and my imagination allowed me to empty my automatic Glock into his private part, but I didn't want to get blood on my uniform, so I had on a white clear see-through raincoat. Yeah, I went straight for the man part and I didn't regret my imagination at that moment. It gave me release and clarity of mind.*

"Good, Sayers." He tossed me the keys. "Wow, do you have PMS?" All I could do until we got another call was to laugh. There was no other choice. What I had just done and said could have cost me my career, my reputation good or bad, and insubordination on my record.

An hour later, we get a call for a hit-n-run. "Clear-right." Farrell said, as we hit the lights and sirens to get through the many intersections. When we get to the scene, we had to call for additional units and block off the scene. Thank God, we got the license plate and witnesses gave a description of the car. A six-year-old child died in the accident. All I could think about was Ashley. I had to block her out for the time being and do my job. Of course, Farrell made me do the report. That night I was so glad to be home. I didn't see Brandon. I just had to be by myself. As an officer, you remember and grieve the tragedies of the day before you can put it all behind you and go to work with a rational mind the next day. It seemed to be like that almost every day. There was always someone getting shot or someone finding someone else dead. I can say the good days made doing the job worthwhile.

~

The next week, I drove every day straight. Farrell started talking to me again. I think he was kind of proud of me for standing up for myself. He could have written me up, but he didn't, and I appreciated him for that. To have a mark or Disciplinary Action on my record that early wouldn't have been good. "I'd like to invite you to my house for a bar-b-que. I believe I owe you an apology. No matter what I think, I should treat you with respect. You are a good person and a good cop. I want to call a truce. Will you accept my apology?" I could not believe what I was hearing. I had to stop the car and pull over to the side of the road.

"Sir, are you serious?"

"Yes, I am serious. I want you to come over to my house and you can bring a couple of friends."

"Okay, I'll bring my fiancé and I might invite his ex-wife."

"Ex-wife! Why would you ask your fiancé's ex-wife to come?"

"Because we've become good friends, and she is single."

"That could be dangerous, don't you think? I think your fiancé is nuts."

"I don't think he's nuts. In fact, you know him. His name is Sgt. Brandon Taylor."

"Oh my god, Brandon Taylor. We were in the same training class together. He's a Sergeant now? He's a good man. I didn't know he got divorced, though."

"Yes, going on five years now. We've been engaged for over two months. When I told him, you were my FTO, he confirmed my first impression of you. However, he also said I'd be learning from one of the best. So, I tolerated you as long as I could. And yes, I accept your apology, even though I know you still believe the way you do."

"Look, Sayers, I give everyone a hard time. Despite being a slight chauvinist, I am attempting to change. I don't want our relationship to be strained, so, I want you to be able to trust me and I want you to have my back since we are partners for now. I know I can be unbearable sometimes, but I respect you as an officer and a woman, and I want you to be the best officer you can be."

Farrell had given me an olive branch and getting the apology meant everything to our partnership. I could trust him now to have my back as well.

~

The Saturday morning of Farrell's BBQ, I arrived at Brandon's house around nine o'clock. I walked through the door and he was looking out the window.

"What's going on?"

"Those people across the street have a lot of traffic going in and out. I don't know, but I think it may be a drug operation or some very wealthy people over there. I need to ask you not to come over here in your uniform until I can find out some more of what's going on over there."

"No problem, I understand. I usually don't come here in my uniform anyway."

"Darn, I just knew eventually it was going to start in this neighborhood. But we're going to just have to put a stop to this now. The exposure to Ashley and the many teenage kids around could get them hooked on selling or using drugs."

"Okay, I will talk to the Captain to see what can be done. But for now, we don't have to go pick up Kimberly and Ashley for a couple of hours. So, I thought we could use those hours wisely."

He grabs her and pulls her close. "I'm so glad you're wise."

"Thank you very much and now make love to me."

"Yes, ma'am."

~

We arrived at the bar-b-que just in time as Farrell was about to burn everything. Brandon and Mike rehashed old memories. Kimberly and I played cards with Mike's girlfriend, Cara. The boys were on one side of the yard and the girls were on the other. I guess I hadn't been a cop long enough to hang out with the *boys in blue*. Not that I minded. I didn't want to talk about work anyway, even though I had to work the evening watch.

~

Monday morning after completing roll call, "Captain, who can I talk to about a possible drug house?"

"Talk to Andrews. He is under cover for Drug Task Force (DTF). He should help you."

"Thanks Captain. Hey Farrell, I'll be right back. I have to go talk to someone."

"Who are you going to talk to? Do I know who this person is?"

"His name is Andrews in DTF. I want to talk to him about a possible drug house on Brandon's street. He said they've only been there about a month now and there's too much traffic going in and out. So, I told him I would see what I could come up with, since I worked in the area he lives in. I'll be right back."

"Let me go with you."

"Okay."

That evening, I told Brandon what I learned from Andrews and he said he would check into it on tomorrow. After talking with Andrews, I knew doing undercover work was difficult. It took time, precision, dedication, and a lot of time spent doing OPS (surveillance). It sounded exciting, but there was no way I could do any of that right now. I had my hands full enough with every day police work out on the street. I had heard about all the special units like Vice, Metro, GED (Gang Enforcement Detail), HazMat, SWAT, and others, but I was too new. Back then, you had to be on the job for at least five to seven years before you could get into the gang unit.

Farrell and I became good friends and not just patrol partners. We would tell each other our problems and he would always say, "I just want a woman's point of view." Of course, most of the time it was me giving him the advice about women. I knew he enjoyed talking to me, just as much as I liked talking to him. He had become my second best-friend, and I trusted him with my life. He even took me one day to a police officer hang out. Often as an FTO, you wouldn't fraternize with P.O.II's. As long as he continued to be my FTO, we got to know each other well. We drank beer and played pool. Boy, could they drink! They would drink me under the table, and yes, some would literally end up under the table, but I couldn't get caught up in all that. I had to stay clear. The pool was fun, but I'd never been into drinking beer or any other alcohol for that matter. I felt like he was finally accepting me, and a lot of the other guys, who had similar ideas as Farrell. It wasn't hard to be a cop anymore. I rather enjoyed my time being out in the field.

When spending time with Brandon, we would talk about work and how the day went for the both of us. I was grateful in a lot of ways he could understand me and could recognize when I didn't want to talk about work. Everyone who'd never been around a cop always thought it was so exciting. Shoot-em'-up, get to shoot bad guy's everyday type of work. And yes, some of those days were fun, when everyone could go home at the end of their shift. Too often, it would get surreal when an officer had to be taken to the hospital for a gunshot wound and the news was that they had succumbed to their injuries. People didn't understand. The things we saw daily could destroy the mental state of the average person if they never put things into perspective and let some of it go. This type of work is not for everyone, and some stories I would soon experience would confirm that.

"So, how did your day go?" Brandon asked.

"You know Brandon, sometimes it amazes me how people live their lives. I mean, adults are supposed to act like adults and they let their kids run rampant."

On a child endangerment call, we arrived at this house and the first thing I see was this one-year-old baby sitting in the middle of the yard, just crying. I stayed with the baby and Farrell goes and knocks on the door. A seven-year-old comes to the door. So, he asks the little girl where her parents were. The little girl opened the screen door and pointed toward the back of the house. No one ever taught her not to open the doors for strangers. I guess in this instance, I was glad she was friendly with us and didn't get scared of having the police at her door—her face said save me. He walked in as she leads him into the bedroom where her mother was. I took the baby into the house and put her in the playpen. The house was a wreck and smelled like a dead carcass of every kind. Why no one had called on this mother before was beyond me. We head to the back room and the mother is lying on the bed with a needle stuck in her arm. I thought she was dead at first, but then I felt a faint pulse, so I called in an ambulance on a drug overdose on a Caucasian female. You can't even imagine the rage I felt. I wanted to take her and just beat her half to death. I've seen some things in my day, but that was downright disgusting to me. And the thing is, I know she's not the only one. Kids are even younger now having babies. She was only nineteen and looked much older than me. Every nationality doesn't matter what color they are—it's happening everywhere. What I don't understand is this: people know what these drugs can do to them and they still try them, anyway. We had to wait for the Department of Children and Family Services (DCFS) to come and get the children, and then we could finally leave. "I don't even know why I'm saying this to you. You know what's going on out there." He gave me this look of welcome to my world. "People get arrested daily for child endangerment, drug abuse, and other crimes. And the thing is, they let these kids go back into these same homes. Most people won't even call to report that type of situation. It's sad, but true. And there is nothing we can do, unless the drug addicts want to change their circumstances and stay clean. Also, you have a system that is not perfect. There is a difference between discipline and abuse. You know, back when we were growing up, parents had control of disciplining their children when they did something wrong. Now, I totally agree that when you have adults or family members abusing children sexually or locking them in closets and those types of atrocities, then those children should be taken from the home. But you have kids now being taken away from their families, because the child says the parents spanked them. The control is no longer in the parent's hands. The control now is in the child's hands."

Time out. I know some of you are social workers and you may have a different opinion about this issue. I know what I'm talking about. I've worked in Social Services, so I know how that side works, too. I am not stating anything I haven't experienced myself. Most of these kids need a spanking, structure, and consequences to their actions, not abuse. There is a difference, but the laws put in place don't justify those differences. Yes, some parents are excessive, but they have taken the rights away from parents who would never go beyond basic discipline. They've handcuffed the parenting system, and that's what's wrong with these kids today. There is no more respect for parents, elders, or authority. Don't get me wrong, I unequivocally do not excuse abuse in any form or any cop usurping their authority in the wrong manner. There just never seems to be a median solution to any of them. There's only extremes to both sides of the issue and that's what's wrong with our society as well.

Chapter 6

Neighborhood Watchers

Brandon and I always talked about forming a neighborhood watch, but never had the time or put in the time to get it started. We decided to do something now. As cops, we had to do something, as caring people with family, we had to think about all the other families on the block. We passed out flyers to everyone within a five-block radius after making them. We set up a meeting in a neighborhood park gym, inviting everyone out.

"Brandon, I hope this works here."

"It will work. I have a good feeling about this. Many of our neighbors care about keeping their neighborhoods safe. They want their kids to go outside and play. I know it's a lot to ask for at once, but we have to start somewhere, before it gets too out of hand around here."

~

Wednesday afternoon, we were down at the gym setting up, making sure everything was in order. "Everything seems like it's going smoothly. I'm sorry, I won't be here to help." He hugged me, and I could feel his love as he kissed me passionately.

"It's alright. I know you have to work. Don't worry, everything is going to go great. Just go to work and tell Mike I said hi."

"Will do. Can I have another kiss goodbye?"

"Whoa, woman, you better get out of here before we set the sprinklers off in here."

After talking to Brandon, the next day. He was glad everything went well. The people responded and were ready to implement the neighborhood watch as soon as possible. Robbers were being caught and drug dealers arrested. What we didn't know was how much we really were affecting the drug sales. Some neighbors were getting threats from drug dealers, but kept the fight going and confronted drug dealers themselves, which was not advised. Knowing we would not stop every drug sale. We were going to make them think twice about selling in front of the kids. Brandon was so proud of the neighbors. He invited them all to a block party. "I appreciate everyone coming. We are here to celebrate the neighborhood watch and its success. All I want to say is thank you for watching my back and I'm sure I can speak for everyone here. We all appreciate each other for the neighborhood watch. Have a great time. Enjoy the food and the music." We enjoyed ourselves until nine o'clock that night. So tired, we didn't even take off our clothes for bed.

~

The next morning, arriving at work, we were to be on the lookout for a serial rapist in Santa Clarita.

"Hey, Sayers, how is the neighborhood watch going?"

"It's going great. I tried to get in touch with you to tell you thank you for all your help."

"It's nothing. This is what I do. Now and then, something positive happens."

"You know, we had a block party for the neighborhood. I was going to invite you, but the Captain told me you were investigating a case."

"Yes, your case as a matter of fact. We found out some information on some runners. A lot of the information and addresses we have for surveillance turned out to be bogus. We have some connections out on the street, checking things out for us."

"Definitely keep me posted... how long did it take you to get into undercover work?"

"About five years. When I joined the department, they attempted to recruit me immediately, but I waited and assessed my career path. Why? Are you interested?"

"Well, I don't know. I was thinking about it, but not right now. I'd probably wait a couple or more years. Brandon and I are getting married next year. So, I don't want to start our marriage off, not being home most of the time."

"I understand completely. My wife and I have a strong relationship. I guess that's why we're still together. Sometimes, you don't go home for days. Be patient and when you're ready, let me know."

"Thanks. I'll talk to you later."

That was a very positive sign for me, and Mike said he would back me up as long as I took him with me. I stared at Mike intently.

"Why haven't you gone undercover before now?"

"Too much into the streets. I was comfortable there. The streets are getting me down now, though. I want to try something different."

"Why don't you do it now?"

"And leave my partner, no way. If I go, we're going together."

 *After training me, Farrell no longer wanted to do training. He wanted to be back on the streets full time and requested to work patrol with me. It was every month, someone was promoting or transferring to another area of work. As long as they needed you, you had a record with little to no blemishes, and/or preferential treatment, you could move up or move on. Not everyone in their positions deserved to be there, and I knew Farrell was on the up and up. He definitely wasn't a brown-nose, but I couldn't say the same for some others.*

"I will not do it for a couple of years yet. So, I know by then, you'll changed your mind."

"I'm surprised they didn't recruit you when you first started. To be as old as you are, you still look in your early twenties."

"You have got nerve, but I'll take it as a compliment anyway and say thank you very much."

"You're welcome." We would laugh all the time. Mike had become like a big brother.

I was so happy Brandon and I were finally getting married. We decided to do it in July. A month before the wedding, we still had watch meetings, and some were getting threats. Some got scared and wanted more police protection, and the others would not back down. We tried to reassure the scared neighbors, not to give up.

The next night, someone firebombed a neighbor's house. Luckily, no one was home, and we think they knew it. They were sending a message and made good on their threats. It was early in the morning, so no one saw or heard anything other than tires screeching. We tried to get some added cops, but they could only patrol for two weeks. The only thing we could do was to encourage them to keep fighting for their neighborhoods and the kids who lived there.

It took Andrews some time to find out the type of operation that was going on over there. Brandon was right, they were selling drugs, but it wasn't dime-bags or crack in a vial. They were moving large quantities of cocaine and black tar heroin. Andrews set up surveillance in Brandon's house a month later. Continuing the surveillance, they would move stuff back and forth from Chicago. It took about a month and a half to find the head players. A part of me was excited, and the other part of me didn't want them to know we were cops, because it would have spooked them off. So, I did what Brandon said and never came over with my uniform on and he never left with his on either. Not that I felt fear for my life. I didn't want DTF to lose their trail.

The neighborhood was very tight-lipped, and if you didn't appear to fit in, they did not talk to you at all. Whenever the other cops left, they would go out the back way and leave through the alley or they wouldn't leave, which was hazardous for our love life. We had no privacy unless we went to a hotel for the night, and that was almost non-existent.

They calculated a time when most of the dealers would be in the house at one time. Not wanting the sellers, people who sold on the street. They wanted those who delivered the dope and the ones who bought the large quantities. Their drop off time was on Mondays. So, that was the time they would move in. At 0530 hours, Brandon and I watched on the video screen as they move into the house. Everything went smoothly. No shots fired, no one died, which was good all around. No one was talking, and no one was getting out of jail until they did. Whoever the detectives didn't need information from either stayed in jail or posted bail.

This was my first time seeing a drug bust so close to home. I waited behind the see-through glass mirror to listen to the interrogation. Two detectives came into the room where the lowest man on the totem pole was being held.

"Hello Mr. Carroll, my name is Detective Jenkins, and this is Detective Harrison. I know they have read you your rights and you now wish to make a statement about the drug operation taking place at the address of 10901 Harvard Blvd."

"Yes, I do."

"Okay, Mr. Carroll, please state your full name and address please."

"My name is John Otis Carroll. I live at 10901 Harvard Blvd., Van Nuys, CA."

"Mr. Carroll. Can you tell me who also lives in the house with you?"

"Some associates and I."

"Some associates! Can you give me their names?"

"Do I have to?"

"Yes Mr. Carroll, you do."

"All right, Robert Adams and Eric Kent."

They just kept drilling the questions and two hours later, they had only the people who lived there and the suppliers. The suppliers were small time. They wanted to know who was backing them, but got no useful information. I don't think they would have, even if he knew. His plan was to testify against the others and then get out of town for good. He was terrified of going back to jail and he was even more afraid to stay in California. Put it this way, he didn't know who the big boss was, but he had heard about him and he would not wait around to get any visitors.

As time went on, they knew this case was bigger than it seemed. They had no proof, no names, or any faces. So, they had to start from scratch. After the bust, everything seemed to go back to normal. No one ever returned to the house because authorities confiscated everything else as evidence. The house was vacant for at least six months or more, and time was waiting for no one. We noticed no one coming to look at the house for a couple of years.

"Brenda let's get married next year."

"I have been waiting to hear you say those words. Do you know how long we've been engaged? Just say your daughter will be seven years old. We've been together for three years. I hope you haven't tired of me yet."

"Well, that's a crazy thing to say. I wouldn't be telling you to marry me next year if I were tired of you. My love for you has grown stronger since we first met. I hope you believe that?"

"I believe you and I want you to know I love you, too. I love everything about you, your eyes, your charm, your muscles, and I especially love Ashley. You know it's not every day you can find a single, very intelligent, sexy, devoted father and man to wait for a woman to get her life and career in order. I appreciate it very much. Come here and kiss me."

"Ooh, I like the sound of that. Say it again."

"No, I will not say it again, because it's going to your head."

"I'm going to go to the store. You want anything?"

"Sure, would you buy me some maxi-pads?" The look on his face was priceless. You'd think I'd just told him to go kill someone. "You said you loved me." I laughed. "I'm kidding. Nothing, thank you."

For me, our love was growing stronger each day. Our marriage would differ from our previous experiences. Deciding on having only two children, Ashley was already talking about having a sister or brother. She would laugh hysterically when she mentioned it. Ashley, funny and smart, had Brandon wrapped around her finger, but she never once took advantage, not that he'd ever stop loving her. Taylor knew his daughter was growing up and like my father, I was daddy's little girl and Ashley was his. I would never come between a father and daughter relationship. I was just glad he had enough room to be in love with me.

Brandon hadn't come back from the store yet and I was worried. I had gone into the room where Ashley was watching television.

"Honey, I'm going to step outside for a second."

"Okay, where's dad?"

"He went down to the corner market and should be back in a minute."

Stepping outside, I looked down the street, only seeing red lights bouncing off the walls. Stopping at the little Mini Market on the corner, my heart just started pounding and my stomach was in my throat. Yellow tape wrapped around the perimeter and the police were trying to keep the crowd back. Pressing my way through, I showed my badge and they let me pass. Not seeing Brandon anywhere, not even in the store, I turned to look some more. I looked again and saw the body covered with a white sheet. It seemed as if I was walking slowly over to the body. "My name is Officer Sayers." I pulled out my badge. "Can I see the body, please?" The officer lifted the sheet. I started screaming. "Brandon. Brandon." I screamed it out as loud as I could. Everyone watching my every move, and no one is saying anything. My head was swimming, almost in shock. I dropped to my knee screaming his name again, "Brandon!" Running from behind the Ambulance, I dropped my head in utter relief.

"I'm all right Brenda."

"Thank God." I hugged him tightly. I think I almost broke one of his ribs. "I knew something was wrong. I didn't see you anywhere."

"No, you didn't lose me. I'm fine."

"What happened here, Brandon?"

"This guy tried to rob the store while I was in there. I did the routine and then he started firing. I shot him in the shoulder at first and then he kept shooting, so I shot him in the stomach, and he stumbled outside. I tried to stop the bleeding, but he died before the ambulance got here. Now, I have to go make a statement at the station. Would you stay with Ashley until I get back?"

"You know, you don't have to ask me. Just be careful, please."

I got back to the house as quickly as I could to reassure Ashley her father was alright. She took the news pretty well.

"Are you alright?"

"I'm fine, I knew something was wrong when you come back without dad. I didn't want to hear any bad news. I'm just glad he's okay."

"He's fine. He should be back in a few hours. We can watch a movie and eat popcorn and pig out on junk food. I don't have work tomorrow."

"Yeah, I would like to!"

"By the way, did you finish your homework?"

"You're sounding like a mother already."

"Oh! Get out of here and go get your pillow."

"Can you tell me a ghost story?" Ashley asked. Eagerly awaiting my answer. I think she had me wrapped around her finger, too. "Sure, I have a good one for you."

Mr. Nevis and the Fate of His Murder!

Mr. Nevis was the ghost of the house my parents owned. The house dates back to 1906. A Victorian family home in the Adams Historic area. A four-story home with a basement and an attic that you could fit an apartment in, and four bedrooms on the second floor. Mr. Nevis and his wife were the first owners of the house and my great-grandmother, Nidessa, was the only one willing to buy it after what happened.

Mr. and Mrs. Nevis thought the house was like a mansion, and probably back then, it was. They had no children to share in the glory of their time. They would have grand parties and invite guests every other Saturday evening to their home. The chandeliers and vases were grand, and beautiful hardwood floors. You could almost see your reflection in the shine and every evening they would have their help buff out any marks.

One Saturday evening after the last guest left, Mr. and Mrs. Nevis decided they wanted to continue the party by themselves and danced once more to show their love for each other. As they finish the dance, they turned off the music from the phonograph and heard a crying noise coming from up the stairs. Both look at each other to confirm what they heard. Upon hearing the cry again, Mr. Nevis investigated. He tells his wife, "I want you to stay here, and I will check to see where the cry is coming from." He kisses her on the forehead as he is comforting her and leaves her side. Mrs. Nevis shook her head in agreement as a reply.

Now Mrs. Nevis was a portly woman with a beautiful face and generational wealth. They met, fell in love, and married within three months of the meeting. Their wedding was the talk of the town, as it was grand. Once married, they bought the house and moved in right away.

So, back to that fateful night. Mr. Nevis walked up the stairs slowly, as Mrs. Nevis nervously watched him walk up the winding stairs. The wood stairs creaked in the night's quietness. He reached the top of the stairs and notices the cry was now muffled. The sound was at a lower pitch, making it hardly audible, but it hadn't moved—whatever it was. He looks up to the ceiling to investigate further and hears it again coming from the attic. In the closet where the stairs to the attic were, he looked for the candle on the shelf. He finds it, lights it, and slowly opens the wooden hatch door to search. Pitch black was all he could see. His first thought was maybe it was some type of animal, a bird of some sort, which had gotten up there and couldn't get out. Maybe even a kitten, but how would a kitten get up there from three stories high? He directed the candle in every corner of the attic. Then he saw it, a doll lying there and being bitten on by a rat. The rat was licking off whatever it was and as it ate. The doll made the crying noises. He flashed the light more toward it and it scurried away. The cries had stopped and then he heard a scream of his name, "MARTIN!"

As he jumps off the ladder from the attic. He quickly runs down the wooden stairs to the dining room, opening the sliding doors to find his wife dead with blood pouring from her veins. A petrified look of horror remained on her face from what she saw as blood was flowing from her body. His mind raced to find the answers. He knew someone was in there. He yells out, "Who has done this thing? Come out you wretched beast, I will kill you." The shadow slowly moves from its space to call out to Martin, "Hello Father." Jonathan's pale skin sagging as though he had been starving to death. His frame moved in closer.

Horrified and startled at what he saw, he couldn't help but fall to his knees. His wife slumped over the chair with her throat slit from ear to ear and her wrists sliced open. Jonathan spoke, "Father, I waited for you at the hospital when you said you would be back the next day to get me. I didn't realize what type of hospital it was, and you coldly and strategically left me in that place to rot my days away! No sooner when my mother is dead from the sickness. You were back on the prowl. Poor sick Jonathan was in your way. What did you think? I was some deranged little boy, and there was nothing you could do for me, but put me in the insane asylum! Father, how naïve of you! Now, I know you didn't love my mother. You married her for her money, and I think she knew that deep down inside of her very soul. Despite everything, she loved you with all her heart and before she died, she told me to make sure I make her proud and to take care of you. Well father, I'm here to take care of you. I'm here to give you everything you deserve."

Mr. Nevis spoke no words and just cried tears in his cupped hands. Jonathan crept behind him—hitting him over the head with a metal bar. He was not dead just yet, but dazed. Jonathan tied his hands and his feet and placed the chains around his neck and body as he struggled with no success to get away. He carried his father up the cherry-wooden staircase and into the closet where the attic was waiting. He opened the wooden latch door and took his father into the attic and hung him there to die. Before he left, he spoke to his father one last time. "Father, I killed your wife to put her out of her misery of remembering her existence with you. She wanted children with you and eventually she would realize that having any children with you would be impossible. Because after me you got a disease that wouldn't allow you to have any more children. You deceived her just like you did my mother. I just want you to know, the hospital doesn't know I'm gone, so when you're dead, all the money will return to its rightful owner. I have waited so long for this day and now that it is here, I think I can get better now and leave that asylum for good. Goodbye, father and have a nice under-life."

Mr. Nevis squirms to get free, but couldn't. They found him and Mrs. Nevis two weeks later. Her dead of the knife wounds and Martin from strangulation and guilt. Jonathan wrote a note explaining they would be on vacation. They never found the person who killed them and never suspected Jonathan of the crime. People claim Jonathan disappeared after being released two years after the murders."

"Brenda, that was a good one, but was it true?"

"Honestly, I don't know. My dad would tell us old ghost stories. I think sometimes they were true." I grab Ashley and tickle her. Screams and laughter filled the house.

My life was full of these kinds of stories. Every Halloween, my dad would play this creepy album with a skeleton face inside the cover. To have two people killed in the same house you grew up in, is interesting and insane.

Ashley's humor was what I needed. I didn't know how I would feel about someone dying I loved and was close to. You expect, we are born and then eventually we die. That kind of situation puts your feelings into perspective. You always pray to God if a loved one dies, they don't die a painful or horrible death. You want them to die of old age or in their sleep. This was a close call for us. Try as you may, the more you're a cop, the harder it is to show emotion with death. I was only three years in. I still had my emotions intact.

With an Officer Involved Shooting (OIS), the investigation interviews could take days or weeks. It was ten hours before Brandon could return home. He would have to go back to Internal Affairs (IA) within four hours, and within the next couple of weeks, to complete the interviews. He was exhausted, so I took care of Ashley and made sure she got to school and back to Kimberly. Life had to continue without Brandon until everything was done. He wasn't a field officer, so there was no need to relieve him from street policing.

Every day, there were babies, teenagers and adults dying for nothing in drive-by shootings, a robbery, or domestic disputes. You put everybody else out of your mind, but when it's your family, that control, that calm, that perspective goes right out the window.

Chapter 7

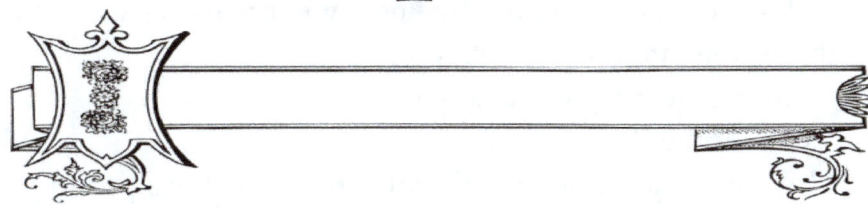

Life in the Balance

July 14, 1995, our wedding day arrived. I dialed Brandon to investigate the evenings events.

"Good morning Mr. Taylor. Are you awake yet?"

"Yes, I am and how are you this morning, my lovely bride to be?"

"I'm nervous, sick, excited, and ready to throw up. Does that explain it?"

"It sounds like you're getting cold feet."

"Cold feet my eye, there is nothing in this world that could keep me from marrying you today, unless you ran off with that striper from last night."

"Striper, what type of striper are you talking about?"

"Brandon, come on, I know Craig and he told me anyway he was going to get you a striper."

"That dirty dog, he told me not to tell you and he goes and tells you himself. I'm going to kill him."

"Don't kill him on my account. I told him to tell me. I'm glad you didn't run off with her."

"You don't have to worry about me running off with any other woman. I've found the love of my life and I would never give her up for anyone. I love her very much and I always will. Now get off the phone and I'll see you at the altar. Goodbye, my love."

I was so ready to be married to Brandon, I could taste it. I loved him so much and I finally knew what real love was. My mother came into the room smiling.

"Are you getting ready honey?"

"Yes, mother."

"I want to say how much your father and I are proud of you. Also, I want to say I know it hasn't been easy for you living here with us, but we want you to know we appreciate you doing it this long. I know it was a sacrifice for you not to get an apartment of your own. Your father said nothing about it, but I'm saying it to you now. I love you very much, my baby girl. Now that we're back on our feet and your father's health is a hundred percent. I want you to live your life to the fullest. And he might not say it, but he is very proud he is going to walk you down the aisle again, this time for true love and for someone he really likes."

"Mom, living here was never a bad idea for me. Needing to heal from an unfortunate marriage, living here gave me purpose, and it also gave me an opportunity to clear my mind and see my way through all of it. You both have helped me so much. I don't want you and dad to worry. This will be the last time I'm ever getting married. I know Brandon is the one for me. I plan on being married as long as you and daddy have been married."

"I know you will. If you need anything, just holler."

"Okay."

Beyond excited, I could hardly wait to be his wife. I never once felt like I would lose who I was or my identity.

Finally arriving to get married, I was inside the little wedding chapel talking to my mother and Kimberly.

"The wedding is supposed to start at three o'clock. I have to stay back here till then. I'm going to go crazy before I even get to the altar."

"Well, I called the house and Brandon said they will leave in the next fifteen minutes. So, don't worry, they will be here on time."

~

At the house, Brandon and Craig were getting ready. The street was quiet, the sun's arrays were beaming.

"Man, I can't believe I'm getting married again. When I got divorced from Kimberly, I didn't even want the word marriage mentioned."

"I know Brandon. Remember, I was there when you filed for the divorce. But I knew one day, someone would open that nose of yours again. I didn't know when, but I'm very glad it was Brenda. She's a lovely woman," Craig said.

"And a good cop, too."

"Man, B., you've got cop on the brain, don't you?"

"Well, that's how I met her, man. I was in-love when she stood up to Kimberly. I knew right then she was the one for me and Ashley loves her, too. So, it turned out perfect."

"I'm happy for you, man. To find love again is not easy. I can attest to that. Now, let's get you married."

"Alright, so how do I look?"

"As good as you're ever going to get," Craig laughs.

~

It was two o'clock and the wedding would start in an hour. The guests were arriving, and the place was so peaceful as the music filled the background with the birds chirping. They would spend the rest of their lives together as one. The Maid of Honor and the Brides Maids were in the back with Brenda as they did final touches to get ready. Brenda's cousin Tanya was the Maid of Honor.

"You know, life can't get any better than this. You are so beautiful in that dress. I have a confession to make."

"What is it, Tanya?"

"For a long time, I felt guilty for introducing you to Cornelius."

"Why haven't you told me this before? You should have never felt guilty. I loved Cornelius, he just didn't know how to love me back. I guess with time, we could have worked things out, but he was just too immature and selfish. We were inexperienced with life. We didn't know how to handle struggle, pain, and disappointment. He was that experience for me to know what true love was not. I found love with Brandon and you need never feel guilty for life being what it is."

"I just want to say thank you because you never made me feel guilty. I just took that burden on myself."

"Tanya, you are my cousin, my sister. I love you and you better never ever forget it."

"Thank you and I love you too. I need to stop before my make-up runs." She said.

"You look beautiful, and you never know, you just might meet your Prince Charming today."

"Well, I have certainly had my fair share of heartbreak, but I will definitely wait on my Prince Charming to show up and sweep me off my feet, like Brandon did to you. By the way, when are they going to arrive?"

"They should arrive soon. They should have left the house already. Maybe you can find Mike to see if they are here yet."

"Okay, I will be right back." Tanya had gone in the opposite direction from Mike.

~

Brandon opening the door to the garage. Shots rang out like fireworks on the Fourth of July. He grabbed the wound as the force of the bullet knocked him backwards. He crumbled into a baby position and then spread out his body, lying flat on his back as he was gasping for air as blood was dripping from his back and his front. One bullet hit Brandon in the chest, with one still spinning in his heart and one exiting out the back, while Craig got hit in the leg. Craig crawled to the car to use the phone to call 911. Just so happens, one of Brandon's partners came by as the smoke cleared and the ambulance arrived.

"Roger, I need you to get to the chapel, and..." Craig said.

"You don't have to say another word."

When Roger arrived at the chapel, he ran into Mike and almost knocked him down. With tears in his eyes, he arrived at the chapel and informed Mike, "Brandon got shot in his garage and Craig got hit in the leg. Brandon didn't survive, and Craig is being taken to the hospital." He was fighting to hold back the tears.

"Mike, I can't go in there and tell Brenda, I can't."

"It's alright, I'll tell her. Just keep a lid on this until I tell Brenda. Do me a favor, compose yourself, tell Brandon's and Brenda's parents to come back here."

"Okay, but..."

"There is no but. Just get them and be quick about it."

Mike couldn't imagine how I was going to take the news. Right then, he didn't know how he felt about telling me, but he knew he had to be the one. Mike knocked at the door hesitantly.

"I'm dressed. You can come in."

"It's me, Mike." Mike's head was the only object through the door and then he came in. "Do I look okay Mike?" Walking into the room, he looked at me and hesitated.

"You look beautiful."

"Do you know if Brandon is here yet? He should be here already." Mike grabbed my hand. "Brenda, you need to sit down." Immediately, my eyebrow turned to concern. "For what, Mike? What's going on?"

"Sit down Brenda. There's something I have to tell you."

"I don't want to sit down, Mike. Just tell me what's going on and I want to know now, please!"

"There has been a shooting."

I was motionless. I don't think I could even move my eyes. It was like I suddenly broke free with every breath I took. "It's Brandon." I was holding on to his hand for dear life. My body was shutting down and so was my brain as he continued. He walks away from me and says, "They were shot in the garage. Craig received a hit in the leg."

Tears roll. "Where was Brandon shot?" I was panting with anxiety.

Mike says, "He received gunshot wounds in the chest and in the shoulder." I didn't move and closed my eyes. "Is he at the hospital? Is he going to make it?"

Mike walked over to me and put his arms around me, and then I knew. He didn't have to say a word. All I could do was fall to my knees. Screaming as loud as I could, my heart and body sank to the floor with my tears. "Brandon, why?" I felt destroyed. My whole body went numb. Everyone came running to the room. Brandon's parents came in first.

"What's going on in here?" Mrs. Taylor ran over to me. "What's going on? Why are you on the floor?" she asked.

"Mr. and Mrs. Taylor, I really don't know how to say this, but someone shot Brandon in front of the house, and he didn't make it to the hospital. I'm sorry," Mike explained to Brandon's parents. I'm sorry."

As Mike was explaining to Brandon's parents about what happened, I couldn't think about anyone else.

"Go get Kimberly." I said, out of breath.

"Brenda!" Mrs. Taylor said.

"Tell her not to bring Ashley in yet. It should come from Kimberly."

Kimberly was told, and everyone was in distress, as she told Ashley. Ashley just cried and cried. She couldn't stop, and I couldn't either. I couldn't talk to anyone. I had to get out of there and out of that dress.

"I'm going home. Would someone call me when the police have all gone from Brandon's house, please?"

"Honey, let us drive you home." My mother said.

"No mom, I'll be alright. I'm going home now. If anyone visits Craig in the hospital, tell him I'll visit him later. I'll see everyone later."

It may have seemed cold, but I was numb to the world. I was numb to my surroundings and to everyone else who existed in the space-time continuum.

~

When I got home, I crawled up into a little ball and cried myself to sleep. I couldn't scream and yell at the bastards who killed Brandon and me with him. I think my body was in shock. Waking up the next morning. Hoping it was all a terrible dream and today was yesterday, I quickly shattered that thought as I was still in the wedding dress. My mother heard me stirring in my room and came in. "How are you feeling?" I never wanted to be rude to anyone except a criminal, but why would you ask a person who just lost the love of her life, how are you feeling? I know my mom meant well and so I let it go, and said, "I would be just wonderful, if you tell me this is Saturday and not Sunday, momma."

"Oh, Honey. I wish this were Saturday."

"Then I didn't dream this nightmare."

"Are you going to be alright? Do you want something to eat?"

"Mom, eating is the last thing on my mind. I need to go over to Brandon's house."

"You can do that later. You need to rest some more."

"I can't, mom. I have to go over there today. Or I won't go at all. I need to do this." The tears fell.

"Alright then, I'm going with you."

"No, you can't. I need to do this on my own. Anyway, I'm going to call Kimberly and Brandon's parents to talk about the funeral. And then I'm going to visit Craig at the hospital and talk to him. By the way, did I get any calls?"

"Yes, quite a few. You were sleeping, so I didn't want to disturb you. Mostly friends and family and you received a call from Captain Hillary. He said instead of two weeks off, he's extending it to three. He also said, check in from time to time, if you have any questions."

"Captain Hillary. I'll call him tomorrow."

My life was not my life anymore. It had totally changed forever. All I had were my thoughts, this room, and this big, beautiful house I grew up in and loved. All of it didn't seem real to me anymore. I stepped into the shower, turned the knob, and just stood there and cried silently. Feeling like a little kid standing in the corner, I knew I had done something bad. I was being punished for all the wrong I had done in my life. No one could console me, no one could take away the pain, and I wasn't about to be pitied by anyone. I thought Brandon was going to be my husband, but now, he has also been taken away from me. I can't pity myself or I'll end up in a Mental Institution. I was close to going, anyway.

The grief, hurt, and pain…it was so hard to describe. It wasn't like I couldn't function as a person, but it was like any feeling of compassion for people was nonexistent outside of Ashley and our parents. I felt like my body had turned into robotic parts. To avoid my joints seizing up—essentially, my existence—I oiled them and kept moving. I was the Tin Woman from the Wiz…a Brandon, a Brandon, a Brandon. With every tear shed, I became rusted. The stages of grief were present, but I didn't know in which I was in. I felt abandoned, not because he wanted it that way, but because it was supposed to be my life. Both my ex and Brandon left me feeling abandoned. No one could convey to me that time would heal all wounds. He had a unique place in my life that could never be replaced. How do you function being in that kind of state? How do you reconcile, the person you were to marry, was the love of your life? I didn't know how to grieve. I had never gone through such a loss as this. Because of all of my immediate family members still being alive, I was unsure of how to handle the anger and desperation. Sometimes as officers, because we lack the knowledge of how to grieve, we may project these emotions onto strangers or our loved ones.

Chapter 8

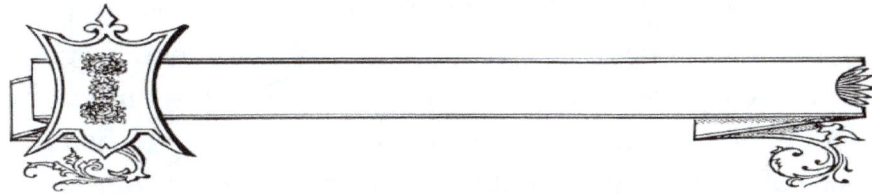

Flag Staph

Standing there in front of the house, staring at the yellow tape surrounding the garage door, and then I turned my face away from all the bullet holes in the garage door. There were some left-over forensics guys collecting any final evidence and wrapping up what they had to do for the case.

Walking in the front door, which was on the opposite side of the house from the garage, I sat down on the couch and wondered if my head was going to explode. I had no strength or energy to even go into the garage, knowing I would probably break down if I had. I did not know where to start. None of this made any sense. Why was I here?

I made myself some tea and then made phone calls to Kimberly and to Brandon's parents. It happened both times when I called. They called out Brandon's name because I was calling from his house. Before I left the house, I recalled Brandon showing me where he stored his important papers and listed the name of his lawyer. I would arrive within the hour to his parent's home.

I rang the doorbell. It startled me unexpectedly, because although I knew what I had to do, my consciousness and my body were still numb. I rang it again, and then it opened.

"Hi Brenda, how are you holding up?" Mr. Taylor asked.

"I'm not doing so well. It took everything I had to go over to Brandon's this morning."

Mr. Taylor grabbed me because he knew I was going to cry, and I did. I held on to him like he was my father. He gave me the comfort I needed. He reminded me so much of Brandon. His walk, the way he talked and the way he had the knack of knowing just what to do and to do it at the right time. We walked to the couch as I sobbed in his chest for five minutes, and then I pulled myself together. "Thank you. I know I called you to talk about the funeral, but I want to wait until Kimberly gets here. What I want to ask is, Brandon told me where he kept his important papers, and his lawyer's name and number were in there. He told me that if anything were ever to happen to him..." I couldn't control the tears, "his lawyer would know what to do. Please call his lawyer and handle that part of it?" "Yes, of course I will."

"Is there anything you want me to do, Brenda?"

"Not right now Mrs. Taylor."

How stupid of me to not recognize that they, too, were grieving. I cried more, "I am sorry. Why am I here?"

Mr. Taylor stops me. "Don't you apologize. We are in this together. I am okay to do this with you. It hurts like the dickens, but we've had much longer to process that something could happen to Brandon as a police officer."

"Honey, you were getting ready to marry my son yesterday. I think it's time you started calling me Anna."

"And you can call me Russell." I knew they were right.

"I'm sorry I never called you by your first names. I guess it's just a habit. Accustomed to addressing individuals by their surnames. I would even sometimes call Brandon - Taylor."

"It's alright honey."

I turned around and picked up a picture that was on the side table near the fireplace. The two of us were on a carnival ride at Evergreen Park. I remembered so vividly, like it was yesterday. The wind blowing through my hair, as we screamed going down the roller coaster. I took the picture and held it to my heart. I could feel the breeze on my face and Brandon's warm hand holding mine.

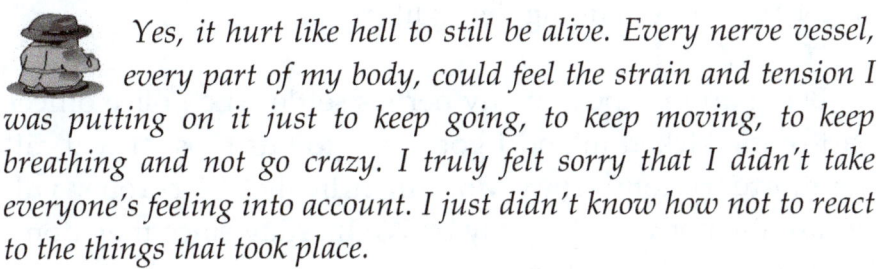 *Yes, it hurt like hell to still be alive. Every nerve vessel, every part of my body, could feel the strain and tension I was putting on it just to keep going, to keep moving, to keep breathing and not go crazy. I truly felt sorry that I didn't take everyone's feeling into account. I just didn't know how not to react to the things that took place.*

"Also, I wanted to ask you about the funeral. I know it is customary for the wife to receive the flag, but since I didn't get to marry Brandon, I thought it would be nice if Ashley could receive it. That's why I asked Kimberly over. I know he would want her to have it." Kimberly drove up, and I let her in. I think I hugged her like she was my sister.

"I drove by the house before coming here. When are they going to take that awful yellow tape from around the garage?" Kimberly asked.

"When they finish investigating and gathering evidence. I can't go in the garage or see anything until they finish. How is Ashley?" It seemed like everyone in the room wanted to know the answer to that question. "She's a tough little girl. when she thinks I'm not around or can see her, she cries. I try to talk to her about Brandon, but she just keeps quiet. I think everything will be all right once the funeral is over."

We all walked into the kitchen and Anna asked everyone did they want anything to drink.

"Would anyone like coffee or tea?"

"No thank you," everyone replied.

"Speaking of the funeral, to bring you up to speed on everything. I've asked Russell to handle Brandon's lawyer, and I want Ashley to receive the flag."

"Why? It's customary for the wife to receive it."

"Kimberly, seeing as I didn't become his wife, I wanted Ashley to have it. Brandon would have wanted it that way. And I am sure I'm doing the right thing."

"Okay."

Being around people, my nerves settle. The police officer part of me kicked in and I got down to business. "I will call the mortuary tomorrow. More than likely, the coroner will release the body on Tuesday or Wednesday since they don't have to do a full autopsy. So, we can view the body on a Thursday night and have the funeral on a Friday morning in the next couple of weeks. Does that sound fine to everyone?"

"Yes," they replied.

"I think that's it for now. I wanted to give you my pager number, just in case you needed to reach me for any reason. I won't be home right away. Craig needs some friends right now in the hospital."

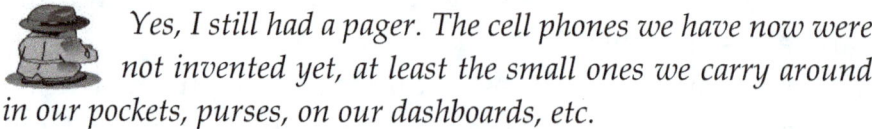 *Yes, I still had a pager. The cell phones we have now were not invented yet, at least the small ones we carry around in our pockets, purses, on our dashboards, etc.*

"If you wait, Brenda, I would like to follow you." Kimberly and I walked out together, and she hugged and walked me to my car.

The Taylor's stood at the door. "Tell Craig we both said, hello and that we'll call him."

Driving to Memorial Hospital, I continued to feel numb. Like a feeling of being lost amid time and you're trapped and can't get out. That proverbial dream of falling and landing nowhere. I felt like I had to be strong because I was a cop, but my insides were all confused and jumbled up. Kimberly and I walked in together. I was in control of my emotions for the moment, until I saw Craig. Just for a split second, I wondered why Brandon couldn't be lying in that bed instead of Craig. I always believed growing up, you have no control over when you die. It's not up to you and when it's your time, it's your time. Only God knows when that time will be.

I cleared my tears as much as I could. "So, you got the room to yourself." I said.

"How are you ladies doing?" His voice raspy as though he had just woken up.

"The question is, how are you doing? How's the leg?" Kimberly asked.

"Well, it will be like this for a few months. The doctor says I will have a limp for a while. The bullet hit a nerve and the other broke my leg in two places. They were able to repair it, but other than that, I'll be out of here Tuesday or Wednesday morning, hopefully."

"Good."

"I hate to bring this up right now, but do you know when the funeral will be?" Craig asked.

"Well, more than likely, it will be held in a couple of weeks."

Craig, the whole time, had a look of concern, and she felt like she needed to remove herself from the room.

"Craig, I'm going to go now. I came to see how you were doing. I'll see you later when you get out of the hospital. Hospitals creep me out. I don't even like to come here for myself half the time."

"Kimberly, thanks for coming to visit me under the circumstance."

"No problem. Brenda, I'll call you tomorrow."

"Oh, by the way, don't tell Ashley what I planned. I want it to be a surprise."

"Sure thing. It's safe with me."

I stood up and walked to the window as Kimberly was leaving. Standing there for a second, staring out the window, Kimberly walked over and gave Craig a kiss on the cheek and then left.

"Come and take a seat on the bed. What was that all about?"

"At the funeral, I'm going to have them give the flag to Ashley."

"That's nice of you. Brandon would be happy."

"I thought it would be a good thing for her to have something personal he earned as an officer." Craig sat more upright in the bed and I fluffed his pillows.

"Not to say I didn't mind seeing Kimberly, but I wanted to talk to you alone. I know this may be hard to hear, but I promised Brandon."

"Promised him what?"

He reared his head back and wiped the tears. The tears draped uncontrollably. "Brandon didn't die instantly. He died in my arms, but before he made me promise to tell you, he loved you with all his heart and he was sorry he died on you. I think he knew he would not make it." All I could do was place my head on Craig's chest and cry. "He loved you so much and he wanted you to know."

'Be strong', I told myself. 'I have to make it through this and survive.' I cried for ten minutes straight.

"I need to know what happened, Craig."

"Maybe we should talk about this later."

It felt like my head was about to explode. Everyone was trying to tip-toe around my feelings. A part of me understood, but if I'm asking, just give me what I want. "No, Craig. I need to know now, please!"

Sighing, "We were in the house getting dressed. He was talking about how he knew you were the one for him when you stood up to Kimberly. He couldn't believe he had found love again." Both of us laughed. For a brief second, a smile showed on my face and Craig smiled when he saw it. I remembered how happy he was when I stood up to Kimberly. That giggle he made tickled me so. "We went into the garage. He went first to open the garage door. I went around him and was more left of him, toward the front of the truck. As soon as he lifted the garage door halfway, shots rang out. They had to have been watching the house for any sign of movement and just sat there in the driveway—waiting. There was no time to react. No time to jump back, forward, or anything. It was instantaneous. The garage hadn't fully gone up before they started shooting. I don't think they even cared who was in the garage. When the bullets hit me in the leg, I was close to the car door. I was going to drive, and you guys would leave in the limo from the reception. So, it wasn't far for me to get into the truck to the phone. The car skids off as soon as both of us fell to the ground. After calling 911, I hopped over to him. At first glance, I couldn't tell exactly where he was hit. Blood was everywhere. I laid down on the ground and put my tux coat under his head and that's when he made me promise to tell you what he said. Roger pulled up as soon as the ambulance showed up. I gave the police the description of the car, but I didn't get the license plate number."

The tears told the story. Craig was his best friend. They were brothers. "Thank you, Craig, for telling me everything. I'm going to go home now and let you get some rest." He looked at me with such sorrow and hurt in his eyes. He wasn't the type to cry much, but you could tell he was hurting inside.

"Thanks for visiting me."

"I'll call you tomorrow to see how you're doing. If I hear anything, I'll let you know. I'm surprised there weren't any media here." He was adjusting the bed once more to get a nap himself. "Well, they were here. So, I asked to be moved. I didn't want to talk about it at all to those gossip sucking reporters. I'd had enough of talking with the detectives." Craig always had a way with words. But I can say he was a loyal friend.

"It was on the news last night and today. They've already put out a hundred-thousand-dollar reward."

"There was one news van at the house, but they didn't see me go in or out to ask questions."

The door swung open, like Attila the Hun was coming into the room. "Visiting hours for this floor is over," the nurse said.

"Thank you. Okay Craig, I am going to leave you to rest, and I'll call you tomorrow. Let me know when you get out and I promise to pick you up."

"See you later, Brenda, and take care."

"I will." I kissed him on the cheek and then left.

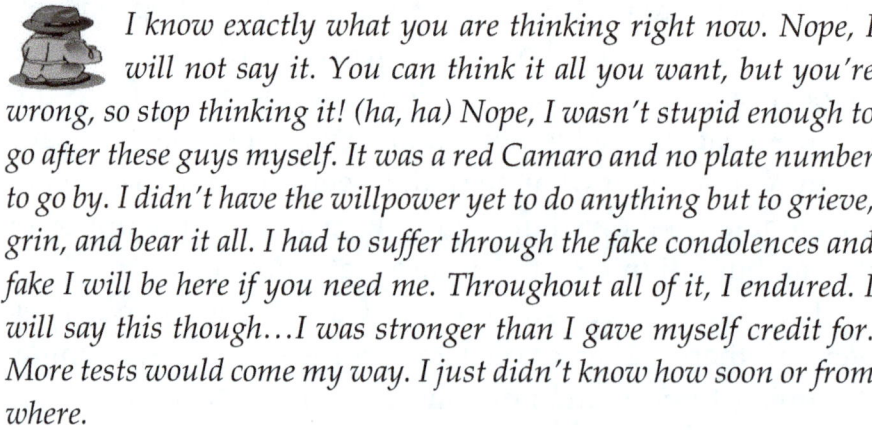 *I know exactly what you are thinking right now. Nope, I will not say it. You can think it all you want, but you're wrong, so stop thinking it! (ha, ha) Nope, I wasn't stupid enough to go after these guys myself. It was a red Camaro and no plate number to go by. I didn't have the willpower yet to do anything but to grieve, grin, and bear it all. I had to suffer through the fake condolences and fake I will be here if you need me. Throughout all of it, I endured. I will say this though...I was stronger than I gave myself credit for. More tests would come my way. I just didn't know how soon or from where.*

Chapter 9

Last Will & Testament

Being a police officer was all I had left. Brandon and I never got the chance to grow old together. We had no children and so I had nothing left of him except memories and pictures. The next couple of days would be one of the toughest of my life. Even though Brandon was no longer with us, I still wanted to keep a relationship with his family. Ashley was over the Taylor's home for a few days, so I stopped by to see her.

"Brenda, you are here!" She was excited and hugged me for a long pause.

"Yes, I am kiddo. How are things going with you?"

"Okay, I guess. I miss my dad a lot."

"I am missing him too and I think that is something we'll have in common always. What do you say, I go and talk to Grandpa Russell and Grandma Anna for a few minutes and when I come back out, we can take a dip in the pool? Would you like that?"

"Yes, I would."

"I'll be right back. Don't go inside the gate until I get back."

Walking through the sliding glass door, Anna hugged me with sorrow in her touch.

"Do you know that is the first positive response we've seen from her in days? You two must maintain that bond and never break it. She loves you like you are her mother." She would always be mine, too. "The iced tea is ready. Would you like some to take outside with you and Ashley?"

"Thank you very much." I pause for a second to see Russell was on the phone with an intent look on his face.

"I'm glad you called me and told me she was over here with you. Who is Russell talking to?"

"He's talking to Brandon's lawyer. He's supposed to give him some information on who is to show up for the reading of Brandon's will." Russell hung up the phone just as Anna finished her sentence. "I just got off the phone with the lawyer. He's asking for you, Brenda, Craig, Ashley, Kimberly, and the both of us on tomorrow morning. He told me Brandon made some changes in his will about a year ago. We have to be there at eleven o'clock," papa Russell said. Anna glanced my way. "You seem surprised?" she stated. "To be honest, I am a little. I figured if he was going to change his will, it would have been after we were married, not a year before." Momma Anna took my hand. "Brandon loved you more than you could ever know. He would do and give you anything in his power to give." I thought no differently inside.

"Craig got out of the hospital this morning, so I'll have to call him to let him know. I'll call Kimberly if you want me to."

"That's unnecessary. She's coming over to get Ashley tonight. In the meantime, take your swim with Ashley and you can tell her about tomorrow," momma Anna said.

The sun shining so brightly. Under a cloudless sky, the breeze brought a fresh scent of roses from around the wooden fence in the backyard. Tranquil, you couldn't help but relax and remember how peaceful it could be amid chaos. It was my chaos to bear.

~

After leaving the Taylor's, I stopped by Brandon's house. I wanted to make sure everything was clean and in order. Upon entering the house, I knew tears would come immediately. I was not afraid to be there because of the shooting. It gave me a chance to be alone in his space. To reminisce on the memories we shared, and to smell him, was hard to take. To lie on the bed, he and I slept on, the bed we wrestled on, the bed we shared our most intimate secrets on. I laid and stared at the ceiling. All I could do was ask God the question, why? Why Brandon? I didn't get an answer.

 *I told you all I was down with God, but I'm not a hypocrite. God was the only one who could give me the answers to my questions. What was His purpose for taking Brandon away from me? I could see why He let my ex go, but what had I done so badly to deserve the love of my life leaving me behind?*

~

The next morning, walking into the lawyers' office, I introduced myself to a very high-spirited receptionist, which could brighten anyone's day. She escorted me into the conference room. It seemed I was the last one to arrive, but I wasn't late. Everyone was in a relaxed mood. The somber faces distracted from the pleasantries that went around the table. A very distinguished and handsome gentleman walked through a side door. I guess leading from somewhere else, maybe his office. He greeted us one by one, shaking our hands and then sat in a thick burgundy leather chair. "I know this is the first time I am meeting all of you face to face, but I've seen pictures of you to know who you are. This meeting will not be very long. I just want to say how sorry I am about Brandon. He was a good man."

Everyone told him thank you and he went on. He went through the formality of speaking about Brandon and what would take place. Questions can be asked after the reading and if there were anything we would like for him to follow-up on, please don't hesitate to let him know. Once finished, he continued with the reading. "This is a matter of a last Will and Testament of Brandon Thomas Taylor. The Will reads: I leave the jet skis, the trailer, and ten thousand dollars of my insurance money to Craig, my best friend and brother. To mom and dad, I leave seventy thousand dollars of my insurance money. I give this to you, so you can take the dream vacation you always wanted to go on. I love you. To Kimberly, I leave ten thousand dollars of my insurance money. To do with it as you please. I know we've had our differences along the way, but in our entire marriage, we did something right. We had a beautiful daughter. To Ashley, my beautiful girl, before you know what I have left you, John has a letter for you. You don't have to open it now. I would prefer it if you read it alone. Afterwards, you can share it with the family if you wish. In the meantime, John will read on. To Ashley I leave two hundred thousand dollars of my insurance money, in a trust fund for college. At the age of eighteen, you will receive twenty thousand dollars for graduating high school. The other one hundred eighty thousand will go toward college. If you choose not to go to college, it is set up, you will not receive the rest of your money until you are twenty-five years of age. You may ask why I did it this way. I have explained everything to you in the letter."

I couldn't imagine how people could truly sit through this. I was squirming in my seat and was ready for this to be over, but I had to be there, because Brandon requested me. "Now to Brenda, my lovely wife," my heart just sunk, tears rushed down my face, so I couldn't see. Everything was a blur. I just broke down. I rushed out of the office as fast as I could. It was unbearable to think we would not be together as husband and wife or together, period. I ran into the restroom and Anna followed me in.

"Brenda, you're going to have to be strong now. I know it hurts, but we can get through all of this together."

"I know. I'm so angry right now. killing whoever did this is all I can think about. It just hurts so much, and I miss him, I want him back and I can't have him back."

"You're going to live and be strong. That's what he loved about you most. You are courageous, beautiful, and smart, a woman he wanted to spend the rest of his life with. You're going to make it, because he's going to be watching over you to make sure of it. Now let's join the others and get this stuff over with." We walked back into the office, hand in hand.

"Sorry, everyone, for the outburst. You can go on with the reading now."

"To Brenda, my lovely wife. Before I proceed, John has an envelope with a letter inside. To Brenda I leave my home and the cars and seven hundred thousand dollars of my insurance money. Any other assets will go to you, including my banking accounts, pension, and investments. This will help with our children's education and take care of anything you need. I love you so much, words can't say, but I did the best I could in the letter."

John read some more information and concluded the meeting. He handed me the letter, and everyone walked out together. I walked back into the office because I wanted to ask a question.

"John, I'm sorry to bother you, but I wanted to ask a question." He sat back in his chair.

"What is it, Ms. Sayers?"

"I wanted to ask... I didn't officially become Brandon's wife. So, does this still stand?"

"Your question is valid and yes, it stands. Your name stipulates the wishes of Brandon. So, it's a perfectly legal document, unless someone contests the Will. He changed his Living Trust a year ago, so if they tried, I don't think anything would happen, although I do want to check in regard to the pension. Since you didn't become his wife, I don't know what the Police Union will do. They may give that to Ashley, but I will let you know as soon as I find out."

"I don't mind if the pension goes to Ashley."

~

The day of the funeral was a difficult day for everyone. Having asked Kimberly to keep the flag a secret from Ashley, I wanted it to be a surprise. Not wanting to dress in black, Russell and Anna agreed it would not be a solemn time. Brandon wouldn't want it to be. He was so full of joy, life, and had a strong character. He made my life full of joy. It seemed the more they talked about him, the angrier I became. He had so much to live for and his life was just snuffed out like he was a piece of garbage. As they handed the flag to Ashley, she looked at me.

"I want you to have it and I think your dad would want you to have it. Cherish it."

"Thank you, Brenda."

"You're welcome, sweetheart. I love you."

"I love you too."

Walking back to the limousine. Someone grabbed my shoulder and I swiftly turned around.

"How are you doing?"

"Hello Captain. I'm doing fine. The funeral helped put some closure to the madness, but you know it won't be over for me until we find out who did this."

"I know. It's tough when you lose a good cop. It's even tougher when you lose someone you love. As they say, time heals all wounds. You'll be okay. You'll be better than okay. Just know that we will uncover the culprit, and we will not cease until we catch them. By the way, I'm giving you a couple of weeks, so take advantage of them. I need you back to work in full force. I can't afford to lose the best team I've got."

"Speaking of Farrell, I haven't seen him in a couple of days. He was at the funeral, but he didn't come to the gravesite. When I call him, Cara answers the phone. She says he's been leaving early and coming home late."

"He didn't want me to tell you, but he wanted to be assigned to the case. For the weeks you're off, he'll be helping with the investigation. When you come back, we will also assign you to the case."

"Why would you put us on this case, especially me?"

"I'm putting my best detectives on this. If I didn't think you could handle this, I wouldn't have put you both on it. There will be no more questions and I expect you to leave it at that."

Like always, he walked away without saying a word. "Thanks Captain." I turned to walk to the car.

Farrell and I got promoted to Detective after passing the test six months prior. I had done my four years of patrol and Farrell had enough years for two detective badges. We worked several cases like this one, but this was too close to home. It wasn't that I didn't want the opportunity to be the one to catch who did this, but my heart wasn't in it at this point. Why was the Captain even using me? The only explanation in this whole situation I could come up with is:

He was testing me. Testing my will and resolve. Or was it a setup for me to fail?

You know what I thought. When I catch up to these scumbags, I was going to make sure they didn't get to a jury trial. They wouldn't get the luxury of being put in a police car. They'd be in a body bag if I had anything to do with it. Of course, I never said it out loud to anyone, but do you really blame me? That's how hurt and angry I was. I mean, think about it. Even if I weren't a cop, you don't think those thoughts would have been the same.

"Can I ride back with you to the house?" At first, I turned around.

"Bran...!" I mumbled. No one heard me.

"Brenda. Can I ride back with you to the house?" I shut my eyes to hold back the tears.

"Sure Craig."

"I had a friend drop me off, since I can't really drive right now."

"You should have told me. I could have had the limousine pick you up as one of the family. You are family Craig."

~

At the house, I tried my best to be cordial to everyone. I laughed when everyone else laughed. Some stories were truly funny and genuine. But inside, I was turning inside out. I looked at all the faces I had never seen before. Ashley's innocent face was the only one I could identify with. She was hurting as much as I was, probably even more so. I had to leave the room and go outside on the patio. I smelled those roses again. They could take your breath away if you let it. God, in that moment, muffled my hearing. I didn't hear the sliding glass door open, but it startled me when it closed.

"You want to talk a little? You don't have to talk if you don't want to."

"It's alright Kimberly."

"It was a nice funeral. I never had to go to one when I was married to Brandon."

"I know, but there shouldn't have been a funeral. Ashley should have a father, I should have a husband, his parents should have a son and even though he was your ex, I know you still had a fatal attraction for him and you shouldn't have a deceased ex-husband." We both laugh. "This world is going to the dogs, Kimberly. And I'm going to make sure the people who did this are going to pay for it. No matter how long it takes." I looked down at my hands. "I've got the letter he wrote me. While I can't let go of it, I cannot read it. I don't know when I'll be able to open this letter." "Do you want me to read it?"

Ladies, ladies, ladies!!! Ex-wives, Ex-husbands, Ex-girlfriends, or ex-boyfriends should never get comfortable enough to ask you to read something so private that you would allow them to read such. Why was she so comfortable in asking to read a letter Brandon wrote to me? Why would an ex do something like that? All I could think was she was temporarily insane. We just had the funeral of the man she ran away with her craziness. Okay, I gave her a temporary insanity pass. I didn't let her have it.

"No!" I closed my eyes for a second. "Sorry, I didn't mean how it sounded," but I meant every word. "I just don't want to read it now." I didn't want to talk either, but I didn't want to be rude.

"Don't worry about it, Brenda. I understand it hurts. Experiencing the loss of a loved one is something I understand. I never told Ashley this, but Brandon wasn't my first husband. I was married at 19. Oh, I thought I was so smart and in-love. My parents told me not to get married, but I didn't listen. I was going to do what I wanted, and no one was going to stop me. I was rebellious and stupid," Kimberly said.

"Oh, that sounds so familiar to me."

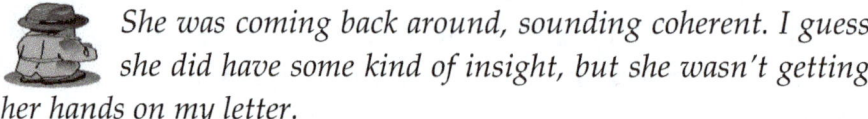 *She was coming back around, sounding coherent. I guess she did have some kind of insight, but she wasn't getting her hands on my letter.*

"Richard and I got married. We were in-love. At least, I thought we were. After the first day, everything went downhill. He was staying out all night drinking and hanging out with his friends. I was so in-love, as they say, love is blind. Well, Jesus couldn't have healed my eyesight. My best friend would tell me she would see Richard come out of this woman's house late at night. Of course, I didn't believe her, and I didn't confront him about it. One day I get a call saying Richard was in the hospital, in a coma. When I got there, I couldn't even recognize him. Someone inflicted severe injuries. In that hospital room, I saw death for the first time up close and personal. His best friend told me the woman's husband found them in bed together. He passed away that same night, and there was nothing that could be done. I was lucky my parents let me move back in with them so I could start over again. Plus, we didn't have any children, so there was no worry there. I vowed from that day forward to never get married again, and I meant it. Then one day, I met this handsome man. He was nice and so genuine, caring, sweet, and honest about his feelings. Totally different from the man I first married and the men I dated after Richard's death. Oh! And by the way, my parents loved Brandon and he could do nothing wrong in their eyes. After getting married a year later, we had Ashley. Our marriage couldn't have been any better. I mean, we were so happy. I didn't know what to do with myself."

 *Was she really trying to help me? I heard her story, and I was trying not to get mad, because I knew what I knew. Okay, this woman is crazy. I just let her keep going. My hope was that soon she would run out of words to say or come back to reality and realize what she's saying. This is not about you.*

"Then he became a cop and started hanging out with his cop buddies. He didn't do it a lot, but the times he did. He never got home the time he said he would. I started accusing him of cheating and not spending time with his daughter and myself of course. To make things better he stopped hanging out with his friends. When we would go out, I'd get jealous of women looking at him. Understanding, he loved me and would do anything for me was somewhere locked up in my subconscious and I wouldn't let it out. I had never known a man who loved so hard, and I haven't found anyone since. When a female officer would call the house, I would have an attitude with the woman. I wanted him all to myself and I smothered him till he couldn't take it anymore. I cried for months when we got a divorce but going to therapy has helped me realize I was the blame and not Brandon."

 *I wanted to smother her right now, but I know she was just trying to help. If I murdered her right now, would I go to jail? She just kept going and going and...*

"Knowing we would never get back together because I hurt him too much didn't stop me from trying. Even though our relationship was never the same, he even agreed to come to some of my counseling sessions. During that time, I would intimidate his girlfriends. Lie to them and say I was still his wife. I was jealous and out of control. To be honest, I hated every woman he got involved with, including you, because I hated who I had become."

Wow, what a revelation. I still think she needs to continue with therapy.

"When I saw you for the first time, I thought you did not differ from any of the others in my eyes. But you were, and Brandon loved you for it, and so did Ashley. She could tell when those women would pretend to like her just because of Brandon. Oh! Believe me, I tried to turn her against you, but I couldn't. Ashley would say you were genuine. It's amazing how she used those types of words at a young age. She would give me this look of disappointment when I said anything about your and Brandon's relationship. And when Brandon and Ashley both came to me and said stop trying to turn Ashley against you. I knew he loved you then and there was no hope for me. He had never done that to me with any other women. What I'm trying to say is, through all the pain and hurt and tears. Brandon was there for us and he's still there for us in our memories. Ashley will always be a reminder of what Brandon and I had once. Now it's time for you to find your memory and hold on to it. I know you want to find the people who did this, but as Brandon used to say, 'It's better to get justice, then to get revenge.'" We both spoke it at the same time. That was the first authentic smile I had cracked all day.

 And for the first time, I didn't think she was totally insane.

"We both knew him pretty well, didn't we? He was a rare open book and hated to keep secrets."

"I guess we did, Kimberly. I will tell you something else. Even if it takes the rest of my life, I will find out who did this."

~

I kept the letter under my pillow for months. I finally had to move into the house myself. My brother was coming home for a few months' leave from the Army and I knew they needed the room. When Ashley and Kimberly came over, we would have lots of fun. I'd sometimes catch her looking at her father's picture, just staring into space. She would be sad for a while, but then she would forget about her sorrow. We had so much fun at an amusement park. We made it a yearly event. I'd look at Ashley and get angry all over again, because someone took joy from her and then I would feel guilty, because I wished it were someone else lying in the grave. Spending most, if not ninety-five percent of my time checking on leads and suspects. Everyone always knew where to find me if I didn't answer my page and call back right away. I was in the gym, letting off steam every day. It would take a miracle to find the killer or killers. We at least knew there was one shooter and a driver. It was frustrating and heartbreaking to go sit in that empty house alone and cry all night. Getting a phone call in the middle of the night from Farrell was common in those days.

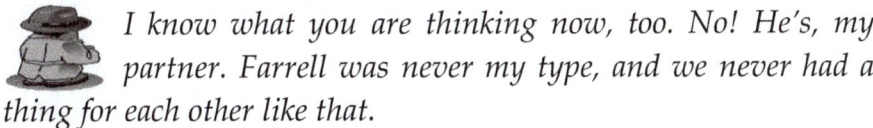 *I know what you are thinking now, too. No! He's, my partner. Farrell was never my type, and we never had a thing for each other like that.*

He would just call to see if I were all right or if I needed anything. It became easier and easier each time to walk into the house and not expect to hear his voice. I had to repair the holes in the house before I would let anyone else over, other than immediate family. I didn't want anyone to feel uneasy or wonder why I stayed there. My memories will always be of love and joy, happiness, and sorrow. All I could do was pray the hurt would go away sometime soon.

Chapter 10

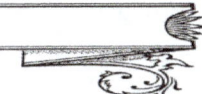

Case of Frustration

One and a half years of frustration in trying to crack the case that changed the rest of my life. I couldn't give up looking. Anger and determination followed me everywhere I went. The thought of losing my mind was ever present, but the drive kept me sane for that moment in time. I trusted Farrell with my life. Though I couldn't claim to trust myself, I was confident he had my back. I hid everything about myself from everyone who mattered. Plus, I had him take the lead on everything.

"Have you gotten any news?" I asked. Of course, I wasn't expecting any, but when he answered, I fell a little lower in spirit each time.

"No nothing. Although, I'm going to talk to Felipe later on to see if he's come up with any information. Oh! By the way, Andrews wants to see you. He said he had to leave but would return around one o'clock."

"Thanks Mike. You want to go have an early lunch?"

He smiled like a big kid. "Just point me in the right direction, but let me go drop off some papers and I'll be right with you. Just give me a minute!"

"Mike, just go do what you have to do, and I'll meet you in the lot."

"Good bet."

~

Coming back from lunch, I checked all the messages to see if there was anything important. "Mike, I am so stuffed. I don't think I'll be eating dinner tonight." I looked into the window of the captain's office. He was eating lunch with his wife.

I recalled the time Brandon arrived at the station with a dozen roses and started singing. After being so embarrassed, this man was incredibly romantic, and no one had ever done something like that for me before. I put my face in my hands until he stopped singing. That was the first time I knew he had a beautiful voice. He had so many gifts and talents.

"Brenda, Brenda."

"Yeah."

"Is everything all right?"

"Yes Mike, just thinking back." I took my eyes off the captain and checked my messages.

"I'm going to talk to Andrews. Don't leave without me. I mean it Mike."

"I won't. Just go talk to Andrews, and I'll be waiting here."

I knocked on Andrews' office door twice before he told me to come in. "Ah, Sayers, just the woman I wanted to see. Have a seat. I'll be right back." It was like I was having a flashback to an earlier job interview. As much as I'd been in there, I never really took the time to look around. The pictures were heartwarming, but I guess what surprised me the most was that it had a nice feeling to it. It wasn't like some of the stuffy offices I had been in. It was personable. I heard the door open. Andrews came in with a file in his hand. "Sayers, I have a file here that is excellent. I have talked to the captain, and he's agreed with my suggestion. We want, I mean, I want you to come to UC (Undercover). You look very young and for your training, we want to put you in a university. This school is notorious for drug pushers and heavy users on campus. There is every nationality in the school, so you won't have any problems fitting in. I want you to know you are the best candidate. You know the type of work it is, and you know the hours. It will be your decision to take this opportunity. Just like the training to become a cop and detective is very hard, think of this training as double. It's not so much the physical, but the psychological stability that is needed. You will think for yourself and for others. We believe you fit the criterion. Like I said before, this will be your decision to make. If you want the position, it's yours. Also, know that if you take this position, you will need to transfer all current cases you have to other detectives. So, think about it long and hard and I will accept your decision when you're ready to give it. So, thank you for coming to talk to me and I'll give your file another look, and then give it back to the captain."

 Just like that, I was being recruited. The whole time I sat there, I didn't have time to say anything. This was an honor to be requested to go to UC, but my first mind was like I just don't know.

We did our goodbyes, and I headed back to my desk. I came back smiling from ear-to-ear, just for getting one up on Farrell. "Guess who just asked me to go undercover? I'll save you the trouble of thinking so hard. Andrews, of course, and he thinks I look young."

I hadn't had a nice compliment about my looks lately. It gave me a little pep in my step.

"You know you sure are talking bad to the person who'll be watching your back while you're in that university."

I threw a notepad at his head "How did you know? Oh, so they asked you first. I feel so betrayed now. They know who the best is, and they ask you first." We both laughed.

"I knew you wouldn't take the job without me, so the Captain gave us both up. Of course, I demanded you come along. I know you wouldn't want me to leave you behind."

"Oh! Give me a break, Farrell. Why didn't you tell me?"

"Andrews wanted to see what I thought of your performance as a cop and a detective. So, does this mean you're going to take the job?"

From the time I'd left the office, I was thinking about the offer. I didn't want to make a snap decision. I really had to think about how my life would change. Would it change for the better or for the worse? I was already on the edge and would be responsible for many other lives instead of just having Farrell's back. This kind of work was up close and personal. "I can't make the decision right now Mike. I want to think about it for a couple of days and I don't need you to pressure me about it. I need to make this decision on my own." He looked at me with a cunning smile. "You won't hear another word out of my mouth about it. This decision is totally yours to make. All I want to say is, you would do great at it, no lie."

~

All the while, on the way home, to the gym, even cooking dinner, the decision was on my mind. During the night, I would wake up and simply stare at the ceiling. I had no one to turn to. I had to decide for myself.

These were the times I wished Brandon were here. He would have helped me by talking things through. But as much as I wanted to believe that. He would give me good advice and leave the decision totally up to me. I guess if he were here, there would be no decision to make. To go U.C. would be too soon.

~

The two days I was off from work. I did the basic things, like washed clothes and went grocery shopping. But one thing I hadn't done in a while was visit Brandon's' parents. I wanted to see them, and I was glad they wanted to see me. I rang the doorbell. Mrs. Taylor answered the door. "Oh! My goodness, we were just talking about you. Come in Brenda. How have you been?" Nothing about them had changed. They were still loving people. "Oh! My goodness, we were just talking about you. Come in Brenda. How have you been?" Nothing about them had changed. They were still loving and caring people.

"I'm doing fine. I wanted to visit since I hadn't seen or talked to you in a while."

"I'm so glad you came over. I was going to call you tonight, because we've decided on that trip Brandon wanted us to go on."

"That is great. When are you leaving and how long will you be gone?"

"We'll be leaving in two days and we'll be gone for three weeks. We're going to the Bahamas."

"Oh! That's wonderful. I wish I had gone. That's where Brandon was taking me for our honeymoon." There was a quiet silence that you couldn't even hear anyone breathing.

Yes, it was an awkward moment, and I was the one who said the stupid stuff this time. Have you ever felt so small after you say something stupid? You want to crawl into a hole, but you can't find one to hide in.

"But I'll be able to go one of these days, even if it's alone."

"Honey, it has been almost two years now and you're not seeing anyone?"

"No."

 *I really didn't want to talk about my love life or the lack thereof, but there was no turning off this road of exploration.*

"Brenda, you're a beautiful woman. You should have a gentleman friend in your life by now. Please take my advice and don't waste away. Brandon would want you to live and not be lonely for the rest of your life."

"Mrs. Anna, I'm not lonely. I have my work."

"And that's all you have." Ouch!! Those few paltry words hit my heart like a ton of bricks. I felt like I was five again. "Listen to me, Brenda, and listen to me well. Brandon was my son and his father, and I loved him very much. I wouldn't wish the pain and hurt of death of a loved one on anybody, but the people we love will leave this earth. We are born to die. What's most important is how we use the life God has given us to live while we're here. Brandon used to come over here and say how happy he was, and he couldn't wait to get married and start a family with you. I asked him did you have the same feelings. Not so much about the marriage I'm talking about, but starting a family. He told me yes. He said that you wanted a family too. Now I want you to tell me if that's still true or not?"

"Yes, it's true. I wanted a family with Brandon."

"Answer me another question. Do you still want a family someday?"

"Of course, I do—someday."

"Well then, you will not do that if you're still grieving over Brandon. You will not have a family of your own if you spend all of your time consumed with your job."

"But Anna."

"Don't but Anna me. I love you and always will love you like you were my daughter. I've worried, Russell expressed concern, and I know your parents have concerns about you spending all your time trying to find Brandon's killers. Don't let your life slip away, and I doubt Brandon would be happy if you used him as a justification for not progressing in life. If you loved him and if you still love him as much as I know, he loved you. I know he would want you to move on. Wouldn't you want the same if the roles were reversed?" Double ouch!! Her words hit deep in my very soul. I knew she was right, but it would take more than that to sink in.

~

After an hour of talking, I left. I didn't want to go home. So, I went to visit a friend. I knocked on the door. It opened slowly.

"Brenda, is that you?"

"Yes Craig, it's me. Were you asleep?"

"No. Yes. Well, I'm up now. Come on in." He yawned in my face before giving me a hug. He did not have bad breath. Shocking. I don't even know why that was a concern for me. It was strange, I know.

"I'm sorry for waking you up. I wanted to visit you since I haven't seen or heard from you in a while."

"You know, I could say the same thing. How have you been, anyway?"

"Oh, I've been doing fine. Just working my butt off trying to find who murdered Brandon. We've had little luck, and it doesn't look like we're going to get any. But everybody at the precinct isn't giving up."

We sat on the couch and talked for a long time and talked about the world, work, and life.

"Before I came over here, I stopped at Russell and Anna's. They read me the riot act and I guess I probably deserved it. I'll probably get it from you too."

Craig gets up from the couch. "No, you won't, because I know why you haven't been around. Self-pity has consumed you, and working day and night on Brandon's case doesn't help at all. You're trying to hold on to every shred of Brandon that you can."

 *Triple ouch!! In just a couple of hours, people who are not my momma and daddy stuck mud on my face. They were bruising me without even throwing a physical punch. Was I just going to take it?*

"Oh! I'm really getting the full ear tonight, aren't I? I don't need to hear any more of this. I'll talk to you later." I stormed out of his house and never once looked back. All night long, tears streamed down my face. I didn't know if I was crying because of Brandon being gone or if what they were saying had any truth to it. Anyway, I didn't want to know the truth. I was content with my life and I wasn't about to change for anyone.

~

By morning I get a phone call. "Hi, Brenda, it's Craig." I was silent for a few seconds on the phone.

 *He's very lucky I didn't slam the phone down in his face. That would be rude, even for me.*

"What can I do for you Craig?" Breathing heavily with disappointment.

"I know I said some harsh things last night and I want to apologize for being out of line. The presentation of what I meant came out wrong. Can you forgive me?"

"Yes, I can forgive you."

 *Whether he was right or wrong, why was I so quick to forgive? Was it because he called me first? Craig was my friend, and I realized he didn't mean to hurt me.*

"To make it up to you, I have two tickets for the Raiders game, not that your second choice, but my friend cancelled on me to be with his girl: she's pregnant and all. So, I thought this would be a good chance for us to become friends again and to have some fun. If you would like to go, I can pick you up in two hours. I know you like football, so do not say you won't go. Please!"

 *I know what you are thinking. You think we are going to go out to this game and I'm going to fall for Craig and stuff. I know what you are thinking. You don't fool me.*

"I would love to go. I will see you in two hours. Do not be late, Craig."

~

The doorbell rings. I opened the door wide. "I'm sorry, I'm late."

"It's okay." I moved out of the way so he could come in. Craig still had a slight limp, but nothing no one else would notice.

"Are you ready to go?"

"Yes, just let me get my cooler."

I loved football. My dad would take me to a professional game every year around my birthday. Brandon used to take me to his old high school football games. I was a true Raiders fan, win or lose, they were my team, especially when Marcus Allen would run the ball.

"This is so exciting. I love football. I watch it every chance I get on television during the season."

"Well, watching it on television is not as exciting as being in the crowd. I get good seats, so it's worth coming. I'm glad you came."

"I'm glad too. This is great. Thank you for inviting me to come along."

"It's my pleasure."

We cheered and cheered for the Raiders. Jumping up and down while screaming is something I haven't done in a long time. It felt good, driving back from the Coliseum. We were laughing and having a good time, because the Raiders had won, 36 to 17.

"That was fun. I haven't had so much fun in a long time. We must do this again." I told him.

"Well, I get home season tickets, so if you want to go to the next game, it's in three weeks."

"Oh! I hope I don't have to work that Sunday."

"Well, if you do, I'll save a spot for you next time. Like I said, I get season tickets, so there will be plenty of more games to go to."

"Okay, you've got yourself a date."

I fixed Enchiladas for dinner, and we sat on the couch eating and watching television.

"I think I better go. I have to get up early in the morning and go to work, and so do you." He stood up and didn't move until I got up. "Yes, that is very true." I walked him to the door, following behind.

"Craig!"

"Yes, Brenda." I didn't want to seem like I was getting all mushy. "I want to say I'm sorry for getting mad at you last night. What you said was true and today made me finally realize I was missing out on life. Not so much the football game, but the company and the friendship. That's something I've missed and I'm glad I've got it back. Thank you."

I kissed him on the cheek, and he gave me a hug and left. I went to bed for the first time in a long time, and had a good night's sleep.

~

Craig was lying in his bed. "I see why Brandon loved her."

As I woke up early, I felt good inside. I had to let go of some of the pain and hurt, finally. I had to make a life for myself. Regarding the rest of my life, I had choices to make, and I will make them.

 *No, it wasn't just because of the football game with Craig. Anna's words were true, and I could finally see. I had only been hurting myself and shutting everyone out. See, I didn't need therapy.*

"Good morning, partner. I don't have time to talk. I have to go talk to Andrews. See you when I come back."
I knocked on Andrews's door.

"Come in."

"Good morning, Andrews."

"Good morning, Sayers. What can I do for you?"

I didn't even bother to sit down. I just said what I had to say. "No, it's what I can do for you. You can have the best female detective on your team if you still want her?"

"You bet your badge we do."

 *Yeah, it was corny, but he was a white dude. He couldn't help it. It wasn't exact words he used.*

"Andrews, you've got her. Where do I sign up?" He shook my hand and sat back down.

"Be in my office at ten o'clock tomorrow morning. I'll have everything set up."

"Okay, I'll be here."

It felt good. I felt free of the quilt of letting go of everything and everybody that didn't pertain to this case. I could have some control over what I was doing to myself and stop it before anything couldn't be done. I had a fresh start, and I could feel the difference. I could focus on something else other than Brandon's case.

He looked puzzled as I asked, "So, Farrell, where are you taking me to celebrate?"

"Celebrate. Celebrate! You accepted the position. I can't believe it. I must apologize to you once again. I never thought in a million years, you would take it." I just laughed.

"Me either." I had a smile so big walking around the station. Receiving all kinds of looks and stares. About thirty minutes later, I was back at my desk across from Farrell.

"There's something different about you today, Sayers. What's going on?"

"I've let go of some of the pain, not all, but some. Mike, I've finally realized and I want to say thank you."

"Thank me, for what?"

"It's been almost two years since Brandon's death, and thank you for your friendship. For being there for me, when I didn't think I needed it. You're not just a partner to me. You're my best friend."

I got up and walked around my desk to his and I kissed him on the cheek and the office cheered. He just stood there with his mouth open. There was no mistaking it was friendship with everyone who was around. Often there were rumors about these two or another. It was par for the course. We worked closely together day in and day out. You just never knew who, until the truth was flying around, or someone got caught with their hands in the cookie jar.

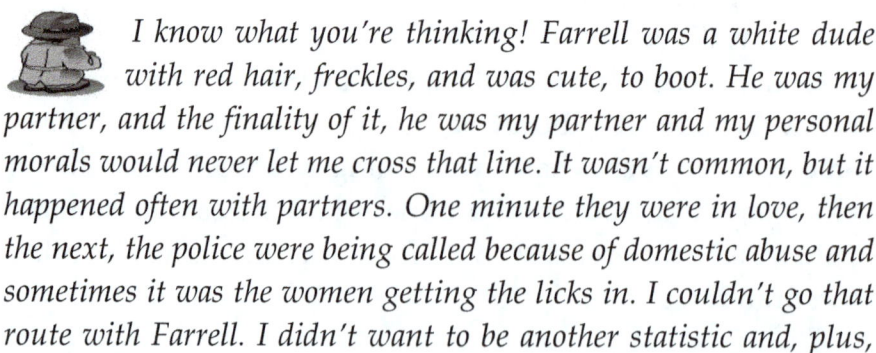

I know what you're thinking! Farrell was a white dude with red hair, freckles, and was cute, to boot. He was my partner, and the finality of it, he was my partner and my personal morals would never let me cross that line. It wasn't common, but it happened often with partners. One minute they were in love, then the next, the police were being called because of domestic abuse and sometimes it was the women getting the licks in. I couldn't go that route with Farrell. I didn't want to be another statistic and, plus,

once again, he wasn't my type.

Someone screamed, "Wow. He's finally speechless."

"I don't know what to say."

I walked back to my seat. "Don't say anything. Let's just go to work."

Then Farrell finally sat back down after the shock of it all. "Okay."

~

While riding around, we received a domestic violence call. It wasn't like we were street cops, but Farrell and I didn't hesitate to take a call when we were in the area. We were detectives, but we were cops first.

"Farrell and Sayers responding, let's go." Arriving at the scene, a crowd had already gathered.

"I'll ask some questions. You call for backup. Ma'am, do you know what's going on in there right now?"

"John, that's the husband. He came home and found his wife in the bed with another man. The man ran out and left. I heard her screaming, so I called the police. Following the screams, I didn't hear her anymore, and I haven't seen them emerge at all. I don't know if he beat her to death or not, but I have heard nothing from her since." I walked back over to the car.

"What information did you get?"

"Well, according to the neighbor. The husband came home and caught his wife in the bed with another man. The lover ran out, and this lady called the police. She said she heard the woman screaming, but she has heard nothing from her since. I think we should go in, but it's your call."

All I could remember is what Kimberly had said about her ex-husband.

"She could be dead or dying in there. I don't think we should wait any longer. Sayers, cover the front and I'll cover the back."

As we were moving in, a primary (A) car arrived. I called Farrell back. We gave them a briefing, and we backed them going in. "Okay." I waited until I heard Farrell bust in the back door before I busted in the front. "This is the Los Angeles Police Department." No one answered. We started checking every room. At the last door, we heard a noise. "Don't anybody move." The man jumps up in his birthday suit. "What's going on here? Why have you busted down my door? What's going on?" the man said. "Oh!" I walked out of the room so fast. I know it was unprofessional to leave my partner alone, but it was a hysterically funny moment. The wife started screaming and so we knew she wasn't dead or hurt. "Sir, calm down. Would you and your wife please get dressed and come into the living room. We would like to talk to you for a minute." I walked into the living room and I muffled my laugh as much as I could, but it wasn't helping any.

"Come on now, Brenda. We need to get this over with. Let Caruso and Maze take it."

"Mike, I cannot believe we busted in on them while they were having sex. They must be into that S & M thing."

"Come on and let's get this over with. You're sick for even thinking like it."

"But you have to admit. He catches her in the bed with another man and then they turn around and have sex themselves. This is a sick couple. We'll just disburse this group."

~

Later, we were celebrating going to a new department. We laughed and laughed about what we had seen earlier in the day. People were staring at us, but we didn't care.

"I've got my partner back. I'm thrilled right now. So, what changed you? And I want all the details."

"Well, on Saturday, I went visiting. I stopped by Mr. & Mrs. Taylor's house. Anna brought some things to my attention I really should have listened to. Then I stopped by Craig's house. We talked for a long while. He said some things I didn't like. I stormed out of his house. The next morning, Craig called and apologized. He asked me to go to the Raiders game with him, so I did. Sitting in the stadium, being around people, laughing. I finally realized I was missing out on life. What Anna and Craig said turned out to be true. I was holding on to whatever I could of Brandon. Closing myself off in the house, just staring and holding his picture. Taking advice from someone I shouldn't have. For almost two years, I did nothing but cry and work. Being with Craig yesterday, I realized what I was missing was my friends, my family, my life, for that matter. I didn't realize what I was doing to myself. To be honest with you, I didn't care what I was doing to myself. I think a part of me wanted to self-destruct to get rid of the pain I felt. Not that I will give up looking for Brandon's killers. I just have a different outlook at this point."

"Sounds like Craig's a miracle worker?"

"We're just friends. Don't read anything into it."

"Okay. I believe in you. I'm just glad you're back."

"I am too Mike. I am too."

Chapter 11

Under the Cover

The first week of training was grueling. I cried at least once every day, but Mike was going through it with me, so that helped a lot. It was a new challenge. We both had to go through. I was glad Craig was there to hold up the pieces when Mike wasn't. Craig and I had really become good friends. He would go with me to Brandon's parents' home and just talk for hours and would make me laugh to no end.

He took me places just to make sure I didn't sit up in the house and my parents appreciated the fact that he was keeping me busy. Craig and I would take Ashley to the amusement park and visit her on weekends I did not have to work. She was growing up so fast. She would be ten soon.

Training was over and it was time for me to go undercover at the University. My first day there, I observed kids smoking marijuana, but we didn't want the drug users. We wanted the drug dealers. It took a couple of days to find the major distributors for the campus.

"Farrell, there are two white males approximately the age of twenty, Daren Stephenson and Elijah Klonick. They sell right out of their room. The dorm was co-ed, so it was easy not to be recognized. I just made my first buy from them, a dime bag. I have to get into the click, to really get to what type of quantity I can purchase."

"You know what to do."

"Find out who is close to them."

Melissa Etheredge, approximately twenty-one years of age and a pot head genius. She was good friends with the two guys. I befriended and won her over, which was the hard part. "I need you to set up a meeting and let them know it would be worth their while." Sergeant Andrews had taught me well. The drug sale went smoothly, and the police arrested them. The trial came because this was their first offense. They got off easily with three months in jail and two years of Summary Probation. One of the boys' fathers got them back into school because of the large contribution he made.

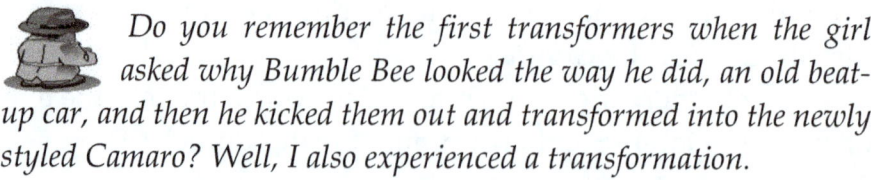 *Yes, these were some rich kids using daddy's money to buy and sell drugs. It was injustice at its best. I have to be honest, had it been kids of another race, money wouldn't have even gotten the father through the door to talk. Maybe I was a little too biased, but there was not much that surprised me these days.*

That part of the training was over, and I was glad. As much as I missed not going to college, the way the schools are now, you couldn't pay me to go back.

Time went on, and the Bumble Bee stung other dealers. That had become my nickname around the precinct because I liked Bumble Bee from Transformer.

Do you remember the first transformers when the girl asked why Bumble Bee looked the way he did, an old beat-up car, and then he kicked them out and transformed into the newly styled Camaro? Well, I also experienced a transformation.

One evening, Craig and I went out to celebrate his new law firm selection as partner at Johnson, Joseph, and now Matthews. We would go to a party honoring him for his work nationally and internationally and they would proclaim his selection and then have a night of fun.

The doorbell rang.

"I'm coming, just a minute Craig."

"Open the door, Brenda, it's freezing out here. The tip of my nose has frostbite." I opened the door and Craig stood there shaking like a leaf.

"Come in out of the cold, although it doesn't get that cold out here. Have a seat by the fire. Anyway, what are you shivering for? This isn't a snow town."

"What were you doing while I was freezing to death out there?" I looked at him for a few seconds before I answered.

"I was putting on my clothes. I did not want you to see me naked."

The look on his face went blank. He turned to the fire and mumbled something under his breath. "Woo th be so bad."

That's all I heard. "What did you say?"

"I said, would that be so bad?" I walked toward him and sat next to him by the fire.

"No, it wouldn't be so bad, but it would be right now. Our friendship means more to me than you realize. I do not want to jeopardize that by trying something I know wouldn't work right now. I have too much baggage to bring into a relationship. You better than anyone knows that. I just want things to stay as they are. Plus, I'm a U.C. now. That takes a lot of my time and energy, and would hurt any relationship."

"Are you saying maybe in the future, you may consider a relationship with me?"

"Craig, I don't know. I can't say yes to something I have no control over."

Right then, I felt like he wanted to make a move, but missed his chance. I felt it and I got up from the footrest just in time.

 *Why didn't I go for it? What did I really have to lose? If I don't try, how would I know if it could work or not? Because I was a basket case and work was the only thing I could focus on intimately. It was easy after a while to turn off the emotions. Don't get me wrong, I loved Craig. He was handsome, but he was too close to Brandon and the memories we shared.*

"You might find someone you may want to marry next week. Let's not try to put expectations on each other. I don't know when I will be ready for a serious relationship."

"Well, I want to put my feelings out in the open. I do care for you and it's more than just a friend feeling, but I don't want to push you into anything or push you away either. Like you, I don't want to lose our friendship, even if that's all it may be. Just know I'm here for you whenever you need me, and that will never change."

"I know Craig and I am here for you too, but not in the way you need me to be right now." I looked into his dark brown eyes, bent down, and kissed him on the cheek. "Thank you." We settled this for now.

"You're welcome. Now let's get to this party. I'm starving," he said.

"Anyway, why did you come over here, trying to look all sexy and not have a coat on? No wonder you're freezing to death."

He smirked to say, 'shut up'. We both laughed and walked out the door.

~

We arrived at the Bonaventure Hotel and it was all fancy as we drove up in one of the many limos.

 *Yes, I must say I was looking mighty gorgeous in my black cocktail dress. Look, just because I was a U.C., didn't mean I didn't know how to glam up when necessary!*

We had a great time, and we laughed so much, because I was looking at all the women who had their eye on Mr. Matthews and to see me with him, they were not happy at all.

"You have all the gorgeous women lawyers around you all the time and not one of them you want to date?"

"Who said I haven't dated any of them. Woman. Just because you are slow, doesn't mean some of these women haven't had their chance. It's just, I know what I want and the women in here are <u>not</u> what I want. When God allows me to find her, then she will be the right one."

 I guess he shut me up!

After eating, they introduced Craig, and he gave a wonderful speech. I knew it was from the heart. He didn't sound like a lawyer. When he brought up my name, I noticed a couple of giggles in the crowd, but I was the first to stand up and give him a round of applause. He walked down to the table, and I hugged him, because I was so proud of him and his accomplishments. He was my friend and only other friend.

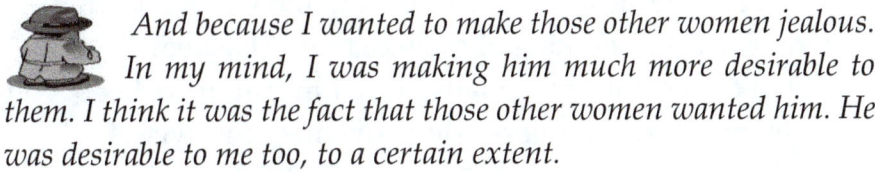 *And because I wanted to make those other women jealous. In my mind, I was making him much more desirable to them. I think it was the fact that those other women wanted him. He was desirable to me too, to a certain extent.*

~

I was never too busy or occupied to think about Brandon and the ongoing investigation. Mike would work on our cases and then, in his spare time, he'd talk to some of his connections out on the street. The Detectives currently on Brandon's case never minded the extra help or connections.

Life for me was slowly but surely moving on. Brandon's memories would always be with me, but he wasn't all I thought about now. Mike and I had been doing undercover work for about a year when they finally got a break in Brandon's case. One of Mike's informants found out some information about a drug dealer who had become well known about six months after Brandon's death. Some people who work for the suspect had talked to Mike's informant.

The boy at the time was bragging and spilt to one of his friends that it was a setup to look gang related. His suppliers wanted Brandon dead because of the neighborhood watch. They put a hit out on Brandon. The precinct now swarming with smiles and finally to me, this case was coming to a head. We would eventually get some justice for Brandon's death.

"Mike, this is great. I can't believe it. After all this time, we finally get a break in the case."

"Brenda don't speak too soon. We don't have him yet. We want both of them, the killer and the one who ordered the hit. It might take a while, so everyone is going to need extra patience for this."

"I don't care about the duration, as long as we apprehend them." I guess Mike could see the determination in my eyes. He looked at me with concern. I was revived, and I was pumped about this news. He looked at me with concern.

"Why are you looking at me like that?" I asked.

"Don't take this personally, but I'm going to keep you away from this case, unless you prove me otherwise."

"What is that supposed to mean? Oh! I see. You don't think I can handle it. You think I'm too close to this and will mess things up. Well, you're wrong, you're wrong. I thought you were my friend, my partner. I'm leaving now and I'm going to give Brandon's parents and Craig the good news. I might talk to you later." I picked up my jacket and stormed out of the office.

The Captain came out of his office as I was leaving. He wanted to know what was up.

"Where is she going?"

"Captain, she's going to go talk to Brandon's family. She's upset and mad at me."

"What did you say to her?"

"That I was going to keep her away from this case unless she proved to me otherwise that she could handle it."

"Well as much as we've all been waiting for this and I somewhat see your point. It wasn't your call to make and next time, I suggest you keep your mouth shut unless you talk to me about it first. Get me, Mike?"

"Yes, sir."

Mike knew I was mad at him. He also knew he shouldn't say any more about it. Even if he thought he was right.

~

I stopped by Craig's house to see if he would go with me to visit Brandon's parents, Kimberly, and Ashley. When I gave him the news, I think he almost cried. He hugged me in celebration, trying to wipe away the tears. He also warned me to give as little information as possible.

"We want both of them. When we get them, not only will we nail them for Brandon's murder, but for attempted murder, too."

"Why?"

"You're a lawyer, think about it. With the extra charge, we'll put them away for a very long time. They had no care about who might be in that garage with Brandon. Think about it, Ashley could have been in there with the both of you. I also want you to be aware you will be under subpoena to testify."

 *Okay, it was a stupid thing to say, but I was in cop mode and wasn't thinking straight, especially after what Farrell*

said to me.

"Have you forgotten I'm a lawyer?"

"I know. Currently, my mind is racing with too many thoughts. I came by to ask you to go visiting with me, to give out some good news?"

"I would be happy to go. Just let me get my coat."

~

The news thrilled Russell and Anna. They said they would be in court every day of the trial. I explained to them we know who they are, but we don't have any evidence. Just hearsay. I didn't want them to get their hopes up too high, because there was a possibility we may never get these guys.

~

Craig and I went back to his place. I guess I was tired, so I fell asleep on the couch. I didn't wake up till the next morning and he had placed a blanket over me.

"Craig. Craig, where are you?" I smelled coffee brewing.

"I'm in the kitchen fixing you breakfast. You still know what breakfast is, don't you?"

"What time is it anyway?" I looked around to find a clock but didn't see one in sight.

"It's about eight-thirty."

"Gosh. I am so glad this is Saturday. I can lie back down."

"Oh! No, you don't. This breakfast will be ready in twenty minutes. So, I want you to go into the bathroom, take a shower and be ready to eat, because you are looking too thin and I remember what you looked like with some meat on your bones. Soon you're going to look like those waif models, without the model."

"Craig, that's mean. I'm not that skinny."

"Anyway, take a shower and be ready to eat when you come out. By the way, there is a new toothbrush in the medicine cabinet you can use."

When I got out of the shower, all I had on was a towel. "Do you have any sweats I can fit?" He gave me a look that only one other person had given me, and I hadn't seen that look in three years.

"Yes, I just bought some uh, uh, some sweats should fit you. They're in my middle drawer on the right-hand side. You should see them on the top. They are black and have a drawstring."

I walked back to his room and closed the door. I got dressed and quietly sat down at the kitchen table.

"What shall we do today?"

"I was going to stop by to see Ashley. You can come if you like."

"I'll pass. I should go into the office and catch up on some paperwork."

"Oh! Okay."

"What if I stop by your office after my visit?"

"That'll be okay. You might get bored, although you're welcome to come."

"I haven't gotten to see the new partners' office anyway."

It was quiet and peaceful at the table.

~

On the way home, and on the way to Kimberly's. I had this uneasy feeling after Craig looked at me that way. Was there a look on my face, which told him something was wrong? If there had been, I didn't realize it, but I knew we needed sometime to cool off. I knew I needed to change my visiting habits for a while and decided not to go to his office after all.

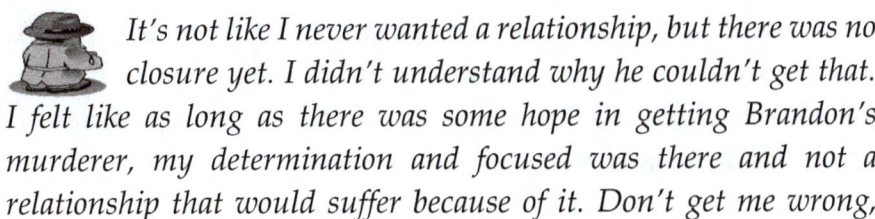 *It's not like I never wanted a relationship, but there was no closure yet. I didn't understand why he couldn't get that. I felt like as long as there was some hope in getting Brandon's murderer, my determination and focused was there and not a relationship that would suffer because of it. Don't get me wrong,*

Craig is such a handsome man. Any woman would be lucky to have him. He was a true gentleman, if nothing else, but I just wasn't ready. Plus, he was Brandon's best friend. Would I experience guilt if I were with Craig? I know what you think. No, I wasn't even considering it. I know your rooting for me to find love, but all in good time.

Mike succeeded in me not having anything to do with the case. Although they let me sit in on the meetings, I could give no input. Only the Captain could change this.

"Come in." I closed the door behind me.

"What is it, Sayers? Wait, a minute. Don't bother telling me. You're upset for being excluded from this case."

"Your darn right I'm upset. Brandon's death happened a long time ago. Mike seems to think I'm probably holding some kind of vengeance for these people. After such tragedy, I don't blame everyone for their concern, but being completely shut out is unbearable. I can say for the first year I wanted them dead, but I don't feel that way now. I'm not holding a grudge. All I want is justice for Brandon."

"What if you don't get justice? What if we can't get these guys?"

"I can live with that. At least I'll know we did our best to make it happen. I can get satisfaction in that, can't I?"

"You know Mike overstepped his boundaries, and I told him so, but the final decision was mine. You and Farrell are to go nowhere near this case. Leave it in the hands of the detectives who are on it now. You can still stay in the meetings, but we will only use you if we have to. Otherwise, I don't want you to do any investigating on this case. You're one of my best. I don't want to put you on suspension. So, please, do what I ask for now and I will evaluate the situation again when we know more."

"Okay." When I came out of the Captain's office, I looked dead into Mike's eyes and walked out of the precinct and he followed behind me. "Go away Mike. I don't want to talk to you right now."

He just kept trying to explain himself. "Brenda, I did it for your own good."

"My own good! My own good! You didn't do this for me, you did it for yourself. From day one, you've hounded this case and I commend you. You didn't give up when everybody else did. Now you want all the glory for yourself. There is no glory in it for you, Farrell. This is not even your case anymore. Yes, your informant provided the information, but you won't receive the credit when they arrest these men. When everybody was saying, you weren't a team player, I wanted and proved them wrong for a while at least, but now the old Mike has shown his two faces again. First, he was a human being gunned down over territory and drug deals, and second, he was a cop who did the right thing for his daughter and his community. These people killed Brandon. Don't you get it yet, Mike? After all these years together, did you even consider my feelings? You have not changed one bit, you're just a wolf in sheep's clothing. The glory hound has found his story. The ball hog has taken over the game. Don't think this is over by a long shot because it's not. I trusted you and you have betrayed my trust for the last time, and I will never forgive you for it."

~

All the way home, I was fuming. I even cried. I couldn't believe my partner could sell me out. There was no explanation he could give me that would ever make me agree to what he had done. I had to find a place of refuge. I had nowhere to go. My parents were out of town. Kimberly was at work and I had no real close friends at the precinct, except

Mike and I definitely couldn't talk to him. So, I had to cry on the only shoulder left.

"Craig, I can't believe they're excluding me from this case."

"Maybe it's for your own good. You don't know how you're going to feel or react when you see these guys."

"You sound like Mike. That is crazy Craig. I want more than anybody to put these people away for a long time. Why would I want to jeopardize the case?"

"I don't know Brenda. Did you talk to your superior?"

"Yes, I talked to Captain Hillary. He agreed with Mike. He would allow me to be in the meetings and he would only use me if needed. I felt so small when I left. It was like I was a rookie all over again. You mark my words, they're going to need me, but in the meantime, I think I'll cry on your shoulder for now."

"Come on, let's watch a movie or something."

Craig held me tight and wiped my tears until we both fell asleep on the couch. It was something about his couch and then I woke up. Surprising enough, it was still daylight. I walked over and stared out the window. I didn't even hear Craig come up behind me. He put his arms around me.

"I'll always be your friend, and no matter what, I'll always be here for you."

"It just hurts. No matter how I felt when all of this happened, I feel like I can never get ahead. I just keep wondering what else in my life is going to go wrong. My ex-husband left me for another woman. They took Brandon from me for no reason, and I can't stop wondering if I'll ever be happy with anyone." He didn't let go. "If we find the right person to love, it will work out." He turned me around. I could not move. Staring into his face, I could see his love for me. I put my arms around his neck. He kissed me and I kissed him back. Was it out of frustration? I don't know. Was there truly attraction from my side of things? It had been a long time without a man's touch, and I wanted it more than I realized. It was passionate, but I knew there was something missing. He was in-love with me, but I wasn't in-love with him. I wasn't ready to be in-love again. I still felt an emptiness inside, as if love alone could never fulfill me. It had to be more than just love. It had to be. He held me in his arms, with my face on his chest. If nothing else, I felt secure with him, but I needed closure.

Yeah, I gave in for a moment, but it wasn't fair to Craig. Because even though I told him I didn't want a relationship, I kept going back to him for support and comfort and I didn't keep it safe between us. To Craig and myself, I was being dishonest. I gave him a moment of false hope. Afterwards, I felt terrible. I know what you thought. Jackpot! They're finally getting together. Wrong!

Days turned into weeks before I could face him again. I picked a restaurant where we could meet and talk. Waiting to talk to him was the longest day of my life. I understood his hurt. Since our kiss, I hadn't seen him, yet the truth needed to be told. I arrived after he did. As I walked to the table, he stood and then kissed me on the cheek. We sat at a secluded booth at Luigi's and I could see on his face he was waiting for me to start. So, I did. "I don't know what the future holds in store for our relationship, but I know what happened can't happen right now. Honestly, I do care for you. I don't want to lose you as a friend. Of course, it will be up to you if you want it to end, but I hope you don't. I need closure before I can move on." I sat there waiting for his response. "Is it my turn to speak now?" I sat back in my seat to gesture I wanted to hear what he had to say. "I knew from the moment you walked out the door, it was a mistake. I rushed , thinking if we just got past that one step, everything would be all right, but in the back of my mind there was doubt. But I don't regret any of it. If you had allowed me to have more, I would have accepted you with all of your baggage, because I know you and it wouldn't be there forever. Yes, I am in-love with you, but I don't want to force you to feel something you don't. Just know I'll always be here for you whenever you need me. Our friendship will always be there, even if you pick someone else to love. I know the memories of Brandon are still strong and I would never want to hurt you. Plus, I know Brandon would come back to haunt me." Grabbing my hands. "Know in your heart I'll be here for you. Just make sure I don't have a woman in the house when you come by for a visit, though." We both laughed. I scooted around the booth, kissed him, and gave him a hug. I think he understood me better than I knew myself. Craig was a brilliant mind and so down to earth it was unbelievable. A Harvard Law School Grad and at the top of his class, he was valedictorian. You couldn't impress him with fancy talk or what type of car you drove. He loved hard, just like Brandon. They were alike in so many ways. He loved his family and would do anything for them in reason. He even donated bone marrow to his cousin and put his niece through medical school. Any girl would be lucky to have him, but it just couldn't be me.

Chapter 12

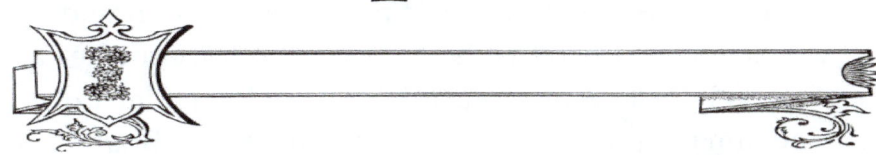

Bait and Tackle

I was still mad at Farrell, but we had a job to do. Another month had gone by and an emergency meeting was called. Only the Captain and Lt. Andrews knew what was going on. I wondered, in particular, why they invited me to the meeting, given my lack of involvement. Everyone sat quietly as the Captain and Andrews walked in. There was another man walking in behind them. "I thank you for getting here on time and on such short notice. We have some important information that needs to be discussed with you. I will let Andrews explain." The Captain stepped back, and Andrews walked up to the podium. "Thanks Captain. As you can see, we have an unfamiliar face in our midst. His name is Bob Dorsett. He is an FBI agent assigned to Brandon's case. This case as of now will be a joint effort. We will pass any information we receive to Bob, and he will do the same. The FBI has been looking into the Kent family for about two years. Some information I have received from one of their operatives is there is only one chance to get both of the men for Brandon's murder. We have gone over this plan all week and weekend.

We will pursue Eric Kent's brother to get the information necessary to crack this case. He loves women. Although he's hesitant to discuss his brother's business with women, he's surprisingly gentlemanly towards them. He may even be a little old-fashioned. The thing is, he knows every aspect of his brother's business. We need to get to him personally. He wasn't in the business when Eric made the hit on Brandon, but we can guarantee from what we know of Eric Kent, he has told his brother all about it. If Eric Kent sounds familiar, police arrested him in the drug bust across the street from Brandon's house. Eric was one boy who lived there. Lawrence, his brother, likes beautiful women and Brenda, that's where you come in. I hate to say it this way, but you are the bait that's going to catch the fish and Jamison, you're going to be her brother and contact for any and everything. We have set up an apartment right down the hall from Lawrence, so when you move in, contact will be quick. We will put this in operation in one week. Sayers and Jamison, I want to see you in my office, A.S.A.P. This is Monday and I want another emergency meeting on Friday. No one in or outside this precinct will hear anything discussed in this room, not even your dogs. Do I make myself clear?"

"Yes, sir," the whole room echoed.

We all got up, especially me, in shock. After the meeting, Farrell followed the Captain into his office. I knew what they were discussing. It was about me, but I guess the Captain set him straight. I was glad I didn't have to do it myself. I was excited and scared at the same time. One minor mistake and everything could go wrong. Jamison and I sat in Andrews' office for a few minutes before he came in. "Let's get right down to it shall we." They picked us for these parts because of our records. Jamison was the best at what he did and number one in doing surveillance. "Sayers, he likes beautiful women, and your record speaks for itself. Not saying any of the other women are ugly, but you best fit the profile he looks for. You can look glamorous, I'm sure." The FBI wanted to use one of their own, but they didn't have anyone that fit what they were looking for. How could that possibly be? But I didn't question it. Just to be clear about things, I know Farrell had some concerns or reservations about me, but they didn't care what Farrell thought. "We picked you because we know you're capable and ready to handle this job. You've handled yourself in every undercover operation you've been in and we know you can handle this one, too. We also picked you both because you look more alike than any of the others." Jamison and I looked at each other and laughed. "You laugh if you like, but you could really pass for brother and sister, and that's what you're going to be. Like we said in the meeting, we have an apartment already set up." I was to work in a lawyer's office as a secretary and Jamison would own an auto body shop. He'd have a partner, who would also be an undercover cop. They'd buy old cars, rebuild them, and sell them for a profit. We 'd have no family other than ourselves. The kicker that may keep the suspicion off of us, and I made this up myself, is that I supply marijuana to some lawyers and their friends. Therefore, that puts me as a beautiful, working and not so innocent young woman. When he feels comfortable with me, if he takes the bait, he'll tell me what his line of business is. "Of course, you get the supply from your brother, so there will not be any suspicion when he comes around. All the rest of this week, I want both of you to concentrate on what you have to do. What I have to ask you to do now will be very hard, but it has to be done for the safety of your lives, the safety of your families and the safety of your fellow officers, and of course, this operation and because the FBI is involved. Jamison, you have been here the longest and have been involved with joint efforts with the FBI before, so you know what you have to do in these kinds of situations, but Sayers, try to follow his lead. Make no mistake, the FBI can take over this case anytime they want, so we can't screw up. You need to contact your family members, close friends, and anyone you on regular basis come in contact with. Make sure you don't exist to them at all. You can have a weapon in your apartment, but you will not carry on your person. We'll get you something from the locker. Your number one priority is this case and this case only. Any information we get you need to know about will come from Jamison. If you don't hear from him at least once a day, do not panic. If he can't get in contact with you, you will hear directly from me. The Captain, FBI Agent Dorsett and I will be the only people who will know your whereabouts. Everyone in this precinct will know you don't exist."

They wanted us to take the rest of this week to get to know each other better and to get our stories straight. The meeting was over, and we had to be back on Friday.

We walked out of Andrews office, and I looked straight into Farrell's eyes. I could tell he was fuming, but I didn't care. I just smiled and walked into the Captain's office. I walked over to where he was standing and hugged his semi-fat neck. It startled him, but he returned the favor. "Thank you for believing in me. That's all I wanted to say." I walked out of the office and Farrell stood up. "Now I see why you got the job."

Even though I had gotten over the fact Farrell didn't want me near this case, I didn't know what came over me. The next thing I knew, my fist connected with Mike's nose and he came to his reality a few seconds later. I just walked out without saying a word. I was okay and ready to deal with the consequences of hitting my partner. I didn't care. All the women cheered, and all the men were laughing. I had had enough of Farrell and his whining.

I called my family Kimberly, Ashley, and even Craig. It was hard explaining to my parents I wouldn't exist for a while. I knew they would worry, but I promised and reassured them, if they did not hear from anyone at the police station, I was all right. Jamison wanted me to come to his house and then we would leave from there.

~

I walked to his door, not knowing what or who to expect. As I was getting ready to knock on the door, it swung open.

"Hi, you must be Brenda. "

"Yes, I am. You must be Mrs. Jamison?" We shook hands.

"My, my. You resemble him, but much, much prettier. Come in. Steven will be right out."

"Okay, thank you."

She walked back into the kitchen and this little rascal ran in and stood there in the doorway. "My name is Brenda. What's yours?" He just stood there, staring. I looked away and then out of the corner of my eye, I saw him sneaking toward me. "Ah, ha, I caught you. You thought you could sneak up on me." I started tickling him and he just started laughing. "Bryan, why are you bothering Ms. Brenda?" Jamison was good-looking, so I could guess why he resembled me.

Hey, if I didn't think of myself as beautiful, then I wouldn't be doing this at all. My confidence and self-esteem would be in the dumps. This is not an ugly duckling story. I knew what my assets were, and I used them for my job.

Jamison had a L.L. Cool J., type of body, head, and vibe, but much taller. He didn't seem the family type, but when you saw him with little Bryan, you could see the daddy in him.

"I'm laughing daddy."

"He's not bothering me, Jamison. I think I just found a new best friend. So, your name is Bryan. Why didn't you tell me your name?"

"I didn't want to tell you, my name. You're a stranger and daddy told me never to talk to strangers."

"So, do I have a new best friend?" Bryan whispered into Jamison's ear. "Daddy, is she a stranger still?" Jamison just laughed. "No, she's not a stranger anymore." Bryan turned around to me. "Yes, you do. Bye." He ran out the room so fast, you would have thought he was Flash Gordon.

"He's so cute Jamison. What happened to you?"

"Hilarious Sayers. Do you have everything?"

"Yes. How does your wife feel about all of this?" I genuinely wanted to know.

"Oh! It doesn't bother her too much anymore. I've done this plenty of times before. She just worries a little. When I leave, she doesn't like me to tell the kids. Jonathan is old enough to know, but Bryan is still young yet. We tell him I'm going on a long trip far away and won't be back for a while. Then he knows I'm on a trip when he doesn't see me. In the meantime, since you have found a new best friend, I'm going to say something to my wife and kids, and I'll be right back."

"Tell your wife I said goodbye. I'm going to wait in the car." I sat outside, thinking about all the secrecy that goes on when you're doing this kind of job. UCs are missing their kids and the kids and the wives and husbands missing them also. I guess I was lucky in that since. I had no husband or children to lie to or to keep secrets from.

~

Jamison followed me in his car to the hotel. We checked in and ordered food from the room. I was so happy there were two beds in there. I think I would have thrown up and switched immediately if there had been only one. We were brother and sister, not husband and wife, thank God! Once we got comfortable, there was a call from Jamison's wife from a neighbor of theirs who called and said he was cheating with another woman and saw us go into a motel together. I couldn't make this up even if I wanted to. Mrs. Jamison told the woman, "I know. I set him up with her." I guess the neighbor was shocked and hung up the phone.

After eating, we got down to the business at hand. The first order of business was what our names would be and from that point, we would call each other by nothing but those names. We decided on the last name first.

"Bravo. Tammy Bravo. What name have you come up with?"

"Sean will do, Sean Bravo. I always use Sean."

"I think that'll do. It's getting late. We can start on why we have no family tomorrow. I'll call Andrews now to get our identifications set up."

"Yes, you really sound like an older sister."

"Older? What do you mean, older?"

"Just kidding, Sayers. I mean Tammy." Laughing hard.

In all honesty, I hadn't laughed that hard in years, but I think I was laughing because I was terrified, too. What if Farrell was right and I mess up the case? I was laughing to hide my fear.

"I'm going to bed. You can do whatever you like, big brother Sean. Goodnight and see you in the morning."

~

During the middle of the week, the only thing we could think of was our adoption and our parents' subsequent death in a house fire. Afterward, we remained without a permanent home. We grew up and out of foster care. What can I say? It was believable, and it was the only way to avoid bringing in any other family members.

~

Friday morning came, and I think I was more nervous than any other time doing UC work. Jamison and I walked into the precinct together. I was the focus of everyone's attention. We both walked to the conference room. I passed Farrell's desk and said, "Good morning," and just walked on. The Captain and Andrews were waiting for some others to come in as I sat there in anticipation. The meeting was short and so we were to go into a procedural meeting with Andrews and Agent Dorsett.

"Just to let you know. We have come up with names and we have no family. This is Sean Bravo my brother."

"And this is Tammy Bravo, my sister. We were adopted and when we were still young, our parents died in a house fire. We have been in and out of Foster care. So, what do you think?" He walked around his desk and stared at us. We stared at each other and then looked back at Andrews.

"It will work, let's do it. Sunday, you Ms. Bravo will move into your new apartment. And by the way Ms. Bravo, we resolved that Monday incident. Do I make myself clear?" He walked out of the door and we were just sitting there. I think that day, Andrews was acting eccentric. It was unusual for Andrews to walk out of his office without a purpose.

"I guess we better go."

"I guess so."

~

Sunday morning came, and Jamison was still asleep. I went and took a shower and got out and Jamison was still asleep. Maybe he had done this so much that nothing bothered him anymore. Everything was riding on me, justice for Brandon and for his family. I stared out of the window for an hour, going over every scenario. There was nothing no one could do or say to prepare me for what I had to do and do it well. I felt like praying. I hadn't prayed in years to God, especially after Brandon died. Regardless, it wasn't like I blamed God or anything. I just didn't understand God's plan. My mother always prayed for me, so I thought at least God would listen to her and that would be sufficient. If nothing else, I knew a little prayer wouldn't hurt. After praying, I heard Jamison groan, so I guess he was finally waking up. "This is the day, big brother Sean." I decided today I would really act like the sister and jumped on Jamison to really wake him up.

"Tammy, why are you jumping on me?"

"Because big brother Sean. This is what little sisters do to their big brothers. So, rise and shine, we have work to do."

"I'm so glad my parents had all boys."

Chapter 13

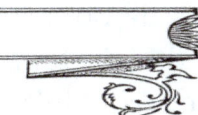

Moving Day

This was my first time doing undercover with a joint task force. So, seeing this huge truck full of stuff for the apartment at the precinct surprised me. Everything I could think of and I mean everything. Some other FBI agents were doing surveillance on the building to make sure Lawrence was there.

~

Arriving at the apartment, we didn't have far to go. I would be on the second floor and it had an elevator, thank goodness.

 *You read about my childhood at the beginning of my story, so you know I was acting like a kid in a candy story.*

Getting all the stuff moved in, Lawrence never showed his face. Jamison and I talked for a few minutes in the apartment. We decided since all the noise didn't make Lawrence curious, I would have to make myself known. We left the apartment so I could get a car registered for Tammy Bravo. I wasn't supposed to, but I stopped at my parent's house before going back to the apartment. We spoke for a few minutes and then I had to leave.

Driving back to the building, I pondered on what I could be up against if he didn't take a liking to me. In a sense, I would be off the hook for this whole thing and another way would have to be found. But knowing me, I would have to come up with another plan of my own. I pulled into the garage, parked, and got into the elevator. The doors open and I walk out as Lawrence opened his door. I pretended like I didn't see him and started opening my door. Just my luck, my key wouldn't work.

"Great! This is not happening right now."

I started kinking the door, and I tried the key one more time. I guess the entire building heard me by then.

"Excuse me, but do you need some help?" he said.

"Only if you can talk this lock into opening for me. This is a bad omen. The day I move in, something has to go wrong."

"Well, I know nothing about omens, but I think I can help you with the door."

"Be my guest."

He wiggled the door a little and then lifted on the door and it opened.

"I can't believe this. No one should go through all that just to open their door. As must rent as we are paying around here. You would think the door would open up on command. I'm sorry to sound like I'm a brat, but this is crazy." He hesitated for a moment and then pushed the door open.

"I'm sorry, where are my manors? My name is Lawrence Kent. I live in 2C and I welcome you to the building."

I stuck out my hand. "Tammy Bravo, it is nice to meet you Lawrence, and thank you for opening my door."

"You're welcome. How long ago did you move in?"

"Well, we finished about an hour ago. My brother and some of his friends helped me. With all the noise they were making, I'm surprised you didn't come out complaining."

"Oh! I was probably in the shower then."

"I just want to say thank you again for opening my door."

"You're quite welcome, again. If you ever need any help with your door, you know where I live. See you around."

"Thanks, bye."

Somehow, my gut said I got his attention. Was I reading something there, or was I just desperate for something to be there? Although it was a good sign, I was not looking forward to taking all that stuff out of the boxes. I just left it here and laid on the bed and went to sleep.

I woke up to the phone ringing. "Hello."

"Hey Tammy, have you made contact yet?"

"Yes, big brother Sean. He opened my door when it wouldn't open after kicking and screaming at it. Sean, you would think these places would have a working door."

"Sister dear, that's the price you pay when you live in Eastwood. By the way, I called to let you know you have to be down at the lawyer's office at seven thirty a.m. They want you there before anyone else, so they can go over your job duties and you can learn how to be a secretary."

"You are enjoying this, aren't you?"

"You should be used to it by now, little sister. You've been getting up at six every morning for the past eight years. Take down this address and I'll call you about seven tomorrow evening."

For another hour, I plopped back on the bed, but I did not fall asleep. I brought very little of my own belongings. I was lacking nothing. Just lying there thinking, in some ways, I knew this would take time. I also wanted things to go smoothly and as fast as possible. To catch Brandon's killer or killers, this was the fastest way. I stayed up till ten, putting things away, trying to get everything in order. "Oh! Forget it. I will not get everything done now, anyway. Go to sleep." And I took my advice.

~

Waking at six, I had breakfast and made my way to the Law Office with five minutes to spare. Having the gist of what being a secretary was about. I was one for a year after I graduated from high school. I walked in and met Mr. Keeble, who would be my boss, for I don't know how long. Right off the bat, I knew he didn't like the idea of me pretending to be there, but the partners of the firm agreed and stuck me with him. I had to make the best of an uncomfortable situation. The only thing he did like was if I had to bring Lawrence there, he would get to act out his part, which was something I prayed to God would never happen.

"Ms. Bravo, I realize this will be awkward for the both of us. All I want to know is, do you have any experience being a Legal Secretary?"

It took every part of my being not to say something wrong. "Yes, Mr. Keeble. I worked as a secretary for a year after high school. My skills include shorthand and phone answering. I just want to make this very clear to you. Laundry and coffee service is not part of this deal. Anything else, I can do it. Oh! And I also type seventy words a minute. Not bad for a U.C., aye."

He straightened his jacket and cleared his throat. "Okay, Ms. Bravo, let's get started."

Yes, I hated every minute of the day. He would walk by my desk and just stare and say nothing and then keep walking. Why did I have to be a secretary? Couldn't I have been a drug smuggler or something exciting on my part? I wanted action, not to be sitting behind a desk answering calls. Okay, I was an action junkie. I was like Farrell, but calmer. Working patrol was enjoyable for me. I had to deal with my issue or it would not go well for me in the office.

Through the day, as long as we stayed out of each other's way and did our jobs, we were fine.

~

My first day, I departed precisely at five. I was ready to be somewhere else. I was used to being free and out on the street. All I could hear in my head was, 'Walter and Associates, Tammy speaking.' Then I thought, thank God, we weren't at Craig's Law Firm. That would have been a total mess.

I had to take a long shower and relax. From the surveillance the FBI had done, Lawrence was not lacking female attention. He was very nice looking. I had to admit, but for him to come after me, I had to differ from the women he was used to dealing with. The only way I knew to get him over here without him expecting me to be the one chasing after him would be to have an 'Apartment Warming'. Invite him, some of the other tenants I met in the building, and Jamison. I would have to set it up for the following Saturday. Jamison called me at exactly seven. I ran the idea by him, and he agreed.

The next day, coming up in the elevator, as I got off, Lawrence was getting on. "Hello. I'm sorry, what's your name again?" I asked him.

"Lawrence. How are you doing, Tammy?"

"I'm doing well. I was wondering if you would come to my 'Apartment Warming' on next Saturday and you can bring your girlfriend or wife."

"I would love to. What time will it start?"

"Six-thirty."

As the doors were closing, he said, "And I don't have a girlfriend or wife."

 *Was he trying to tell me something? Of course he was, but I still couldn't pursue him. He would have to come after me. That meant trying to play hard to get. This would not be easy (ha, ha).*

The next Saturday morning came, and I knew I had to get an early start to get everything together. Grocery shopping, something I hadn't done in a very long time. Surprisingly, during the week, everything was situated and out of the cardboard boxes. That achievement deserved a pat on the back. I was ready by six.

At six-fifteen, the doorbell rang. "This must be Sean trying to be funny." I opened the door. "Lawrence! I thought you were Sean. Come on in and have a seat."

"Thanks for inviting me." He exuded confidence, but his expression was one of surprise, or he was thoroughly impressed. "You fixed this place up nicely. Did you have any help?" Now, I didn't know how to take his comment. All I could think about was I had to be different. "In fact, I did this all by lonesome. It took me a while in my head to figure exactly how I wanted everything. The living room and my bedroom were the hardest for me to decorate and to find who I was in those rooms. I like space and having something in every corner of the room is not my style. Would you like to see the bedroom?"

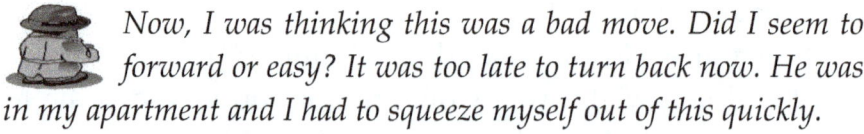 *Now, I was thinking this was a bad move. Did I seem to forward or easy? It was too late to turn back now. He was in my apartment and I had to squeeze myself out of this quickly.*

"Yes, I would like to see your bedroom." As we walked down the hall, I had to save myself somehow. "This is my bedroom. Of course, you can see I love purple. I had to have at least one room with my favorite color in it. I love the spacious closets. They're roomy and cozy and not all closed in." I walked out of the room as fast as I could and he followed. "I'm surprised you came early. Everyone else seems to want to be fashionably late."

"Who did you invite?"

"Well, of course, I invited you, Sean, some co-workers of mine, and some people in the building."

"I hate to be nosy, but who did you invite in the building?"

"Well, let see. I invited Warren, Jerry, Samantha, Kim, Sharon, and Karen."

"Karen! You invited Karen!"

 *Sorry, I had to interject here. No, she wasn't one of those types of Karen's we know of today, but Lawrence was not happy.*

"Yes, what's wrong?!" I asked.

"I know you've only been here a few weeks and you don't really know everyone who lives here, but Karen is a gossip column. She's goofy and very flirtatious with every man she comes in contact with. Karen is bad news."

"I'm sorry to hear that. She's been so nice to me. Maybe she's changed."

"Please don't think I'm rude if I don't speak to her. I must keep my distance."

"Alright. I won't."

Everyone started showing consistently after that. I introduced Lawrence to everyone. Then big brother Sean showed up with a date no doubt. I'd never seen her before, but I guess that was a good thing. If I didn't know her, then she didn't know me. As they walked in, I gave Jamison a big hug and told him in his ear we needed to talk. They both came into the living room. Lawrence stood as I introduced him to Sean. "Lawrence, this is Sean, Sean this Lawrence." They shook hands. I looked into Lawrence's eyes. I really didn't know what to think. "Excuse me Lawrence. I have to speak to Sean for a second. You and Tiffani can grab something to eat and we'll be right back." Jamison and I stepped out onto the terrace.

"Tell me where in the world did you find her?"

"I met her around the corner from the shop. I needed a date, so I asked her."

"Sean, you didn't have to bring a date. You could have come by yourself."

"Well, I didn't. So, let's party, if you don't mind. Don't forget, little sister, I've been doing this way longer than you have."

"Well, that's good to know. You don't have to keep rubbing it in, you know. What kind of woman would go out with a man after meeting two hours ago?" I stopped in my tracks and realized what I had just said. With Brandon, I did the same thing. I guess there was no difference.

 *I just want you all to know, I am good at discerning my shortcomings, but it was different with Brandon, though. I felt an instant connection with him, and I know Ms. Tiffani felt nothing, or Mr. Sean was fantastic with the ladies and his acting.*

We walked in and I saw Lawrence with his head in his hands. Tiffani had left Lawrence to mingle, and Karen swooped in and was yapping at the mouth. I guess he didn't want to be rude. Maybe I could win some brownie points if I rescued him from Karen. "Hi Karen, I am so glad you could make it. If you don't mind, I'd like this agreeable gentleman to help me with something heavy." I could see the relief on his face. He mumbled to me, "Thank you," without her seeing. As the night went on, everyone started heading home. Sean and his date were the last to leave. Lawrence had just left before them. As I was straightening up a bit, my doorbell rang. I looked out the peephole, but I didn't see anyone. "Who is it?" I wasn't expecting anyone to come by that late. "It's Lawrence. I have something for you." I opened the door, and he had changed. "My apologies, but I should have given you this earlier. Despite your request for no gifts, I couldn't resist buying you something I saw in the store." I shook the box. "Don't shake it too much. It's fragile." I walked back to the living room and left the door open, hoping he would follow behind me. He did and closed the door behind him. I sat on the couch and he sat on the chair. "Believe it or not, I wrapped it myself." I know he was fishing for a compliment. "The bow is beautiful. I love purple. It's my favorite color." I looked back at him with an aww seduction.

"I know," he said.

"How did you know?"

"I'm very observant. The two times I've seen you, you had on some portion of purple and your key chain is purple."

"Oh! My, this is beautiful. I have nothing on my dining table. This will go perfectly. Thank you, Lawrence. I love it. Now I have to get some flowers." Looking as if he was concerned, or he wanted to say something. He hesitated for a second and then spoke.

"I wanted to ask you something."

"What is it?" I sat on the couch.

"I wanted to know if you were seeing anyone?"

I didn't want to seem anxious, so I said, "Well." Before I could finish, he started talking, "Oh! I understand. The guy that was here, you're interested in him."

"Who are you referring to?"

"What's his name, Sean? The one you went out on the terrace with."

"Oh, no! You think I'm interested in Sean. I see you've jumped to conclusions. I thought you knew."

"Knew what?"

"Sean is my brother."

"Brother! I thought… I am sorry. I jumped to conclusions."

Again, I didn't want to seem anxious. "No, I'm not seeing anyone, and you don't have to go. It's my fault. I thought I introduced him to you as my brother. That's why you thought, well, what you thought. I was fusing at him because he just broke up with his girlfriend a few days ago and he's already on the prowl again. Men can be so selfish and insincere sometimes."

"Excuse me, but some men. Not all."

"I stand corrected. I know… I guess I just want my brother to be happy."

"What about your happiness?"

"Me! I haven't found true love yet, but I haven't given up." It hurt me to say those words, because I had found the perfect love of all for me and his brother murdered him. Of course, I kept that bit of information to myself.

"It's late. I better get going. Hopefully, I'll see you sometime tomorrow," he said.

"Thank you for the beautiful vase."

"Your welcome. See you later, Ms. Bravo."

"I hope so, bye."

He walked out the door and closed it behind him. This was working out better than I had hoped. I didn't know whether he would go for it, but tonight was the break I needed. At least I knew he was interested in me. I had to let Jamison know, but now was not the time. I was tired and ready to go to bed.

Chapter 14

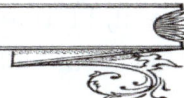

Dance of Deception

I woke up to the doorbell ringing again. My plans were to sleep in late, but that didn't happen. "Who is it?" I looked out the peephole again. "Flower delivery ma'am." This time, I could see the delivery man. I drew my gun, remaining cautious. I couldn't allow my act to go to my head. To avoid blowing my cover, I had to prevent being recognized. After I asked for identification, I asked the delivery man to wait a second while I put down the gun. I opened the door wider, and he handed me a box. "Please sign here ma'am." I signed and closed the door. I opened the box. The smell was exotic and intoxicating. There was a card sticking out the side. 'Here are the flowers for the vase. Be ready at twelve-thirty, if you would like to join me for lunch. I will pick you up then.' "Gotcha!" Now was the time to let Jamison know. I called him down at the shop. "This would be a good time to get in his apartment and put the bugs in. He wants to take me to lunch. I know we'll be out for a while."

"Okay, I have to call Andrews to see if the FBI will set it up. I'll call you back in thirty minutes."

"Okay."

At eleven o'clock, Jamison called back. "Everything is ready. So, all you have to do is go to lunch and keep him gone for a couple of hours." I explained to him it wouldn't be a problem.

At twelve-thirty, Lawrence rang the doorbell. I must admit, I looked smashing. I opened the door. "Oh! Wow. You look great." I thanked him for this wonderful compliment and then asked where we would be going.

"This place is quiet and cozy. It is a restaurant very few people get into during the day...you have to make reservations. Just so happens, they had an opening for our lunch date."

"Thank you very much." And then I asked again.

"Where are we going to lunch?"

"It's a surprise, but I will give you a hint. It's quiet, cozy, and private."

"That sounds nice. I love quiet, cozy, and private."

We left at 12:35 p.m., and the Feds moved in.

~

As we drove up Mulholland Drive, we reached what looked to be an old historical mansion. It was about five stories high and the doors to the entrance looked to be about ten to twelve feet tall. He opened my car door and then opened the double wooden doors to the building. It was beautiful inside. He held my arm as we walked down the corridor to some wide angled stairs. At the top of the stairs, a maître-d' stood.

"Mr. Kent, it is nice to see you on this lovely day."

"Nice to see you too, Philip. Is the table ready?"

"It's ready. I'll show you to your table."

As we walked through the door, a huge smile was on the young man's face. The ceilings were high, with gray and pearl marble floors and posts. We arrived at the table and no one was in sight.

"Did you rent this whole place just for lunch or is the food that bad?"

"Well, to tell you the truth. This place doesn't open until six-thirty. They only serve dinner. Breakfast and lunchtime, it's rented out to private parties or groups. Today was open, so I took it."

"And what would have happened if I had declined the invitation?"

"I guess I would have had the whole place to myself. I guess I'd have to dine alone, dance alone and just be alone. But I must say I'd much rather have company. Beautiful company, I might add." He raised his hand to the server, in control, calm, and sure of himself. In that aspect, he seemed much like Brandon, but they were on different sides of the law, although he intrigued my curiosity. He was not at all as I expected. I guess what surprised me most was he didn't flaunt his money, like a lot of the drug dealers I had seen and dealt with. The car he drove was nice, but reasonable.

I had seen the brash type who had gold on every finger and around their necks. The drug dealer that showed off the girls they had on payroll, because it certainly wasn't love. As much as they did to make it rain in the strip clubs. They were just detestable men with no class or manners.

He was suave and debonair instead of haute and loud. He lived the finer life, yet he kept his wealth and status very private.

"So, tell me about yourself, Mr. Lawrence. I'm pretty sure you want to know something about me. So, to make the conversation interesting and fun, I will ask you a question and then you can ask me one. Does that sound fair enough?"

"It sounds fine to me, but let's save the questions for later. I brought you here to have lunch."

"Are you ready to order, sir?"

"Yes." He turns to look at me. "Do you mind? I'd like to order for both of us."

"Great. It's fewer brain cells I have to use."

"Two lobsters, pasta, bread sticks and special Chablis. Do you drink wine?"

"Yes, once in a while. I don't drink often. I'm not a smoker or a drinker and I especially don't do drugs. Not that I have anything against other people using them, I just don't do the stuff myself."

"Well, that's good to hear. My last girlfriend became an addict. Facing that again is something I don't think I could do. I tried to help her, but she couldn't stop. I even paid for her to go to rehab for six months. Last I heard, she was prostituting herself to support her habit."

"Wow, what a sad situation." And I wondered how much he had to do with it. "She started before we met. It got worse after a couple of months of us dating."

The meal came just as he finished his sentence. "This looks great. I hope it tastes as good as it looks." The lobster was tender. I could get used to this, but in the back of my mind, I knew I had a job to do. We ate in silence, with an occasional look my way seeking approval. "The lobster was delicious. It was so tender and not overcooked. Thank you for lunch."

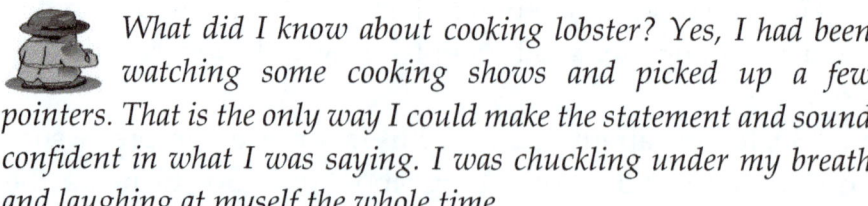 *What did I know about cooking lobster? Yes, I had been watching some cooking shows and picked up a few pointers. That is the only way I could make the statement and sound confident in what I was saying. I was chuckling under my breath and laughing at myself the whole time.*

"You're quite welcome. Would you like some dessert?"

"Oh! No. I don't think so. I would probably burst if I ate another bite. You can eat dessert for the both of us, if you like, or we can stop for some ice cream on the way home?"

"No, no. I won't eat any dessert. I'd rather do something else." We sat there talking for another fifteen minutes, then he stuck out his hand. "Come with me, malady." He leads me up some spiral stairs from the entrance of the dining room. They were beautiful ivory colored, spiraling to the next level above. We entered a room. It was huge, and I knew right away what it was. He left me standing in the middle of the floor, like you would see in those old movies. He had disappeared into the music booth. There were blue satin curtains hanging from the ceiling to floor and you couldn't see out, but you could tell the light from the outside was bright. Music started playing, and then I really knew what was going on. He walked back out to me. "I wanted to dance with you at your party, but now there's no one here to ask you to dance. I know I have a better shot of you not turning me down. So, may I have this dance?"

In my mind, I thought this was going a little too fast, but I couldn't back down now. In any normal setting, when a boy meets a girl, would someone really say that it's going too fast? So, I had to play along. "Yes, you may." We danced for a few songs and then the music stopped, and the lights go out. It was still daylight outside, so we had a little light to go by from a small port window. I stood by the window as he went to check the switches in the music booth.

"Mr. Lawrence, are you all right in there?"

"I'm fine. A flashlight is what I'm searching for." I was standing there and then the Maître d' came in the door and stood next to me.

"Is everything all right up here?"

"Everything is fine. Lawrence is in the booth looking for a flashlight. Are all the lights downstairs out also?"

"Yes, except for the backup generator lights in the kitchen. We may have blown a fuse." I stood there hoping he hadn't turned on some of the equipment and it shorted out everything.

"I'm going to go downstairs and call an electrician if I can find one open on a Sunday. I'll leave you this flashlight, miss."

"Thank you. Lawrence, you don't have to look anymore. I have one." As the Maître d' walked out of the room, Lawrence walked out of the booth.

"Lawrence, were we even supposed to be up here?"

"I don't see why not. I paid enough for the day."

"You don't think, I mean." It was like I was tongue-tied or something. "They won't hold you responsible, except for a fuse."

"I won't doubt it. I pay every time something breaks around here."

"Wait. What did you mean by that?"

"I own this place, Tammy. This restaurant and dance club is my baby. Are you surprised?"

"Why didn't you tell me you owned this night club?"

"Because I wanted it to be a surprise, and it was, wasn't it?"

"Yes, it sure was." I handed the flashlight to him.

"Do you mind if I kiss you?" He was bold and knew what he wanted and wasn't afraid to ask for it.

I hung my head down, being coy, and I looked up to him. "No. I don't mind at all. In fact, I know I'm going to enjoy it." Never forgetting this was a job and not an adventure, the kiss would be something I would never forget, either. Walking out of the room, it was pitch black. The flashlight illuminated the walkway. He braced my hand as we walked down the stairs and through the dining room area. Walking through the kitchen doors, the lights came back on.

"Thank goodness it was just a fuse," Philip said.

"Thanks, Philip, for finding the problem. You saved us a lot of time and money."

"So, do I get a raise?"

"You just received a raise last month."

"I'm kidding."

"We're leaving now. And you don't have to pretend anymore. She knows I own the place."

"Oh! Thank you. Now I don't have to kiss up to you anymore."

"Lawrence, you have a nice and comfortable relationship with your employees."

"He's not an employee. He's my brother Philip."

"I should have known. Your features are very similar, but Philip is much cuter. It is very nice to meet you, Philip."

"Likewise, Ms. Tammy and you are much prettier than the rest as well."

"Alright Philip, I saw her first. Go get your own girl." They both laugh. "During the summer, he's employed here. He goes to college. He's the first in his family to study medicine. His mother is very proud of her son." Lawrence squeezed Philips's cheeks like he was some five-year-old Italian kid.

"Oh! Go home. By the way, are you coming back tonight?"

"I don't think so. You can handle it for one night. It's just routine procedure." Philip looked shocked.

We left and drove back to the apartment. He walked me to the door. He looked at me and I looked at him. I got close to him. "I have to get ready for work tomorrow, but if you would like, you can come over for a movie, some popcorn and some conversation, only if you're interested."

"I'm very interested. What time would you like for me to come over?"

"About six will be okay."

"I'll be there, I mean here."

He kissed me on both cheeks and then kissed me on the lips. It was sensational and spine tingling. He spoke into my ear softly so the neighbors who were walking down the hall couldn't hear him. "I'll see you at six o'clock." I almost felt like a schoolgirl again, but I had to come back to reality. All the questions I had running through my brain. I wanted answers. I got on the phone and called Jamison.

"Hello."

"Big brother Sean, this is your little sister Tammy."

"So how did it go?"

"It went fine. We had lunch and then danced and then came home. But I have some questions I need answers to. You don't have the answers, so you're going to have to get them from Andrews or Dorsett. First, how is it we didn't know he had a younger brother named Philip who goes to college? And please don't tell me his brother is the same Philip that was Farrell's informant? He works in Lawrence's restaurant and nightclub during the summer."

"What night club?"

"Exactly! The night club in the pictures is Lawrence. The restaurant is called the Golden Swan, and the nightclub is called the High Life. I want all the information about his family. Who is his mother, father, sisters, and brothers, and if he has a dog staying at his parent's house? I want no more surprises." I wasn't understanding why this hadn't been thoroughly searched. I was putting myself on the line and not having simple information like this was bothering me to no end. Was I being left out in the cold or was this genuinely an oversight on the FBI's part? "By the way, no one paged him all day. No one called him on his car phone either. So, if you can get me that information as soon as possible, I can know what my next move is and how fast we want this to go. Oh, by the way! Has there been any information on the wire in his apartment? I believe we are being kept in the dark about some pertinent information. Any news on Eric?"

"Apparently, he has been on vacation with his girlfriend. They're supposed to be back tonight. The FBI has had some people on him since they've been gone. We haven't been privy to any other information either. So, I know I won't get any until tomorrow. My partner and I have to finish this car."

"Okay. Just get back to me as soon as possible. I'm not sure if he's hooked, line and sunk just yet. If today was any indication, he's definitely interested. Bye." I hung up the phone before he could even finish. "Wait, a..." Knowing exactly what he was going to ask. I didn't feel like explaining.

Around five-thirty, I changed into something more comfortable. There was nothing sexual about it. I didn't want any misunderstandings. Sweats and a T-shirt did the trick. Lawrence showed at exactly six o'clock. If my clothes disappointed him, he didn't show it.

"Come in. Have a seat. Would you like anything to drink?" He sat but didn't answer right away.

"Just some juice, if you have it."

"I have Grape, Apple-Raspberry or Orange Juice."

"Let me have the Apple-Raspberry."

"Coming right up, by the way, I have an extensive video collection. I have a list in the book on the table. Pick something you haven't seen before." I brought out the drink, and he stood up. "Sit down, you're my guest. Just sit back and relax. Did you find a movie?"

"It wasn't hard. I haven't gone to the movies in ages. The last time I went to the movies, I saw Alien the first one."

"It sure has been a long time. We definitely need to change that. I hope you don't spend your every waking moment at the restaurant. Do you?"

"I spend about ninety percent of my time there, but I don't mind giving some time for the right reasons."

"I'm glad to hear it." I sat on the couch next to him after putting the movie in.

"Because I plan to make sure you live life to the fullest." I kissed him. I think he was just as surprised as I was.

Around nine o'clock. He received a page.

"Can I use your phone?"

"Sure. Use the one in the kitchen." I tried to hear the best I could. My unwired apartment prevented taping. He walked out of the kitchen.

"I'm sorry, but I have to leave. I have to go see my brother."

"Philip, the cute one I met today?"

"No, my other brother Eric, it's important."

"I understand. I have to finish getting ready for work tomorrow." I walked him to the door, and he kissed me on the cheek and then left. I had thought about them tapping into my phone, but I didn't want them to invade my privacy. Ha, ha! The Police tapping in on the Police. I would hope to spend most of my time at his apartment, anyway. There, the wire, and video were in place.

Chapter 15

Brother or No Brother

A few weeks had passed. I never really saw Lawrence during the week, just on the weekends. I only saw him on Saturday and Sunday mornings. According to the tapes, he spent a lot of time with Eric. Within the next couple of weeks, we had someone to infiltrate the organization. The following Saturday, after the infiltration, he invited me to dinner at his apartment. This is when I would try to gain his trust. I didn't know this would go, but all I could do was wait and see. I knocked on his door. He opened it slowly.

"Come on in."

"I hope I'm not too early."

"No, you're right on time. Have a seat."

Looking around, observing everything I could. It was Sheik', as some would put it. It wasn't overly or under decorated, but you could easily tell he had someone decorate for him. As I entered the apartment, I noticed the black Italian leather couches. I didn't know why this was important, but you're taught to observe every detail possible. Tan drapes adorned the ceiling, and his kitchen boasted the most modern appliances imaginable. His business and his apartment received more attention and money, than he had on himself, but I guess all of that was for him in the long run, anyway. The carpet was black with a tan and crimson pattern right under the coffee table. I clearly saw family pictures covering the walls. I trusted the celebrities he had adorned on his wall were from the restaurant and not at his home. There were many faces I had not seen before, but I recognized Eric and Philip right away. As I looked at the pictures, my curiosity got the best of me.

"You know, this is the first time I've stepped foot into this apartment. You're not hiding some woman in the closet, are you?"

"Not at all, but you can check the bedroom if you like."

"No, thank you. I will just stay in this general area right here. Your much too cute. I don't want to be tempted."

"Some wine?"

"No, thank you. Do you have juice? Whatever you're cooking in there, it smells delicious." I didn't know how this evening was going to turn out, but one place it couldn't end up was in his bedroom.

"Here is your juice, and we can sit while dinner is finishing. Everything should be ready in twenty minutes."

"You know we never could talk in depth." I wanted him to open up.

"We can talk now." And there was my opportunity. "All right, you know I work for a Law Firm and I have one brother. I like to be honest with the man I'm dating. We are dating, aren't we?"

He chuckled. "I would say, yes, we are only dating each other."

"You mean, exclusive, exclusive. Meaning there are no side chicks floating around?"

Ladies, if a man doesn't define your relationship and state to you emphatically only dating each other. Please don't take it upon yourselves to believe he is yours alone just because you have sex with him! I've seen too many broken hearts. Assume nothing is exclusive unless they say it. It's bewilderment on the side of the woman thinking sex defines what you are together.

"No, not one, and you seem surprised there are no other women in my life."

"I am very surprised. You are a smart, intelligent and a very handsome man. You own a hot club, and you tell me there is no one else?"

"Absolutely not, that's not how I role."

"I am so happy to hear you say those words, because a lot of times, women fall into this we are exclusive thing, when the man hasn't really said they were. Some women lose all consciousness when they find out the man never thought they were officially dating because they never stated it." I know it sounds weird, but I've seen a lot of relationships go sour, when people just assume they are dating someone exclusively, if they have sex with them or they've gone on several dates or they have introduced them to their mothers.

"I know what you mean, but I am officially saying we are not just dating, but I am exclusively dating you and no one else. Was that clear enough for you?"

"Yes, it was so clear and what I have to say makes this much harder to do. So, I will just get right down to it. Now some men can handle what I'm about to say, but a lot of them can't. When I first started doing this, it was just to make a little extra cash. Now it's like twice a month I do it because I have a job."

"Do what? You're not telling me what you do." I stood up to make like I was nervous.

"I sell pot to some of my co-workers. There, I said it. I hope you don't hate me for not telling you sooner."

He sat there quietly for a moment and then he stood and walked close to me.

"Do you smoke it?"

"No, I can't stand the smell. It gives me a headache, like I told you at the restaurant." He grabbed my face, and then kissed me like he couldn't stop, and then the timer went off in the kitchen. My body wanted him so badly. I could taste it. (Sound familiar?) This was déjà vu all over again. His eyes gazed into mine as though he were testing me. He slowly pulled away. "Let's eat." I could breathe again without delay. I thought, 'That went well.'

We sat, ate, and never spoke a word during dinner. It reminded me so much of Brandon and our dinners together, it was scary. We would just enjoy the silence, the meal, and the fact we were in the same room with each other was enough. "That was delicious. Did Frank prepare it and you brought it home?" His reaction was priceless. "Such language you have. I prepared every savory morsel you put into that lovely mouth of yours. My training was at the Cordon bleu. I see you enjoyed it. You left nothing on your plate. I will clear the dishes later. So, let us go into the living room and you can tell me all about how you started selling marijuana." Having never really thought that far ahead, I didn't think I would have to go into my life story. I had to think of something fast or I was going to sink with the ship. "I get it from my brother. When I first started at the Law Office, I also started dating one paralegal. From time to time, he would smoke it, but he never did while I was around. Apparently, the person he got it from was getting it from my brother. So, the man I was dating cut out the middleman. That's when he came to me. I liked him, so I talked to my brother about it. Sean wasn't having it at first, but business grew because of my ex-boyfriend. I'm not naming names, but there are about five people in the office that smoke it. Now that my brother owns his own shop, we don't do it very often, unless something unexpected comes up and we need cash right away. So that's the complete story. I know it seems a little crazy for people in a law office to take part in such illegal activity, but it seems to wind them down."

"I'm glad you trust me enough to tell me about it."

"Well, like I said, I like to be honest with the man I'm officially dating. I want nothing hanging over my head. Well, enough about me. Tell me about your family. What are your mother and father like?" He stood up and walked over to some pictures and took one from the mantle over the fireplace. "These are my parents in the picture. They had three boys: Eric, Philip and, of course, me. They wanted a daughter, but never had one. You know Philip goes to college. Although Eric and I are close, he's estranged from the family. I'll tell you the story someday. For three years now, my restaurant has thrived. I like to be involved in what I have money invested in. Running my business myself is a must for me. I believe in family. I do whatever I can to help anyone in my family. Frank is my uncle."

"Is there any more of your family working there?"

"Just Philip and Frank. My mother and father come to the restaurant every once in a while, but my mother prefers to cook at home. You name it, she can cook it."

"It sounds like you have a lovely family. You are very lucky. I just have my brother, but I know that he's always been there for me when I needed him. He's all I have left." He pulled me off the couch. "I hope that won't be so from now on." We kissed passionately as the time passed between us.

"That was very nice."

"There's more where that came from, but for now, I have to go down to the restaurant. If you like, you can come with me for the ride."

"I would like that. Let me get my coat. I'll meet you back here in two minutes." I called Jamison to inform him we were going to the restaurant.

~

As we walked into the Golden Swan, Philip warned Lawrence that Eric was there. The look on his face was disturbing, but he pulled himself together. Walking in, I spotted him right away. He also spotted us and waved his hand for us to come over. Although I had seen his pictures, my mind wondered back to when Brandon was alive. I didn't remember seeing Eric in the neighborhood, only when the bust took place. I prayed he wouldn't recognize me at all.

As we arrived at the table, Eric got up and hugged Lawrence.

"Lawrence, introduce me to this gorgeous young woman."

"Tam, this is my brother, Eric. Eric, this is Tammy."

I shook his hand and said, "Hello." I knew right away these two men differed from each other. One was a loudmouth, and the other was Lawrence.

"Come join us. We haven't ordered yet."

"We'll just sit for a moment. We've eaten already."

"He prepared dinner at home for us."

"What? Are you guys living together?"

"No, Eric. We live in the same building. I think we're going upstairs now. Of course, you know dinner is always on me, big bro. Enjoy your meal, Patricia."

I noticed Patricia had not said a word the whole time we were at the table and looked away. When Lawrence said for her to enjoy her meal, she turned her head away. I couldn't pinpoint the reason and I wasn't sure what type of relationship she and Eric had. Lawrence grabbed my arm to help me out of the chair. "I'll talk to you later, Eric." Instead of going to the dance floor, we went through the kitchen to some stairs. "Where are we going? Are you okay?" He kept walking, and I kept following up some stairs we went. He pushed on this charcoal gray steel door and I felt a gush of warm air hit my face. We were on the roof. He took my hand and stared at the moon for quite some time before he said a word.

"I come up here to get away from everything and everybody."

"I assume you mean your brother, Eric?"

"Yes, my brother. I love him with all of my heart, and I would do anything for him, but he gets on my nerves. He's a control freak. When I opened this place, I didn't want any help. This is something I wanted to do on my own, but Eric wasn't having it. He always had to put his nose where it didn't belong." He told me that Eric always had to be the winner in everything, even with women. Either they agreed with his advances and started seeing him, or they wanted to have nothing else to do with either of them. Patricia went for Eric. "I confronted him about it, and he just laughed, saying, 'It was part of the game.' He also said if they really wanted me in the first place, they wouldn't have gone out with him. I'm surprised he didn't hit on you immediately."

"I'm sorry I poured all this out on you."

"It's all right. I'm getting to know the person inside the suit." I hugged him and we just stood there in each other's arms.

"Trust me, you will never have to worry about that with me. I would never get with your brother, ever."

~

Four months we had been dating and not once did he bring up making love. I guess he was an old-fashioned gentleman after all, but I knew soon or later it would come up and I would have to deal with it professionally and calmly. A few weeks after, Lawrence confided in me about his brother's relationships. He came to me about ours. He came over to my apartment on Saturday night. I let him in the door.

"How is the club doing tonight?"

"It's fine. They didn't need me, so I came to visit you."

"Well, I'm glad you did. I didn't see or hear from you all this week and I was kind of missing that deep, sexy, and provocative voice of yours. You want something to eat or to drink?"

"No, thank you. I ate at the restaurant."

"Well, I'm fixing tortillas and cheese."

He came into the kitchen as I stood by the sink. He started kissing my neck. I knew this couldn't happen, but a part of me didn't want him to stop. I turned around to face him and he put his fingers up to my lips. At first, I thought maybe he knows who I am, that's why he's covering my lips to keep me quiet, but that would be ridiculous. If he knew, we certainly wouldn't be standing here together. I just think, I was trying to rationalize my thought and the actions that followed. He carried me to the bedroom. I could have said no and come up with some excuse, but I didn't want to. He laid me down on the bed and looked at me with such sincerity. He lay on the side of me. His touch was invigorating, and he left no part of my body untouched. I put my arms around his neck to kiss him. There had been no one since Brandon. Arching my back to accept him, I couldn't resist the forbidden.

The next morning, we woke up in each other's arms. I knew what I had done was wrong, but it was what I wanted. No one would have to know, but him and I. Then and there, I realized I was falling for him or starting to. I couldn't shout it to the world, and I couldn't tell a living soul, but my heart felt like it had life again.

I know what you are saying. She was stupid, and she should have known better. My behavior is inexcusable. I was fulfilling my duty, but I also indulged in some pleasure. I thought. The reality was it also hurt me because I knew it had to end. It was based on a lie. God, how could I be so stupid? This would be the first and last time we would be in each other's arms like this, and I had to make sure of it. As the old cliché goes, I found love in the wrong place. I stared into his face until he woke up.

"Good morning, Mr. Kent."

"Good morning, Ms. Bravo."

"Would you like some breakfast?"

"I would love some...I'm starving."

We made love again after I put a mint in his mouth and mine. Yes, I was stupid again, but since we had just been stupid, and it was in the same period, why not?

Fixing breakfast, a knock on the door rang out so loud my heart skipped a beat. Panic almost overcame me. I was on the edge. I thought maybe Jamison was checking up on me and Lawrence would come out of the bedroom and then Jamison would know. My heart was pounding like a racehorse. Anguish was instantly on my face. I walked to the door and looked out the peephole, but I saw no one. Then they knocked again.

"Who is it?"

"It's Eric. Is my brother here?" I opened the door. As he walked in uninvited, he eye-balled my apartment like a hawk.

"How did you know where I lived?"

"Karen told me. I presume my brother is here."

"You presume right. He's taking a shower at the moment. You may have a seat and wait if you like. If not, then you can wait outside in the hall." Anyone in his or her right mind would know I was being sarcastic. Eric had the brains to become a big-time drug dealer, but he had no common sense in saving his own life.

"No, I'll wait here. Thank you."

"I was afraid of that." Lawrence walked out of the bedroom dressed.

"Eric, what are you doing here?" Eric stood up. "Well, I've been paging you all night and all morning. We have some important business to discuss for next week. I need your expertise on the matter." Lawrence walked over to me.

"I have to go talk some business with my brother. I'll see you later."

"Okay."

But before he left, I gave him a kiss, goodbye. I knew it would get his brother's goat and made him wait even longer. In his ear, I whispered. "I will miss you." I couldn't know what they were talking about in his apartment. The surveillance tapes later revealed their discussion.

"Your little girlfriend has you wrapped around her little finger, doesn't she?"

"Don't start with me, Eric, about Tammy. She's a very beautiful, intelligent woman and I don't have to worry about her falling for you I might add."

"Look Lawrence. We have a big score to run next week. I don't need your head in the clouds when it should be on business."

"Eric, you don't have to worry about me. My relationship with Tammy has nothing to do with your business. What you should be worried about is the people you're getting the stuff from."

"I hope that's true about you and your girl because this is a big score. This could be the one that puts me over the top and I need nothing to go wrong. Do you understand me? And you don't worry about my connections. I handle that part of things. I'm leaving now and I'll page you later."

~

I hadn't seen Lawrence for a couple of days, and he hadn't called, but according to the tapes. He was hardly at home and rarely used the phone. Friday evening, Jamison called me with some significant news. "Tammy, I just received word from Andrews. Eric and Lawrence delivered the biggest buy of their lives. Somehow, it went sour. They haven't seen Eric or Lawrence. If you hear from Lawrence, try to keep him in his apartment." I was terrified inside. Completely shocked, I didn't know how to react. I didn't want him to be dead or even hurt. Another person taken away. "Oh my! I am in-love with him!"

In my mind, this wasn't supposed to happen, but my heart said otherwise. Was I desperate to have someone? No, it couldn't be. I could have had Craig. What was it? Why had I lost my mind and fell for the wrong guy?

"If I see him, I will keep him over there." I couldn't tell if he noticed the terror in my voice. As I was heading for the kitchen, I heard a door slam. It startled me at first, but I knew it was too close to be my other neighbors' apartment door. I checked to see if there was anyone in the hallway, and then I crept over to Lawrence's apartment. Pressing my ear to the door, I listened to see if he was inside. I heard rambling, and I knocked on the door. He never answered and then I knocked again.

"Lawrence, I know you're in there. It's me Tammy." I kept knocking, and he kept saying nothing until I knocked again.

"Tammy, I can't talk to you right now."

"Lawrence, please let me in. What's going on? I'm not leaving until you let me in." A minute passed, and the door opened. I walked through and he was pacing the floor. Closing the door behind me and locking it, I could see he was worried.

"Lawrence, what's going on? I've never seen you this upset before. Have you had a run in with your brother again?"

"No, it's nothing like that. Tammy, I need to talk to you about something."

"What is it, Lawrence? You know you can tell me anything." He just kept pacing back and forth.

"Come sit down. What I'm about to say could destroy our relationship, but I hope it doesn't. I know you told me about selling the marijuana, but I haven't been honest with you. Just know I love you and if you decide not to continue this relationship, I will understand completely. It's something I'm not proud of, but it was something I couldn't get out of once I got in." He walked around and paced some more. I guess he was wondering if he should really tell me, but it was too late to back out now. He confessed that he and Eric sold drugs. He wasn't talking about marijuana, but the hard-core stuff. Today they were going to do the biggest buy of Eric's life. Somehow, everything went wrong. It happened so fast and things didn't go the way they planned. A shootout occurred, and he believed Eric was hit. "I haven't sold drugs since I've had the business, but Eric has been the head of the organization from the beginning. Believe me, I tried every way to start my business legally, but no one would give me a chance." Eric had long been in the drug game before

Lawrence came into the picture. This was his only chance to get a piece of the pie. Upon his arrival, Eric's position was secure, so Lawrence assumed control of the manpower. "I really didn't want to be involved, but he told me I was the only one he could trust. So, I went along. Believe me, Tammy. This is not the way I want to spend the rest of my life. Living, always having to look over my shoulder, isn't what I want out of life. I want to grow old with a wife and have children." I stood and walked over to him. I caressed his face and kissed him. Secretly, I whispered into his ear to avoid the surveillance tapes.

 *This was a dangerous game I was playing. I didn't know how deep I had gotten until I said...*

"I love you, Lawrence Kent, and nothing will change that. So, how many kids do you want?" We both laughed and hugged, but I could tell he was still worried. Still, having a job to do, I had my assurance I loved him. After this was all over, I couldn't honestly say he would still love me in return, because I knew someone would get hurt in the end. And the night went on quietly.

Hurt was the least of my problems. I wasn't thinking of the consequences, the true consequences of my actions. I was a damaged person. There was no coming back from this, but at least I could hide from everyone else what I had done and what I was feeling for Lawrence.

The next morning, I woke Lawrence up early. I knocked on the door. It took him a while to come to the door and then he opened it.

"Good morning Mr. Kent. Are you up for a big breakfast?"

"I'm not hungry, but I appreciate and need your company. I've been trying to call Eric all night. Come in and make yourself at home. I'm going to take a shower."

"I'll fix some coffee. It should be ready by the time you get out."

"I hope so. I need something to wake me up right now."

As I was scooping the coffee out of the jar, someone knocked on the door. I opened it. "Hello, Eric." He didn't even acknowledge I was even there. He just barged through the door, looking, and searching for Lawrence. My confirmation Eric wasn't dead had come. Eric threatened me with a gun. "I need to speak to my brother."

Of course, I could have taken him in my head, but I had to play it cool. I didn't want to show my hand if I didn't have to. I especially didn't want to have to answer Lawrence's question about how I beat up his brother. So, I stayed cool, and collected.

 *I know you are laughing right now, but you all don't know I am a 3rd Degree Black Belt in Tae Kwon Do and Hop Ki Do. I am a bad Mama-Jama.*

"Honey, is the coffee ready?" As soon as Lawrence saw his brother, he stopped in his tracks. "Eric!" He pushed me down on the ground and punched Lawrence in the mouth. The look on Lawrence's face said death and then I knew in Lawrence's heart he wanted to kill him, but he just stood there in shock that his brother would punch him with such disdain.

"Hello, little brother. I'm sorry to interrupt this love fest, but we must talk. Can you ask your girlfriend to give us some privacy?" As he was saying this to Lawrence, he was pointing at me the whole time.

"You don't have to Lawrence. I finished the coffee, so I'll let you two have your privacy."

"No, Tammy. You can stay. Eric, I will only say this once and I don't plan on saying it again. Don't you ever in the life you have left, put your hands on me or Tammy." The look on

Eric's face said it all. The rage in his eyes was terrifying, but I couldn't move. It looked as if things were going to come to blows right then and there and we would have the information I was doing all this for. "Eric. Tammy is my girlfriend. Whatever you have to say, she can hear it." Eric looks back at me.

"Are you sure you can handle it?"

"Eric, she knows what we do. I told her everything."

"Okay. Can you explain what happened yesterday?"

"I don't know what happened yesterday, only you do. When we drove up to the site, I told you something didn't seem right, but you just said I was being paranoid. It's my job to be paranoid, fool! You put me in charge of the personnel to have your back, but you constantly undermine me, and I hate it when you do it in front of the men!"

"All right, I will give you that, but how come you didn't back me up when everything was going haywire?"

"Because, Eric, when they started shooting, in order for me to back you up, I had to be alive. I had to take cover. I didn't see you anymore. Despite my calling your name, you didn't answer. I thought you might have gotten out. I hated to admit it, but I thought you were hit or dead, but I guess you escaped before me. So, if anyone didn't have someone else's back, it was you, you selfish prick! You left me there, and you didn't care whether I was alive or dead. I walked for miles after everything cleared. So, don't come down on me for something that wasn't my fault. I told you something wasn't right, and you just ignored me. You had to do it your way, no matter what. They played you, Eric. Deal with it."

"Okay Lawrence. We will discuss this further at another time. All I have to say for now is, you better get your head out of the clouds and back on business." And then he left. Yes, they were brothers, but they were looking at things in a whole different way. My heart started slowing down, and then I started breathing again. Lawrence walked over to me to help me get up.

"Are you all right Lawrence?"

"I'm fine. It just makes me angry when he tries to blame me for everything that doesn't go his way. I had no control over what happened yesterday and because he did not listen to me in the first place, there are two of my men dead and he's never going to admit to it." He kissed me on the forehead and sat on the couch. I felt bad for him because he was right. No amount of talking would change that. Why was I sympathizing with this man? Was it just because I was in love with him or was it something else?

Man, you don't know how much I was relieved things didn't come to a head. The FBI knew what was taking place. They sabotaged the buy. I just knew they were going to kill each other right then and there, and then we would never get justice for Brandon. Just a little tidbit before I go on with the story.

I knew nothing about it, but that night Lawrence and Eric had a big argument over what happened because he told me everything. According to the tapes, Eric was furious with Lawrence. He couldn't control him anymore. Lawrence was finally breaking free from his brother's grip. Eric called his second in command bully into the office.

"It seems my brother is tired of this lifestyle and I am going to need someone to take his place."

"Eric, he's your brother!"

"Brother or no brother, I can't afford any more mistakes. You're my number one man now, Hammer. My brother trusts you, and now I trust you. I know you are my brother's best friend, but I need to know I can trust you to keep your feelings out of this matter. It's business. I trust you will make the right decision because your life depends on it. My brother is going in another direction and I need my men to stay on top of their game. I never want another problem like we had the yesterday."

"But Eric, you know that wasn't Lawrence's fault. We didn't find you, so we thought you got out."

"Once again, brother or no brother, he needs to be taken care of. He knows too much."

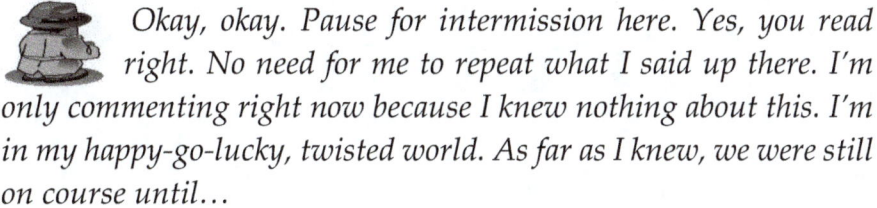 *Okay, okay. Pause for intermission here. Yes, you read right. No need for me to repeat what I said up there. I'm only commenting right now because I knew nothing about this. I'm in my happy-go-lucky, twisted world. As far as I knew, we were still on course until...*

Chapter 16

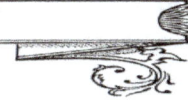

Busted

There was an emergency meeting secretly held, and no one knew why. I had to be careful in my planning. No one could see me leaving the office. No one could know my destination. They set the meeting at one o'clock. Everyone was on time and eagerly awaiting the news. Andrews, the Captain, and FBI Agent Dorsett walked into the room. "I thank everyone for showing up on time. Each of you knows this operation has been a joint effort. The FBI has been doing the surveillance and we have our own U.C. Sayers and Jamison. We all know we've been on this case for a very long time. We brought you here to let you know this operation has come to a head. I'm going to turn it over to Agent Dorsett to fill in the rest." Not understanding what was coming. Farrell was never far from my mind. I wasn't able to see him before the meeting to make sure he was all right. Of course, he couldn't reach out to me because I was undercover. Although he had betrayed my trust, I still cared about him and didn't want any harm to come his way.

"Thank you, Lt. Andrews. We know Eric Kent was the man to carry out the hit on Sgt. Brandon Taylor. We also have the surveillance tapes from Lawrence, the younger brother, confessing to Sayers about what they do for a living. We also know we can't bust them unless they are in the act. But we've got something better. On last night, an informant in the organization said Eric and Lawrence had a big argument. They hollered a lot, but after Lawrence left, Eric summoned Jonathan Woods, known as Hammer, told our informant, which was wired at the time: in so many words, Eric has put a hit out on his brother." My heart, my stomach, and my whole body could have dropped to the floor. My disbelief at what I heard was overwhelming, and my feelings remained hidden in that room. I was not only playing undercover to Lawrence, but also to the men and women I was working with. "Sayers, this is where you come in. You're going to have to tell him who you are. We want you to let Lawrence hear the tape and see if he'll testify against his brother. I know this is a risk, but this is our only chance. We don't know when or where this will take place, but until we find out Sayers, just play your normal role. This may come at any time or place without our knowledge, so we have to be prepared and ready for any situation. It would be preferable to know, but we may not count on that."

"Sayers and Jamison, we will let you know as soon as possible if we hear any word. If we get when and where, then, Sayers, you will go to work on Lawrence. Does anyone have questions for me?" He waited, and no hands went up. "No. Then I'll turn it over to Lt. Andrews." My ears were reeling with white noise. "That is all. There's nothing further to add. Sayers and Jamison, make sure you're not seen when you leave."

When I saw everyone getting up from their seats is when I realized I had better go to. Numb was the only word I could describe. Knowing Eric put a hit out on his own brother made it surreal. I made it back unseen and unmissed from the office. I had to leave the law office and there was no way they could stop me.

 What could they do, fire me? I don't think so!

~

I sat in my room all day, and night, tears rolling down uncontrollably. I prayed with sincerity of heart for the second time in my life. That we could know when and where this was going to take place. My dread would be to tell him I'm a UC and that I loved him and wouldn't expect him to understand. You know that old cliché.

There was that thing lingering over me again, prayer. God heard my prayer, and they were able to get the information needed and that dread hit me like a red house brick. I would have to tell him who I really was and that his brother was going to have him killed. I wouldn't even know where to begin.

My feelings for him were deeper than I wanted them to be. This time I knew the heartache was coming, and I had to do everything in my power to get him to understand and continue to love me for the sake of sanity. Even though I knew what he did for a living, I also knew the other side of him, and he wanted out. I had no one to turn to once again. Everything was riding on my shoulders. I heard a knock on the door.

"Who is it?"

"It's me Lawrence. Let me in." My role was not over yet. I opened the door wide and brisk.

"Come in."

"I don't have a lot of words to explain. I just need you to get dressed and come with me. We're going to celebrate."

"Celebrate what?"

"Please, don't ask any questions right now. You will know soon enough."

"Okay. Let me get dressed."

"I would like you to wear the purple dress I bought you. You haven't worn it, have you?"

Yes, purple is my true favorite color. There is no denying it. I watch the Purple Rain movie every time it was on, just because it had the word purple in it. If I thought a purple car would be cute, I'd do it. Yes, sometimes I even have to laugh at myself.

"No, I haven't. I'll be just a minute." I came back out into the living room.

"So how do I look?"

"You look beautiful, sweet, and sexy, I might add. All the qualities I love in a woman."

"Well, if you want to keep going, you can add smart, too." He stood and came close to me. "You are a very smart and sexy woman!" He kissed me with enthusiasm. A kiss I'd never known from him, something about him had changed. He wasn't holding back. It was like he was free and then I realized why. He had left his brother for good. That's why we were celebrating. I couldn't really celebrate with him on the inside, but on the outside, the play had to go on.

"Are you ready?"

"Yes. Where are we going?"

"We are going to the restaurant. I closed for the night. Dinner was prepared for us and I told everyone they could have the night off. We have the whole place to ourselves. Just come on."

We left, and for the night, I had forgotten my job. When we walked into the restaurant, there was one lone table in the middle of the room set for two. After dining, he stood up and walked around the whole place.

"I'm free. I'm finally free from my brother, the drug business, and I'm free from looking over my shoulder all the time. You can't imagine what I'm feeling right now." He walked over to the table where I was sitting.

"Will you marry me?" He really wanted to marry me. Words failed me. I was in trouble and there was no getting out of it. "Tammy, I'm asking you to marry me." He got down on one knee and pulled out a ring the size of Mount Everest. How could I say no? He was going to be heartbroken enough.

"Yes, I will marry you."

 *That night was real for him, but a fantasy for me. We danced and kissed like there was no one else in the world. We held each other tight, and he talked about the life we were going to have, and he had no clue I was going to ruin his life, like his brother had ruined mine, on purpose so many years ago. To be honest, we wouldn't have been there if it hadn't been for his brother. Why wasn't his life being ruined inside out? Jail was too good for him. I wanted him dead for existing in my reality.*

The following morning, reality hit me once again in the face. I woke up in his arms, but I couldn't stay there this time. He was asleep. I had to leave and get away so I could beat myself up without waking him. A method of informing him about the current situation had to be conceived. I loved him too much not to tell him the truth. I reached my apartment, and the phone was ringing while coming through the door.

"Hello."

"Tammy, where in God's name have you been? I've been trying to reach you all night."

"I was out with Lawrence last night. We were celebrating. I went for an early morning run too."

Yes, I lied to Jamison. I couldn't let him know what was up. I was stupid, but I had to cover my tracks and my feelings. No one had my trust at this point. I didn't trust myself for getting me into this mess.

"Celebrating what?"

"Well, apparently, he's out of the business. Sean, he asked me to marry him last night."

"And of course, you said no, right?"

"Actually, no I didn't. I said yes. I mean, what was I supposed to do? If I had told him no, he would have become suspicious and shut down. I know this man and to tell him no last night would have put us back, way back."

"Tammy, you know this makes things more complicated, but we can't talk about this right now. I just heard that they moved the drug deal up to next weekend instead of two weeks. Eric wants this done, and he wants it done as soon as possible. Apparently, he has someone spying on you two. So, you're going to have to go to work. You're going to have to put your feelings aside. You have a job to do first. Feelings come second."

"I know Sean. I always knew I had a job to do. It still doesn't make it any easier."

"I know Tammy. I was in your shoes once. It wasn't pretty, and it's something you never forget, but the job comes first. So, if you go down to your mailbox. The tapes will be in there. I couldn't reach you last night to tell you and I didn't want to take the chance of leaving a message on your answering machine. Sayers, between you and me, I know you're in-love with him. The right love is out there for you somewhere and when all this is over, you will find it. You're going to have to be strong, like I know you can be."

 *Yeah, he caught me. He knew and if he knew over the phone, how could I hide it from anyone else? I was so lost. I didn't know if I could ever redeem myself for this one.*

"Jamison, thanks for being a friend and my big brother. You are right. You have been doing this longer than I have."

"I know, and you are welcome. All I ask is you do your job. I have a wife and kids to go home to and you also have a family to go home to, an actual family."

A real family, Jamison said. Those words haunted me. The pain and reality of the whole situation was before me. I hung up the phone, headed down to the mailbox, and came back, seeing no one. Quietly, I walked back to my apartment. Inside, I looked at the envelope. I opened it and put the tape in the stereo. Confirmation of everything I'd been told arrived, and I knew then there was no turning back. I didn't see Lawrence at all that day or night. He called me on the phone to tell me he was in bed and asked if I wanted to come over. I couldn't face him just yet. I had to come up with a plan. To save our relationship, I had to figure out a way to tell him who I was and where I worked, hoping against hope that we could salvage it.

"Lawrence, I can't come over tonight. I'm not feeling very well. A migraine has been plaguing me. I should be okay by morning. First thing, tomorrow, I promise to call you first thing. I need to get some rest."

I couldn't come up with a better excuse than that? As a woman, I was a Bond girl. I was undercover, FBI, CIA, and MI6, all rolled up in one. My style should have been much smoother. My head was in a fantasy basket case.

"I love you, Tam. I hope you feel better."

"I'll see you in the morning, Lawrence. Goodnight and don't let the bedbugs bite." I couldn't tell him I loved him back. He called me on his house phone, which was tapped. All the memories of old times had rushed back in. I was crying to sleep. I loved Brandon so much and now I was doing it because of Lawrence. I would lose him and the love we shared once again and that hurt the most.

The morning of tell all to end all things, all I knew how to handle these situations, had gone out the window. The only thing I could think of was to play the tape. At eight o'clock in the morning, I called Lawrence to my apartment, already putting the tape into the stereo. Waiting for twenty minutes in agony, before he would show up at my door. His knock was terrifying, but fear would have to subside. I opened the door, and he knew by the look on my face something was wrong.

"Lawrence, come in."

"Tammy, what's wrong? What is it? Oh, I get it, you don't want to marry me."

I closed the door behind me and walked over to him. I kissed him long and hard, hoping the bond we shared would remain after I told him the truth. Hoping against all hope he would know I was truly in-love with him. "Lawrence, what I have to tell you is going to hurt you. I love you more than you know, and what I'm about to say won't change that." He stood there looking at me as though he knew what I was going to say, but he didn't know. Maybe he thought I was going to call off the engagement, but after hearing what I had to say, he just may do that on his own. His look was though I had shot him and maybe I had, even from the beginning. He shuffled his body as though he was waiting for an Ali boxing blow. I could not make him suffer any longer.

"Lawrence, I built our relationship on a lie. My name isn't Tammy Bravo, it's Brenda Sayers. I'm an undercover police officer for the Drug Task Force Unit for the L.A. Police

Department. My job was to get information about your brothers' drug operation. I was to use any means necessary to get that information."

"Even pretend to fall in-love with me?"

"Lawrence, I'm not pretending where my love for you is concerned. That's why telling you all this is. Why? It's beyond imagination. You may not believe that, but it's true. I love you, which is the one thing I am truthful about. They tapped your apartment, so I did this here, but that isn't all. I was in-love once before, to a man that was indeed rare to find these days. His name was Brandon Taylor."

"What the @#%&!"

"By the look on your face, you know who I'm speaking of."

With his hands interlocked on top of his head. "I heard about it."

"We know your brother was the shooter that killed Brandon. He and I had been engaged for several years. Your brother murdered Brandon the day we were to be married. For three years, we had been trying to find any kind of lead to Brandon's killer or killers. That day came and the next week I was moving in here. Believe me, I had no intention whatsoever to fall in-love with you. As a matter of fact, I hated you even before I met you, because of what your brother represents to me."

"This is truly happening to me. So, now you want me to turn in my brother? No way! You people must be crazy!" He was furious, like he could kill me right on the spot.

However, I hadn't finished, and I couldn't gauge his tolerance. "Lawrence, I'm not finished. I have something you need to hear." I walked over to the stereo and I played the tape. The hurt in his eyes was overwhelming. Tears rolled down uncontrollably. I reached out to him, but he jerked away.

"Don't touch me. Don't you ever touch me again, Tammy. I mean, whatever your name is."

"Lawrence, please. Believe me. I love you."

"You don't know what love is." I know I couldn't get through to him right now, but I had to say it.

"We need you to go through with the drug deal. We want you to testify against your brother for the murder of Brandon and the attempted murder of you. This is the only way we can put him in jail for the rest of his life. We need your help, and we can't do this successfully without your cooperation. If you don't help us, they are going to charge you as well. Your brother is going to jail whether or not you do." He turned and walked out of the door. I didn't run after him because I knew my words wouldn't and couldn't help him decide. He had his own spiritual principalities to face and so did I. Knowing I had lost his love forever. It didn't hurt any less than when I lost Brandon. I explained to Jamison what I told him and what transpired. I explained they needed to make sure he didn't visit his brother and shouldn't touch him otherwise. He relayed the message and now it was a waiting game.

~

The day after the disaster of my life going up into flames, I took a walk. I hadn't walked on the beach in years, since my first date with Brandon. I told Jamison where I would be and to page me if they heard any news. The sea air was vigorously refreshing. It was civil, calm, peaceful, and tranquil and totally opposite to what my personal life was. 'Two different men, but I fell in love with both. Why?' I guess that was the biggest question of all. This heartbreak was all mine to claim. "Why God?" I screamed to the heavens because no one was on the beach with me.

"Because true love knows no boundaries and no matter what happens in our lives, nothing can ever destroy what two people share, even if it's just a memory. The thing is, do we just let it slip away?" I turned to face Lawrence.

"How did you find me?"

"Your big brother Sean. I did a lot of begging when I went to his shop."

"I'm." He put his fingers to my lips once again.

"Say nothing. Just say you will still love me and when all this is over, we'll get married."

"Yes, we will. I love you so much." I held on tight. Nothing could ever tear us apart again. We would finally get Eric and put him in jail. I finally get the happy ending I deserved. I had Lawrence back, but the worry and anxiety were still real. It wouldn't go away until this was all over. Lawrence had agreed to a deal for his testimony. The dangerous part would be the attempted execution itself and making sure that not only Lawrence but everyone else came out alive.

~

On Thursday, there was a debriefing. They briefed Lawrence on what he needed to do. He knew he had to get all the information he could about Brandon's death. We had one night together before all of this was supposed to take place. Committing ourselves to each other and this process was all we could do at this point.

~

On Friday, we were in my apartment. He was being fitted for a wire and briefed once more. I could talk to him alone without the other officers hearing me.

"Lawrence, don't forget there will be police everywhere and whatever you do, don't panic. Remember, this is your life on the line, and you can't afford to do anything stupid or daring. We need you and your brother alive. I need you alive.

We shouldn't have to take any shots, unless absolutely necessary, but we would rather it not end that way."

"You don't have to worry. I have a lot to live for. It's just amazing to me, after all this, the years we've spent together, money is what it all came down to. He would rather have money than his brother. I just pray my parents can handle all this. This is going to break their hearts." He looked up at me and smiled. It was time. He had to meet his brother at noon. They would meet at Eric's house and then would drive to the sight together.

As they were in the car, Lawrence got Eric to talk about Brandon's murder.

"Eric."

"What?"

"Would you promise me this is the last time?"

"I promise, Lawrence, this will definitely be the last time."

"A part of me is going to miss it, but I want to spend the rest of my life making a family. I was thinking the other day about how you really got big time by killing that cop over there on Harvard Street. After that, you were an unstoppable man. You were exceptional. Your business has grown and look at you now, not a care in the world."

"Lawrence, I care. I care about my business staying profitable. Killing that cop was just part of the game. He was messing with my boss's business out on the street and taking customers away. Something had to be done, and I was the one who had the guts to carry it out. No matter what anyone else thought about that move on the cop, the boss was happy I took care of business. It was a massacre. When he lifted that garage door, I sprayed him with no hesitation. I almost had a two for one deal. I think his name was Taylor or Baylor or something like that. We're here. Let's get this over with. I have to be in Palm Springs in two hours." The wire was still functioning, and everything was going smoothly. We got him on tape admitting to killing Brandon. As soon as Eric gave the signal to Hammer, we were to move in.

As the deal was going down, everyone was cautious not to move too soon or too slow. The purchase was complete, and the buyers disappeared. FBI agents, who were waiting for them out of sight, stopped them and made a clean bust. We knew this was where it would go down.

"Lawrence, my little brother, I'm sorry to say I can't afford to let you out of the game. Now you have a choice. You either stay in the game or your dear sweet mother is going to have to bury you without having a body. What's it going to be?"

"Eric, I know you're not doing this. You can't be serious."

"Oh! Little brother, I'm very serious. I can step in and fill the void. Mom always favored you over me, anyway. With you out of the picture, she can love me again. You've got five seconds to decide. One…, two…, three…, four…"

"You're just going to kill me, then."

"Hammer, you know what to do."

"Hammer! You're going to let him use you like this. We grew up together, man. You were more like a brother to me than Eric ever was. Don't put yourself in this man. Think of your mom." Hammer loved his mother more than anything in the world. She was the only one around for him. His father had left when he was three and she had no family to help care for him. She did what she could to raise him the best that she could, and he loved her dearly for it. Not because she was his mother, but she cared enough to keep him and not put him up for adoption. "I can't, Eric."

Eric pulled out a gun and shot Hammer in the chest. The police moved in and all hell broke loose as Eric then shot Lawrence in the stomach. It was total chaos. Things I witnessed. I didn't want to be a part of. During the time of the shooting, most of the guys who worked for Eric were dead, except for maybe four or five men. Some of the FBI officers took two of the men and just killed them in cold blood. They had given up, but they just killed them, anyway. They finally stopped, but it was too late. I went up to them and asked why? "Because they killed an officer and I don't mind if there's two less drug dealers around," one officer said. I wished they had gone crazy or something, but they hadn't. They knew exactly what they had done and unfortunately, no one was going to say anything, even me. An ambulance was called. In fact, two or three were on standing by. I went back to stay with Lawrence. As I caressed his face, he seemed more peaceful than I was at this point. I wanted him to wear a vest, but he refused. He said it would make Eric suspicious. "Stay with me Lawrence. You're going to be all right. Don't forget we have a date at the altar." Looking out of the corner of my eye, it was like I saw it happening in slow motion again. It was an apartment complex across the street from what had just happened with the bust. A teen-aged girl, who couldn't have been only about fourteen, was pointing a gun at her mother and pulling her four little sisters outside the door. I told an officer to stay with Lawrence. Having called Jamison over, I told him what I saw. I ran across the street and tried to talk to the girl, but she just stood there with this blank look on her face. She pulled the trigger and shot the smallest girl and then the next one and then the next one. She paid no attention to me or anyone else as I was yelling. I ran up behind her and tried to grab her. Before I could get the gun away, she shot the last little girl, right through the mouth, as she was screaming. I finally got the gun away, and I wrestled her to the ground. After cuffing her, I sat her up, and she just sat there, rocking back and forth, not saying anything. All I could do was fall on my knees and ask God why? Why did this happen? I was crying uncontrollably, and I couldn't stop. Every hurt and pain I had ever felt all came crashing down on me at once. What purpose or reason was there for four young babies to be taken away in such a tragedy? A torrent of images of every dead child I'd ever seen flooded my mind. Every child nearly beaten to death in a hospital bed in a coma I saw so clearly. Every child living in filth and squalor could not be driven from my mind. Jamison called some other officers to take over. The mother and father stood there in utter shock, holding each other. It was terror on their faces, but only the mother was crying. Jamison picked me up and walked me to the other side of the street. Everything happened so fast. I fell down next to where they were putting Lawrence on the stretcher. I had fainted. They put us both in the same ambulance.

~

The next thing I remember was waking up with all these bright lights glaring down at me. I asked the nurse what happened, and he said I had fainted. The nurse said he would get the doctor. He came in, looking at my chart.

"Ms. Sayers," he says, "You're pregnant."

"My ears must have deceived me." I asked him to say it again, and he did. At that moment of my meager existence, all I could think about was Lawrence and how I promised him everything was going to be all right. I broke out crying uncontrollable tears. Overwhelmed by life's unexpected twists, I felt like screaming. Death would have been a preferable alternative. I finally calmed down.

"Where is the man they brought in from the drug bust?"

"Which man are you referring to? They handcuffed most of the men and treated some wounds before returning them to jail."

"Lawrence Kent, it was from a drug bust this afternoon."

"Let me find out ma'am." He came back. "A nurse said he had come out of surgery about an hour ago and they didn't think he was going to make it through the night."

"How long have I been out?"

"For a few hours, at least according to the time on this chart, but that doesn't mean it wasn't earlier."

I had to see him. He had to pull through because he was going to be a father. When I arrived at the room, I showed my badge to the Agent, who was standing at the door. I went in. His mother and father were in there with him. "Who are you?"

I walked closer to the bed. "My name is Officer Sayers. I'm the one who tried to help your son get out of his brother's business."

His mother asked demandingly. "What business is that?"

"Ma'am, your son Eric was selling drugs, and he tried to have Lawrence killed. Lawrence didn't want to be over his men anymore. He wanted to be free of the drug business altogether."

The mother cried. I asked Lawrence's' father, could I have a moment alone with his son. He hesitated for a second and then took his wife outside to comfort her. As he opened his eyes, I sat on the side of the bed and kissed his perfect lips. I was pretty sure he didn't recognize me, so I waited about ten minutes before I spoke. I had to tell him. Because you cannot talk now, I don't expect you to try. I want you to blink your eyes if you can understand me, and you know who I am." He blinked his eyes twice. "First, I want to say I'm sorry for what happened. It wasn't supposed to turn out this way. Your parents are here. They're waiting outside to see you. They were in here earlier to check on you. We also have your brother in custody. He will go to jail for a very long time. So, you don't have to worry about him or anyone else." His smile was comforting. "I am very proud of you. You were so brave and courageous, and I love you very much. All I want you to do is get well, get well, to see our baby grow up." I saw his eyes get bigger as I put his hand on my stomach. His eyes suddenly closed, and he took a deep breath. An elongated sound pierced my body. Instant panic drove me to a split second of insanity. All his lines were flat. "No God, no. Lawrence." I screamed for the nurses, I screamed for the doctors, and I screamed for anyone to help. It had to be a curse. Every man I had ever loved left me, my ex-husband, Brandon, and now Lawrence. There was no hope for my life. I cried until I couldn't cry anymore. The doctor came in and pronounced him dead after trying to revive him for fifteen minutes. The doctor had to give me a sedative to calm me. I didn't know if I was going to go crazy later on, but the insanity lingered, and the hurt was indescribable.

Chapter 17

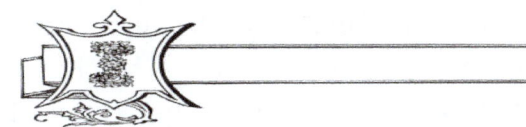

Trust or Betrayal

I know what you are thinking. I completely lost it and there was nothing left to live for. You were absolutely right. It all came crashing down and there was nothing I could do about it. Except...

Two weeks went by and Lawrence's funeral took place. From the gravesite, everyone was walking back to his or her cars. Of course, I stayed back and didn't show myself until it was over. "Mr. and Mrs. Kent, I need to speak with you privately. Not today, but sometime later this week or next week. I need to talk to you about Lawrence." She stopped in her tracks and slapped me. She looked at me with a look of hatred. I was unaware of the reasons for her hatred. "Ms. Sanders or Sayers, whatever your name may be, I don't think we have anything to talk about. I know all the facts. You got my son killed, and you have put my other son in jail for no reason at all. I want you and your police department to stay away from me and my family. I never want to talk to you or see you ever again." They both walked away. Somehow, I had to talk to them and tell them they have a grandchild on the way. Everyone blamed me for Lawrence's death. I couldn't understand why.

~

I waited a week before I had the courage to knock on their door. When I stepped onto their porch, I looked around. No one was in sight. I knocked. "Ms. Sayers, we don't want to talk to you now or ever. I thought I made myself clear at the funeral of my son. Please leave us alone." I had to step in now or never because he would not give me the chance. "Mr. Kent, I know the police aren't telling you much right now and all the information you're getting from Eric and his lawyer is false. I know the truth, Mr. Kent, and I think you know the truth about your sons." He looked at me long and hard and then he opened the screen door. "Thank you, Mr. Kent." Mrs. Kent sat on the sofa quietly and still and not once did she look at me. It seemed as if she had no strength to look up at me or acknowledge I was even there. She stared blankly, with no motion to her body. "I thank you for this opportunity to tell you the truth. I should probably start at the beginning. After befriending Lawrence, I got him to talk about his brother and their drug business. As time went on, I knew Lawrence and the person he really was. He didn't want to be in it anymore, but Eric became the head of his own organized drug operation and kind of forced Lawrence to stay in. I never expected or wanted to, but I fell in-love with your son. I was in turmoil over the job I had to do and the love I had for him would not go away, even though I knew it was wrong. A few months down the road. We find out Eric wanted Lawrence dead. In the process of telling him his brother wanted him dead, I also told him who I was. To put it lightly, he was furious to the point I could see in his eyes the hurt and pain I had caused him. I didn't see him for hours, wondering if he would come back and he didn't. He found me at the beach the next morning. I knew then he had forgiven me. He later expressed to me he had suspensions about his brother. Eric was leaving him out of meetings and would never call back when Lawrence would call or page him. He knew his brother had to be stopped. If Eric could have his own brother killed, he would stoop to do any and everything. It took little to get him to testify after he heard Eric conspiring to have him killed by Hammer. We wanted to get Eric for attempting to have Lawrence killed." I cleared my throat and then proceeded. "Things went bad. It wasn't supposed to happen how it did, but nothing ever happens the way we want them to." I sat there a moment, staring at his picture on the coffee table. "Ms. Sayers. We appreciate you telling us the truth. I hate to rush you, but my wife needs her rest." His voice was bitter, like he believed it, but he didn't want to hear it from me. "I know you may not believe what I'm saying, but there is one more thing you should know. Before Lawrence passed away, I could at least tell him he was going to be a father, which is something he wanted badly. I am pregnant with Lawrence's child, and I wouldn't tell you all this if it weren't true." Mrs. walked with a smile, which at least told me she believed what I was saying. "Thank you for seeing me, Mr. Kent. I appreciate it very much. I think I better go now."

"You know that's going to be our first grandchild. Don't be a stranger, Ms. Sayers. We want to see our grandchild grow up."

"I plan to, Mr. Kent, which is why I'm here. Despite everything, I loved Lawrence, and he loved me."

That day I felt great about being alive and, for the first time, I realized I had something precious and wonderful growing inside of me. Then everything started piling on me at once. The preliminary trial for the fourteen-year-old girl who killed her sisters began. My mind wasn't even on her trial, but I was called to testify. I was two and a half months pregnant, almost three. No one knew about the pregnancy, except the Kent's and my parents and the doctor, of course. I knew I couldn't hide it much longer.

"Detective Sayers, can you tell the court what happened on the day of November 17, at two-twenty p.m.?" The Prosecuting Attorney asked.

"On November 17th, I was working on another case in that area. At two-twenty, I observed the defendant holding a gun in one hand and pulling four other girls away from a woman and a man, apparently the stepfather and the biological mother. I tried to talk to the girl, but it was like she couldn't hear me. She kept screaming at the mother and the stepfather not to come closer or she would shoot. I just kept trying to calm the girl down, but she wasn't listening. I kept my distance as much as possible, to not make the girl more edgy than she was already. Suddenly, the mother lunged forward, and the girl just started shooting. As I went for the gun, she shot the last girl as I was trying to hit the gun in an upward position. I got the gun away, but she was just standing there. I knocked her to the ground and started cuffing her, and a partner of mine finished cuffing her. There was nothing else I could do."

"No further questions, your witness, counselor."

Now it was the Defense Attorney's turn. "Ms. Sayers. Can you tell the court whether the defendant was pointing the gun at the mother and stepfather, or was she pointing the gun at her sisters the whole time?"

"From what I recollect, she was pointing the gun at the mother and stepfather the whole time she was pulling the other girls away from them. Once the mother tried to get closer to the girl, she then started pointing the gun at the girls and then shot them point blank."

"Well, can you tell the court if you can recall exactly what the girl was screaming to her mother and her stepfather?"

"She was screaming at the parents that they would never hurt her or her sisters again. She gave no specific information about what the parents were doing to the girls."

"No further questions, your honor."

"Detective Sayers, you may step down." I was glad that was over. Soon there would be more to come with Eric Kent's trial.

~

I stayed locked up in the house by myself. Other than going to the doctor and buying food, I didn't go out. I would remember Lawrence's funeral and how all the family looked at me with disdain. That day I had to relive Brandon's funeral all over again, but this time I had to grieve by myself. The same man had killed two men I had loved deeply, and no amount of justice could bring them back, but I knew he couldn't get off this time. He had to pay for both Brandon and Lawrence's deaths. I didn't know how much longer it would be before the trial would begin. I couldn't allow anything else to jeopardize this investigation than what I had already done.

~

About five weeks after Lawrence's funeral, I was called into the captain's office. I knocked on the door.

"Come in Sayers."

"Yes, sir, you wanted to speak to me?"

"Yes, come in and close the door behind you. Take a seat."

"What is it, Captain?"

"Sayers, we could have a catastrophe on our hands and we're going to need as much information as possible about the Kent. I'm going to only call Andrews in here and then we'll start." Andrews came in and sat next to me, but facing toward me, the look of worry was on his face.

"Am I getting ready to be interrogated now?"

"No Sayers, nothing like that. We just need to know the answers to some questions that only you can answer."

"Okay, I'm listening."

"I know this may be difficult for you, but can you explain to me, why Eric Kent's' Lawyers are claiming you're pregnant by Lawrence Kent and they know this before we do?"

In utter shock, I could do nothing, but explain.

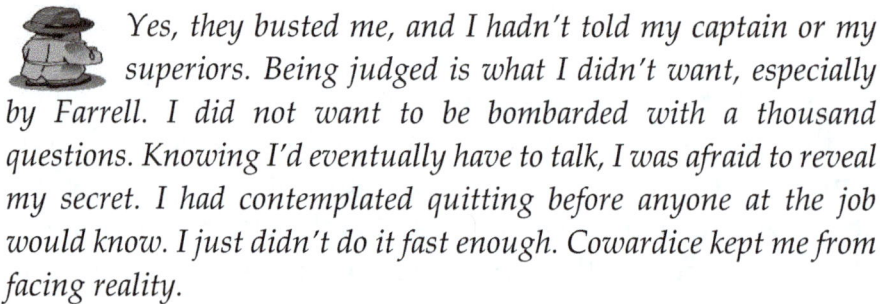 *Yes, they busted me, and I hadn't told my captain or my superiors. Being judged is what I didn't want, especially by Farrell. I did not want to be bombarded with a thousand questions. Knowing I'd eventually have to talk, I was afraid to reveal my secret. I had contemplated quitting before anyone at the job would know. I just didn't do it fast enough. Cowardice kept me from facing reality.*

"He knows, because I told Lawrence's parents and I didn't tell you right away, because I didn't know how you or the department would take it and I was contemplating what I was going to do. Quit, take the hit, and move on and have everyone around here questioning everything about me."

"How I would take it. This could be disastrous. How in the world do you figure this was something you could keep from us? We have a murder investigation at hand here. What in God's name were you thinking, Sayers?" He never gave me a chance to answer. "Answer me this. Did Lawrence know about the baby before the bust?"

"No, he didn't know. I didn't even know until after the bust. As a matter of fact, I didn't know until I woke up at the hospital."

"Well, then. Why did you tell the Kent's, and you did not tell us this was Lawrence's child?"

"I wanted them to know the real side of Lawrence. They had to know the truth other than what they were hearing from Eric. They were blaming me for his death. Eric was telling them lies." Andrews took my hand gently to comfort me. "You were in-love with him, weren't you?" Andrews asked. From my chair, I walked over to the window. "I knew going in I had a job to do and I never once forgot that, even to the end. I did everything necessary to get the job done, except fall in-love. Even when we first made love, it was my job, but it didn't end that way. I didn't use protection once, and I knew afterwards it was a mistake. That mistake turned out to be love in the end and that resulted in the child I'm carrying and that's something I don't plan on changing. I know I screwed up, but my being pregnant shouldn't negate the fact this man admitted to killing Brandon on tape and killed his own brother."

"Sayers, I believe you and we are here for you. We're going to have to get to that doctor before Eric's lawyer tries to use this as a ploy. Sayers, I'm putting you on desk duty because of the baby. I just want you to know we have to report this little situation. Internal Affairs will then determine what will happen after that."

"Captain, I get it. I feel somewhat relieved. I thought, once you found out, you'd suspend me."

"I know it was a onetime mistake. It could happen to anyone. I just want you to be aware, this case could go media and if it does, this pregnancy will come out. Every kind of accusation in the world could manifest. I just need you to take this time to prepare yourself for the tornado that could break loose. On that note, if things get heated, you may have to be put on suspension or leave with pay until everything cools down. Until then, you will be on desk duty. We only now hope that he pleads guilty for everything and we don't have to go to trial. If he doesn't, then we go to trial and waste taxpayer money. Either way it goes, he's going to jail for a long time. Now Monday morning, you start desk duty. It won't be fun around here. Some cops already suspect with the clothes you've been wearing, but I know at least you'll be safe off the streets."

I walked out of the captain's office and sat at my desk across from Farrell. "Look at you, having a drug dealer's baby. I didn't think you could go that low to find a man."

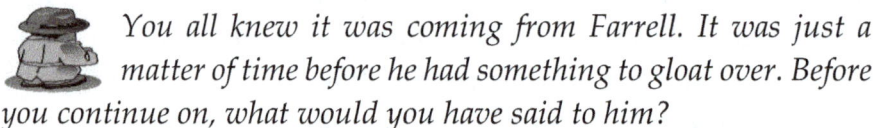 *You all knew it was coming from Farrell. It was just a matter of time before he had something to gloat over. Before you continue on, what would you have said to him?*

"Well, at least I have had love twice in my life, but I can't even recall you being in-love once. That's why Cara left you, you self-righteous son of a @#%$," he looked at me with contempt, but I didn't complete the sentence.

"You could have blown this case being careless. From the start, I warned them against assigning you this case."

"But I was Mike, and I was better at it than you could ever be. From day one, you've hated the fact I was better than you were. So, what I made one mistake, I did my job and nothing you or anyone else can say can change that. As they say in the movies, I always get my man. Can you say the same? I think not. Oh! And another thing, and this goes for anybody else in here. If you have a problem with me, you come to see me. Don't go behind my back. Come to me if you have something to say and if you don't, then fine. I am almost five months pregnant, and I expect a baby present from all of you. Excuse me, only from those who don't condemn me to the gas chamber. Now I'm going back to work. Thank you so much for giving me your undivided attention."

Things were quiet for about a week. I truly found out who my friends were. Jamison was one of them. He would come and visit with me and I would go to his house and have a woman to man talks. Of course, he and I talked a lot about the baby and even his wife took me in and treated me as if I were a human being.

I dreaded to tell the rest of my family and then, I finally got nerve enough to see Anna and Russell. I called them on the phone, and they invited me to dinner. Walking to the door, I felt somehow everything would be all right. I knocked on the door and Russell answered. He greeted me with a big hug and a kiss. "Who is that in there?" I didn't know how they would react to my news, because a part of me felt like I had betrayed Brandon and if I felt that way, more than likely they would feel that way too. "Come in, come in. We are so happy to see you. I hope you're hungry, because dinner is about to be served and I see you're eating for two now."

"Good, I'm starved." I would rather have done anything than tell them the news right then. After dinner, they both were putting away the dishes, and I waited for them in the living room. It was as if Brandon were standing by me, cheering me on. They both walked into the living room, as I was looking at Brandon's picture. "I really appreciate you inviting me over for dinner. This is hard for me, but I have something I need to tell you and I need to explain everything, so maybe you will understand."

"What is it, child? This sounds serious." Mrs. Taylor said.

"It is serious. It's very serious. Believe me, I wouldn't tell you any of this if I didn't have the utmost respect for you both, and I think you have a right to know. You already knew I was doing undercover work on Brandon's case, but what you didn't know was I was the bait. I know you're wondering why? It was because I was to go in and get any information I could from the drug dealer's brother that killed Brandon. In the process of gathering information, I came to know the man he truly wanted to be. After, the FBI, who was also in on the investigation, taped proof of his involvement in drugs and illegal activity, meaning Eric Kent. Lawrence was only in it as manpower. Don't get me wrong, I make no excused for him, but he never wanted to sell drugs and he didn't after he got enough money to open his restaurant, but his brother wouldn't let him out. So, one day Lawrence confronted his brother about getting out and this time he wasn't taking no for an answer. After their argument and Lawrence left, the next conversation Eric Kent would have would be about having Lawrence killed."

"I can't believe what I'm hearing. What has come of all this?" Mrs. Taylor asked.

"I know it's hard to believe, but that's not all. During this entire process, I fell in-love with Lawrence. Knowing his brother was going to kill him, I had to tell him who I really was. Believe me, I never expected in a million years I would fall in-love with this man, but I did. The day of the bust, things went sour and his brother shot Lawrence and later died in the hospital."

"So, what does that mean? He gets off now?"

"No. Eric will go to jail for a long time. It's just if he doesn't plead guilty, then this goes to trial and then something about me is going to come out. Something I would rather you hear from me. After I have told you, you can make your own decision and I will respect your wishes." I stood there with a blank look on my face and was pacing the floor, but my mind was running a hundred miles per hour. "After the bust was over, I blacked out and woke up in the hospital, and the doctor told me I was pregnant." Everything in that house was silent. I didn't want to move, but I had to. I think they intuitively knew what I was going to say, but truly wanted to hear it from me. "By the look on your face, I think I should leave now."

"Yes, I think you better." Mr. Taylor said.

"Russell. How could you be that way?"

"It's all right Anna. I understand his feelings. My father reacted the same way. I'm going to go now."

"Let me walk you outside," she said.

"No. You don't have to."

"But I want to, dear."

Walking to the car, I couldn't help but cry. There was no peace in sight for me. Even though this was an innocent child, I was not innocent of the things I had done. I had to suffer the consequences of my actions and no one could comfort my grief. As much as I wanted everything to be all right, it wasn't, and it would not be for a long time.

"Honey do not cry. For what it's worth, I appreciate you telling us. Your honesty prevented my hurt and disappointment. I don't blame you for falling in-love. Love reaches everyone's heart and allows it to come in. The one good thing is that you have finally let go of the past and have tried to move on with your life. I don't know this man you loved, but if you loved him, there must have been good in him, because I know there is nothing but good in you."

"I really wish I could believe that about myself, Anna."

"Why is it so hard for you to believe there is good in you, too?"

"Because of what I've suffered over the years. I haven't always made the right choices and now this child. This child is going to have to live with the stigma of being a drug dealer's child."

"What about you, Brenda? You have turned your life around so much. You are a detective who loves hard and fights even harder for those you love. I don't know about you, but for you to truly love someone like my son and this man, love has to be in your heart. This man must have been someone special."

"Anna, he didn't want to be in his brother's business anymore, but because he wanted to keep peace in his family, he stayed. When he told his brother, he was getting out. That was the happiest day of his life and he still wanted to be with me, even after I told him who I was. Just know that I understand Russell's reaction. I'm going to go now. I'm sorry if I've caused you any pain."

"I just want you to take care of the baby and yourself and call me anytime."

"Thank you, Anna."

"Go now and be safe. I will talk to Russell and set him straight."

~

The feeling of failure crept back in. I didn't have to hear words. My father's and Russell's face said it all. As I knew he would be, my father was very disappointed. I was daddies' little girl and hurting him tore me apart each time I did something I knew he wouldn't approve of. Disappointing my father was the last thing I wanted, but forging my path and making my own mistakes was necessary. I felt growing up he had put me on a pedestal and once I graduated from high school and didn't go to college. I felt as though I could never measure up to his expectations. This time did not differ from any other. My mother was forgiving, like Anna. My mother never judged me, which was a quality I knew I needed, but I also knew I wouldn't get it from others. They would let me know lovingly what I had done was wrong but wouldn't condemn me for it. The love they showed remained prior, during, and after. Kimberly understood, and Ashley was more excited about the baby than anything else. I think as long as it wasn't Eric's baby, people could swallow the proverbial pill.

Chapter 18

Trial, Redemption of Truth & Forgiveness

Eric didn't plead guilty, and the preliminary hearings completed. I had hoped and prayed this pregnancy wouldn't come out, because Eric's Lawyer knew Lawrence, nor I knew nothing about the baby. So, what could he have up his sleeve?

The trial had come quicker than I had first thought. After picking the jury and the trial started. I was getting calls from Eric's family members who thought I had entrapped Lawrence to testify against his brother. They knew only one side of the story and my day in court would come. Even some cops were making prank phone calls in the middle of the night. Boy, that thin blue line had Farrell's name all over it. I had to leave my phone unplugged and had the number changed twice, so I could at least get some sleep. Truly, I understood where they were coming from. I had messed up, but it was done.

The trial had been going for five weeks and I knew then I was supposed to be the last witness they had to get on the witness stand. By this time, I was six months pregnant and not hiding it at all. I had been feeling the baby kick for a month now and was getting excited about the pregnancy. I remained in touch with the Kents regularly, but couldn't see them in person until this trial was over. I was called to testify on a Thursday afternoon. I would be the highlight of the circus for the day. "Your honor, I would like to call my last witness for the prosecution. I would like to call Detective Brenda Sayers to the stand."

The courtroom got so loud. The judge hit his gavel about fifteen times. "If I ever hear an outburst like this again, I will clear this courtroom."

"Raise your right hand. Do you promise to tell the truth, the whole truth and nothing but the truth so help you God?"

"I do."

"You may be seated."

"Now please, can you give the court your name?"

"My name is Detective Brenda Sayers."

"Can you tell the court how long you've been an officer?"

"I've been with the Police Department for ten years. Four years as a detective and undercover."

"According to your police file, you have an exemplary record, do you not?"

"Well, Mr. Niece, my record speaks for itself, but we all know if you make one mistake, which is all it takes to send a good record straight to hell. One mistake scars you for life, because the media never reports facts or positive things about a person. People believe what you tell them or what gossip they hear, but they never take the time to investigate or go straight to the source to seek the truth for themselves. You fight for the truth or you die in it, physically and career wise."

"Okay, now we've gone through the formalities. You were the Undercover Officer to go in and get information about the alleged drug operation of Eric Kent and to collect information about an alleged murder of a Lt. Brandon Taylor of the Police Department. Is that correct?"

"That is correct."

"What information had you received that made you divulge your identity to Lawrence Kent?"

"Only from what I heard from the tapes and was told from my Commanding Officer and Lawrence himself, he was finally out of his brothers' business and that the defendant and Lawrence had an argument. Following the argument, Eric directly threatened Lawrence's best friend, ordering him to kill Lawrence unless he, Lawrence, reversed his decision to leave, or Hammer himself would die instead, if he didn't follow through with it."

"Objection." The defense asked that the last remark to be stricken from the record. Mr. Niece's rebuttal ensured that the jury only heard a portion of the tape, but the last statement the witness made was on the surveillance tape. The surveillance tape would corroborate my testimony.

"Overruled. The statement is to stand. We will now here the finality of the tape, but next time, counselor, make sure this court hears the tape first. You may continue, Mr. Niece."

"Thank you, your Honor."

The tape was played, and you could hear the gasps in the courtroom, but no one got out of order. Mr. Kent put his head down on the table. That's what I couldn't understand. Eric's lawyer had access to the tapes, but they decided not to plead guilty!

"Now, Detective Sayers, there have been reports of an alleged pregnancy by Mr. Lawrence Kent. Can you tell this court whether this is true?"

"Well, as you can see Mr. Niece, it is true."

 *Look, everybody on our side, meaning the prosecution was aware I was pregnant with Lawrence's child and so, their defense plan was to bring up entrapment. I entrapped Lawrence. What a load of you know what. I was dishonest in the approach, but Lawrence walked away from me. He could have just said he was going to jail for the rest of his life, but he returned to me and we were working it out. We were going to make it together. Did that sound cliché? Does that explain? Well, as a defense attorney, they have to do whatever they can within the confines of the law to get their client off, whether innocent or not. They had to put that doubt in the jury's mind.*

The courtroom went into an uproar. When the judge warned them, he meant business about outbursts in the court. The judge ordered only family members and television crews to remain in the courtroom. All the other spectators would need to leave. It took a few minutes to clear it, which I was glad about. I needed to catch my breath. The baby was kicking something fierce.

"You may finish Detective Sayers."

"I loved Lawrence. Yes, I went to do a job, but in the end, I found him to be a special person. He loved his brother, which is why he didn't leave his business sooner. Lawrence didn't want to cause any problems for his family."

"No further questions, your witness, Mr. Deitz."

"Your Honor, may I treat Detective Sayers as a hostile witness?"

"Mr. Deitz, what kind of request is that? You haven't even started questioning her yet. No, Mr. Deitz, I deny your request. Just ask your questions and get on with it and heed my warning. This woman is pregnant."

"Yes, your Honor. Detective Sayers, you say you went in to do a job, but then you fell in-love with the deceased. Is that correct?"

"Yes, correct."

"Detective Sayers. You described Lawrence as very devoted to keeping the peace in his family. Is that correct?"

"Correct."

"Then can you tell this court why he disrupted the family at this time, knowing full well leaving this alleged business would do just that?"

"Because, for a long time, he wanted to get out and because his brother gave him the money to start his restaurant, he finally decided that enough was enough and he wanted out permanently."

"Well, Detective Sayers. Do you think his decision had anything to do with your relationship?"

"I do not know. When he went to go talk to his brother, I knew nothing about it."

"Okay, well do you think him knowing he had a family on the way had anything to do with it?"

"Objection, speculation. The deceased is not here to speak on his behalf."

"Sustained, Mr. Dietz. Let's stay with the facts of the case."

"Detective Sayers, you want my client to go to jail, don't you?"

"I go to work every day to protect and serve. If someone is breaking the law, there are consequences."

"Yes or no, Detective Sayers. Do you want my client to go to jail?"

"Yes, Mr. Deitz, I do."

"Can you tell this court why?"

"Because Mr. Deitz. Your client is a cold-blooded killer, and he has murdered the only two men I have ever loved."

The tears rolled down uncontrollably. I didn't expect it, but they showed up anyway.

"No further questions."

"Your honor, I'd like to re-cross examine the witness."

"Detective Sayers, are you okay?"

"Yes, your honor, I'm fine."

"You may proceed with your re-cross counselor."

"Detective Sayers, when did you find out about the pregnancy?"

"On the day of the drug bust, I woke up in the hospital and the doctor told me then."

"Did you have any prior knowledge of this pregnancy prior to the day of the bust?"

"No, I did not. I just thought it was stress from the job that my menstrual cycle was late. It's normal for my cycle to sometimes not show up for three months at a time. I thought no different this time. My gynecologist can confirm what I'm saying."

"One more question. On the day someone murdered Lt. Brandon Taylor, where were you?" That whole day flashed before my eyes. All I could see was my body falling to the floor. I had silent tears. At the chapel, I waited for Brandon so we could get married. I never saw him alive that day, and I didn't get the chance to say goodbye.

"No further questions of this witness your honor." The judge dismissed me, but Mr. Niece had one last witness before the prosecution would rest its case.

"He is on the witness list your honor."

"Okay, Mr. Niece. This is your last witness, isn't it?"

"Yes, your honor. I promise." The judge allowed for the prosecutions last witness. "I call Dr. Jordan to the stand." He was a typical-looking doctor. Fashionable plaid overcoat and trousers were what he was wearing.

"Do you promise to tell the truth, the whole truth, and nothing but the truth? So, help you God?"

"I do."

"Okay, Dr. Jordan, just a few questions. Do you work in the Emergency Room Department of Hope Hospital?"

"Yes."

"What type of medicine do you practice?"

"I am an OB/GYN."

"Were you working in the ER Department on November 17th, and did you examine Detective Sayers after the ER staff brought her in?"

"Yes sir, I was and yes, I examined her."

"When Detective Sayers woke up. What did you say to her?"

"Well, first she asked me what happened. I told her she had fainted. I also told her she would be fine, but that she was pregnant."

"Can you tell the court her reaction to the news?"

"She was shocked. It was as if she didn't want to believe it at first, plus, she asked me to repeat what I had just told her."

"Can you tell us how she reacted after the news had some time to set in?"

"She cried a hard, silent cry. She didn't scream out loud, but her cry was hard. Once she calmed down, she wanted to know where the man was. They had brought in with her. She was eager to tell him he was going to be a father."

"So, for your first-hand knowledge, she did not know of this pregnancy and telling the deceased man he was going to be a father was the only thing on her mind at the time?"

"By her immediate reaction, I'm sure she didn't know, and she didn't hesitate to go find the gentleman she was looking for, to tell him."

"Objection! Goes to the reading of the witness' mind."

"Sustained. We will strike the last statement."

"No further questions, your witness, counselor."

"One question, can you absolutely say for sure, Ms. Sayers did not know she was pregnant?"

"No. I can't, but..."

"No further questions." It was understandable to see why the defense ended the questioning there.

"The Prosecution rests, your honor."

"Okay. It's four thirty. We will recess at this time and reconvene at nine a.m. Monday morning. The defense will present its case." The judge adjourned court. "All rise! The honorable Judge Stokes presiding, case number 0619."

My testimony was the longest and the most strenuous thing I had to deal with at that point and time. Everyone in the courtroom and in the department was questioning my life and the way I did my job. My mother was there to support me, but my father would not come to the courthouse. I think someone else I knew felt disappointed in me, too. He never came to the trial other than to testify. I thought at least he would come and be my friend, but Craig never came.

The trial had gone on for about another six weeks, with no end in sight. I knew I had to stay till the end. I had to make sure they sent Eric Kent to the electric chair. Life in prison was too good for him. One thing I was glad from the beginning was they had decided on asking for the death penalty early. They asked for it during opening statements, and only Erik's family protested this decision.

My mother was sound with what was going on and really helped me prepare for the baby. With six weeks to go. I had taken Lamas classes, which was hard doing alone. Especially with everyone looking at you funny, knowing who you are, and whispering behind my back. I never gave into quitting. If the force taught me anything, it was never to give up. After all the false testimony, the defense rested its case, and closing arguments would follow the next day. Then it would be a waiting game. They would be in deliberation for however long it took.

~

I think those days I spent time in church, more than I had in my entire adult life. I sat on the pew seat, and I picked up the Bible and it turned to Titus 3: 4-5, But—When God our Savior revealed his kindness and love, 5 he saved us, not because of the righteous things we had done, but because of his mercy. He washed away our sins, giving us a new birth and a new life through the Holy Spirit.[a] I talked to Him. 'God, I know you hear sinners' prayers and I know it's up to you to answer my prayer. First, I want to say my mother taught me you are a just God. I know my life hasn't gone the way I may have wanted, but it is what it is. Lord, my life is in your hands now. My peace of mind is in your hands. Brandon and Lawrence's justice is in your hands. Lord, I know I messed up and I ask your forgiveness for my sins. Bless this child. It didn't ask to be born. Let Brandon and Lawrence's love shine through this child. Lord, make everything right again. God, help me be the person you want me to be in You. Help me understand life's challenges and help me stand through this trial and the trials to come. Guide my life's footsteps and pick me up when I fall. I accept your son as my Savior and turn my will over to You. This is too much for me to handle alone. I need your help and God, whatever happens in this trial, I know your justice one way or the other will prevail.'

As I was getting off my knees, wiping the tears from my eyes, I felt a tap on my shoulder.

"I heard someone was praying in here?"

"Craig! I can't believe you're here. What are you doing here?"

"I'm here and here to stay, if you'll have me?"

"Oh! You know I will."

"Besides, little baby in there's going to need a man around, and your father tells me you need a delivery coach."

"You would do that?"

"Brenda, I told you once before I loved you and would be here for you when you needed me. Nothing about that has changed. I will admit I was more than a little disappointed, greater than anything. I've seen you stand strong in what has taken place. Plus, I wanted this little bundle to be mine and not some other man's. I wanted you to be mine and not some other man. I had to let you find your way. My trip to Europe prevented me from seeing you after my testimony. I didn't get back until last night, but if you only give me a chance to prove it to you. All you have to do is say yes and we'll take it one day at a time." With the utmost sincerity, I knew he would be there for me. I knew because he loved me. "Yes." Perhaps I hugged his neck too tightly. I nearly choked him. I couldn't let go. My life had been full of loss. I didn't want to let him go, but I had to realize that even though I wanted Craig to be in my life, God would have to show me he was more than that for me. As Craig looked like his veins were popping out of his forehead.

"I think I may pass out in a few minutes if you keep holding on any tighter."

"Oh! I'm so sorry." His smile was as big as hers.

"Thank you so much for being here and wanting to be there with me." Through the tears I expressed what had just taken place, "I just accepted Christ in my life, and I asked God to make everything alright. Right now, peace and release washed over me. I can't even explain it. I have lost so much and now all that doesn't seem important anymore. Then you walk in. I know God heard me, because I didn't know what I was going to do or how I was going to make it through this. I thank God, he sent you." Tears rolled. He wiped them and hugged me again. Tears rolled. He wiped them and hugged me again. "It's okay. Let me take you to get some dinner. I'm pretty sure little baby is hungry, and you can tell me all about it." As we are walking out of the church, I had to know.

"Craig, are you sure you're up to going to the delivery room with me?"

"When the time comes, Brenda, just hope and pray I don't faint."

We both laughed. I don't think I had laughed in months. My life had changed drastically in one day. Instantly, in a split second, I knew I had made the right choice in giving my life over to God. I knew everything wouldn't be peaches and cream, but everything was starting off in the right direction. There was still one more hill to climb, Eric's conviction. If nothing else, justice had to be the victor. The war and the battle had to be won in this case. I didn't envy the jurors. They had to be locked up in that room for as long as it was necessary. Craig helped me tremendously in those two days.

~

Monday at twelve forty-five in the afternoon, I received a phone call from the Captain.

"Brenda, the jury has reached a verdict."

"Wow! I didn't expect them to come back so soon."

"Well, I expected as much. Just be at the courthouse at Two o'clock. They will start then."

"Thank you, Captain, for calling me, I appreciate it. I also want to thank you for backing me up when everything went haywire."

"You're welcome. I know you're a skilled detective and no one can dispute that for one minute, not even Farrell. So, I'll see you there at the courthouse."

My stomach was all the way in my throat and the baby wasn't helping any. Of course, the reporters were waiting for us. There was no getting away. All I could do was hold on to Craig and pray. If my faith were going to grow in grace and mercy, this sure would be a good start in practicing it. God, faith, my baby, my mom and now Craig, was all I had to hold on to. Finally getting away from the reporters, I sat waiting intensely on a hard-wooden chair. It seemed like the chatter intensified as time went by. "Please rise, the Honorable Judge Stokes presiding." He walked in, always confident, and very sure of himself, but not arrogant or self-righteous. Throughout this whole trial, he had been fair. He gave only one warning to those who interrupted his courtroom. I heard once you violated it a second time. He banned you for life. They mounted your picture on the banned list outside the courtroom. You could never come back to his courtroom, even if you were the plaintiff or the defendant. I'm pretty sure the situation was exaggerated somewhere along the way. Judge Stokes sat in that big black leather chair and swiveled around to the jury and just stared for a moment. As he looked, I stared as well. I hadn't noticed before, but there were four African Americans, four Caucasians, two Hispanic, two women from the Orient and my peace of mind was in their hands. I stared back at the judge as he spoke. The court bailiff went through the motions as they do, in reviewing the court number and state vs. defendant. "Has the jury reached a verdict?" As the lady stood, you could see satisfaction on her face. Untroubled and energetic. That's how she looked. She was an older woman with snow-white hair. She unfolded the paper and handed it to the Bailiff to give to the judge. "We have your honor." Receiving the verdict back, the judge says, "So say ye. Would the defendant please rise!" That courtroom was as quiet as a church mouse. "We, the people of Los Angeles County, find the defendant Erik Kent as follows. We find Erik Kent guilty of four counts of drug possession, sale of illegal chemicals, and sale of handguns to suspected gang members." There was not a stir in the building, except the reporters. "Three counts of first-degree murder. For the murder of Sgt. Brandon Taylor, Lawrence Kent, and Anthony Woods A.K.A. Hammer, we find the defendant, Erik Kent GUILTY, on all three counts." If you ever wanted to hear a pin drop, this wasn't the place to hear it. The judge hit the gavel to quiet the crowd. "Eric Kent, your peers have found you and this court to be guilty of the above-entitled charges. We will hold your sentencing in one month. Please remand the prisoner into custody." It was loud as the Kent Family expressed their dissatisfaction with the verdict. But how could they truly not see he was guilty? If nothing else, he had killed his own brother. How could anyone want to defend that? All I could say was thank you, God. I had no words to express what I felt inside. Craig pulled out his handkerchief and wiped the tears and he held me all the way out the door. That chapter of my life was finally over, and nothing could take that satisfaction away.

My father met us outside the door. I reached out my arms to him and he grabbed me with all the love he could muster. "Daddy, I love you and I'm sorry I disappointed you." He pulled me back from him. "You have nothing to be sorry for. I should be the one apologizing to you. I'm sorry for abandoning you when you needed me the most. Can you ever forgive me?" I hugged him dearly. "I forgive you, daddy. Can we go now?"

I know what you're thinking. It's all over now. She lived happily ever after. She got justice and Craig. Well, I have to disappoint you right now. It wasn't all rosy from here. I had to go before a Board Review and the fate of my career would be at the hands of some who were not always on the up and up themselves.

One month to the day had passed, and the court would sentence Eric Kent. I did not speak to Eric that day, but Mr. and Mrs. Taylor said it all eloquently. Eric chose not to speak to those in the courtroom. He had no remorse for what he had done. Eric's parents had learned the truth about their son and could not support him because of the senseless murder he set for his brother and the others. His stern look of contempt for us all said it all. You could see evil within him, and I knew only God could help him now. It was a victory for Brandon, Lawrence, Anthony, and closure for everyone else.

Chapter 19

 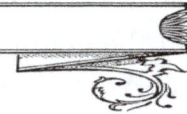

Family

As we walked down the courthouse stairs, I had one arm around my dad and the other arm around Craig. I stopped dead in my tracks. I felt something warm run down my legs. Craig and then my dad looked at me as though they were in instant panic. I had instant embarrassment, because of a stream of liquid slowly but surely, falling from one step to the other like a slinky. There was no hiding it and there wasn't a mop in sight. I asked God, "Why did this have to happen in public?" I looked up at my dad and Craig. "You guys better get me home, I think. My water bag just broke." My father panicked for a second, and then immediately took control of the situation. Craig wanted to seem brave, but his acting wasn't very convincing. I think my father yelled Craig's name twice before he even responded.

"Craig, help me get Brenda to the car."

"Okay, Sir."

I had a plastic bag in the back seat, which would start using it just in case my water bag broke while I was out. My father knew I wasn't ready to go to the hospital yet. If he knew anything after six children, Sayers' children were never early bloomers, and this one would be no exception. We arrived at the house, and I could take a shower and then the first real contraction hit me like an eighteen-wheeler, diesel mac truck, as I was coming out of the bathroom. Craig rushed to help me up. I fell to my knees. I asked the Lord to forgive me because I didn't have any clothes on and Craig could see all my business. The pain at that point made sure I didn't care. He did the gentlemen thing and grabbed my robe to put it over me. At that very moment, my mind went back to Adam and Eve. How could they be so stupid and so naïve to eat that fruit? What possessed them the go against God's Word? The contraction finally subsided, and I could speak at this point.

"This isn't supposed to happen for another week."

"Well honey, it could happen two weeks before or two weeks after your due date. I guess a week before is just fine with the baby."

"Oh! I don't think a bullet hurts worse than this."

My father was in the room by then and just started laughing at me, because he said, "You remind me so much of your mother." I think Craig's focus prevented him from finding anything humorous. He even made me laugh. "Craig, relax. You must stay calm. I need you in the delivery room, now more than ever. I don't want to do this alone." I think my words kind of sobered him up and he was okay after.

"OH! OH! OH! Another one is coming."

"That's been eight minutes. Honey, come on and do your breathing. It will help you get through the contractions easier." I guess the look I gave him was a look of, if you don't leave me alone, I will kill you and then ask God for forgiveness afterwards. Of course, I didn't say it aloud, but I was thinking it, so I had to ask God to forgive me anyway. Craig tried to explain.

"What? I read it in a baby magazine."

"It's easing up now. So, answer me one question."

"What is it?"

"How long have you been reading baby books?" I guess he was surprised when I asked that question. I wanted to know for my own satisfaction. "For a few months now and while I was in Europe, I knew I needed to get up to speed." I thought to myself that maybe he needed more time to think about what he would get himself into, if, I had accepted being with him of course. I also thought that I was a very blessed woman this day to even have someone in my life right now, who is willing to be there for the baby and me. Of course, I had God in my life and if I learned nothing else while I was in church as a young person, was that God supplies all your needs and I knew God had sent Craig back to me.

A few hours had passed, and the contractions had only gotten six minutes apart. From there, I knew I had to head to the hospital. I didn't want to wait any longer.

"A contraction is coming and this one is harder. I need drugs!"

"Okay, Craig. Let's get my baby to the hospital. We may not have long now."

"Okay, Sir. Honey, tell me when the contraction stops."

I breathed so much, my lips became chapped and crusty. "It's stopping. We better go now. Daddy, go get, mom. You know she will be very upset if you go to the hospital without her. Craig let's go." He could hear the irritation in my voice. He never said a word to me all the way to the hospital. I had about three contractions while in the car and I had another one on the way into the hospital. If you've ever had a baby, you know how I felt and how I looked. If you've never experienced childbirth, just wait and consider yourself blessed.

In the hospital room, they were coming four minutes apart, and I knew it wouldn't be long now.

"I have to push."

"No, no. You can't push yet. Breathe right now."

"Look nurse. I've been breathing for 8 hours already. I'm finished with breathing. This baby is ready to come out, and it's coming."

"Okay."

"Brenda. Please don't get stressed out on me. We need to be calm." He put his lips to my ear and said, "I love you. We're going to get through this." I panted, breathed, and drank water. A scream, not my own, erupted after my own screaming and pushing. I laid my head back in utter exhaustion. I think if I hadn't wanted to see the baby so badly, I would have fallen asleep without delay. "Brenda, it's a boy, a beautiful baby boy." They laid his little body on top of mine. They clamped the cord and handed the scissors to Craig. He had that proud father look already. Even though he was not his biological father, I knew Craig would be his father, because he was just that kind of man. He cut the cord and then he kissed me. "I'm very proud of you. I was going to wait to give you this, but I don't think I will." He knelt down on the side of the bed. "Brenda, I love you. I've loved you ever since that day in my house, even when you didn't want to have a relationship with me. I know what I feel, and it feels right. Brenda, will you marry me?" I didn't even hesitate. "Yes. I will marry you, Craig." He was so excited. He ran out into the hallway. By the time he came back in, I was asleep. My mom and dad showed up after an hour. I received at least an hour's worth of sleep. Everyone from the Captain on down showed up, even Farrell. I had no hatred toward him at all, even before I had given my life over to God. Now, I had forgiven him, and even more so. I just knew that we could never be partners again. I could not trust that it wouldn't happen again with him.

After all the commotion, everyone left except for Craig. He was the last one to leave. I had to know his feelings about the name I had decided on for the baby.

"Craig, I need you to come and sit next to me."

"Sure, honey. What's going on? I can tell by the look on your face you want to tell me something." I sat up in the bed and cleared my throat. I took his hand as I began. "Craig. I need to know your feelings about something I have decided upon. Before I tell you what it is. I need to explain something to you."

"Brenda, just tell me what it is."

"I want you to know that I love you and I want to marry you. Nothing has changed about that. I know you will love the baby like he was your own, but I have decided on a name for him. To avoid problems, I won't mention the name. I want your feelings to count on this matter because you will be his father." I paused for a second and then continued. "I want to name him Brandon Lawrence Matthews. Before you say anything, I also want you to adopt him. I have thought about this long and hard for the last three hours. I want us to be an actual family. This is, I realize, a considerable request. I want to know your feelings, and are you willing to go through with the adoption?"

He stood up and walked out of the door without saying a word. His actions broke my heart again, but I couldn't blame him. I just slid down into the bed and cried. With my eyes closed, tears streamed down my face with every sniffle. I heard the door open, but I was sure it was the nurse, so I just laid there with my eyes closed. I felt a kiss on my lips and as I opened my eyes. He held a pen in my face.

"What is this for?"

"Where do I sign the dotted line?" I kissed and hugged him until they brought the baby in for feeding. Craig picked him up and held him in his arms, and then handed him to me.

"Brandon Lawrence Matthews, this is your daddy."

~

We were married one year later and two years after that. We were in the delivery room again. The scream I heard was not my own and then another scream I heard was not my own.

"Mr. Matthews, you're the proud father of two baby boys."

Our love had grown into something lasting. Two more babies. God had been so good to me. As I lay back on the bed in utter exhaustion again, I motioned to Craig to come closer.

"Wonderful and helpful, husband. You have the privilege of naming your sons this time. I only have one desire."

"What is it, dear?"

"That you don't name them Richard, Howard or Eric."

We both laughed, but he was not in pain. So, I just chuckled a little. They brought in Brandon and as soon as he saw them, he wanted to play with them or at least bounce them like a ball, but I was glad.

~

Throughout the years, there was no sibling rivalry, and Craig treated all the boys the same. Craig and I have been married for twenty-one, almost twenty-two years now. I look back and think about the opportunities I had as a young woman and realize that I held my life down by making poor decisions. If nothing else, I wanted my children to make better choices than I had. I knew from experience. You can't decide for them. They have to make them for themselves and live with the consequences of their actions, especially when they are adults.

Brandon is about to graduate from college to go into Law School. Bryan and Brett are going to be sophomores in college.

They don't know what they want to do with their lives, but whatever they decide, I'm pretty sure they will do it together.

Both my parents, Anna, and Russell, passed away several years ago. I stayed a detective for ten more years. Happy and content with the life God had blessed me with. I remained on light-duty after getting shot in the leg. Although I was fine afterwards, my husband and children want me out of detective work. So, I agreed and I'm working at the front desk. They got me away from the streets, but they couldn't get me away from the job.

Ashley's a professor at Harvard and married with two children. She calls me about once a week. Kimberly remarried and was traveling around the world with her husband and could get over her insecurities about men.

Farrell's teaching training classes for officers and has changed little. He later confessed he was jealous and in-love with me at the same time and didn't know how to handle his feelings. Boy, was that a shocker. We talk every once in a while, but not like we use to.

Captain Hillary retired from the force. They gave Andrews his position, and Jamison now holds Andrew's former position running DTF.

~

They sentenced Eric Kent to death by lethal injection. He wasn't shocked and vowed to appeal. He filed an appeal, and after its denial, they sent him to death row. Someone executed him before his transfer to San Quentin State Prison.

As of August 4, 2023, there are 656 Condemned Inmates and out of those 656, 80 of those inmates have 2 to 7 multiple execution convictions. Their age ranges from 31 to 93 years of age. There are 636 males and 20 females currently on Death Row. The top four ethnicities are: Black 224 males/2 females, White 211/11 females, and Mexican 126 males/4 females, and

Hispanic 44 males/1 female. It's amazing, isn't it?

The CDCR is looking to close San Quentin & Central California Women's Facility, so the death-sentenced could have more access to job opportunities and be able to pay victim restitution and take part in rehabilitative programs. https://www.cdcr.ca.gov/capital-punishment/condemned-inmate-summary-report/

~

I thank God every day for what I went through. God's mercy, I understand now, protected me then. I deserved death, but God gave me a second chance to accept Him and live the life I was supposed to, God's way. I could have very well died that day in more ways than one, but I know now God had a purpose and a plan for my life. Learning from many of my mistakes and going through the storms. Although it was tough, I wouldn't change a thing. Just looking at the end results, I don't think you would either. It was God's Mercy Undercover.

Who would have all men to be saved... It is the will of God that all men should inherit eternal life, but it is also the will of God that people should accept Jesus Christ, and persons refusing to do so will give up their inheritance? Another factor enters consideration is the will of man. God having granted to all people the freedom of their will, and, where man's will is unresponsive and rebellious against God's will, there can be no salvation. God DESIRES the salvation of all, but the RESPONSIBILITY for accepting salvation rests squarely upon every man.

The End

About the Author

Social Media:
FB: nitanaesbooks
IG: nitanaesbooks
Twitter: NitaNaesBooks
Pinterest: nitanaesbooks

For Other Author Interviews, NNB Author's Point of View Blog & YouTube Channel
NNB Author's P.O.V. BLOG | nitanaesbooks.com and YouTube Channel https://youtu.be/OePi-LCJz_A

For more book information and editing consultation, web address: www.nitanaesbooks.com
e-mail to: nitanaes_books@yahoo.com